A GOOD LESSON

"What's eatin' on you, Cal?" Smoke asked the boy.

Cal couldn't look Smoke in the eye; he gazed up at the stars as he spoke. "I reckon it's rememberin' that Indian I shot back yonder, Mr. Jensen, remembering what he looked like with that big hole in him . . . knowin' I done it."

"Killin' a man is never easy," Smoke said gently. "Sometimes it's necessary. Those Apaches were coming after us, and you did what you had to do in order to save your friends. That's part of accepting the responsibility of being a man."

"I wish I could be more like you, Mr. Jensen," Cal said. "I seen how you stay calm, like it don't rattle you none when you kill somebody."

"There's some men who need killin'," Smoke said. "They break the law and bring harm to other folks who can't defend themselves. You do it when it's necessary, when you have to defend what's yours if somebody tries to take it. I think you realized for the first time how final death is, after you took another man's life. Understandable, to feel that way. It may keep you from becoming a killer yourself, unless you've got a good reason to kill."

Smoke turned back toward the fire. Cal would understand today's incident, given time. "You did yourself proud, Cal, and you may have saved a life . . . maybe mine."

"I hadn't thought of it quite like that," Cal said.

BOOK YOUR PLACE ON OUR WEBSITE AND MAKE THE READING CONNECTION!

We've created a customized website just for our very special readers, where you can get the inside scoop on everything that's going on with Zebra, Pinnacle and Kensington books.

When you come online, you'll have the exciting opportunity to:

- View covers of upcoming books
- Read sample chapters
- Learn about our future publishing schedule (listed by publication month *and author*)
- Find out when your favorite authors will be visiting a city near you
- Search for and order backlist books from our online catalog
- Check out author bios and background information
- Send e-mail to your favorite authors
- Meet the Kensington staff online
- Join us in weekly chats with authors, readers and other guests
- Get writing guidelines
- AND MUCH MORE!

**Visit our website at
http://www.pinnaclebooks.com**

Battle of the Mountain Man

William W. Johnstone

PINNACLE BOOKS
Kensington Publishing Corp.

http://www.pinnaclebooks.com

PINNACLE BOOKS are published by

Kensington Publishing Corp.
850 Third Avenue
New York, NY 10022

All Kensington Titles, Imprints, and Distributed Lines are available at special quantity discounts for bulk purchases for sales promotions, premiums, fund-raising, and educational or institutional use. Special book excerpts or customized printings can also be created to fit specific needs. For details, write or phone the office of the Kensington special sales manager: Kensington Publishing Corp., 850 Third Avenue, New York, NY 10022, attn: Special Sales Department, Phone: 1-800-221-2647.

Pinnacle and the P logo Reg. U.S. Pat. & TM Off.

First Printing: July 1998
10 9 8 7 6 5 4 3

Printed in the United States of America

One

Smoke Jensen rode his big Palouse, Horse, into Big Rock, Colorado, just as the sun peeked over the mountains to the east. As Horse cantered down dusty streets, Smoke's eyes flicked back and forth, checking alleyways and shadows for potential trouble. Though his days as one of the West's most feared gunfighters were behind him, old habits died hard, and old enemies seemed to live longer and outnumber old friends.

As Smoke passed the jail, Sheriff Monte Carson stepped through the door and tipped his hat. "Howdy, Smoke. Gettin' an early start this mornin'?"

Smoke smiled at his old friend and pointed back over his shoulder at a buckboard following him. "Got to set an example for these young punchers, Monte. Otherwise they'd sleep half the day away."

Monte grinned and glanced at the wagon. Pearlie, foreman of Smoke's Sugarloaf ranch, was riding slumped over, his hat pulled down over his eyes, snoring loud enough to be heard over the creaking of wheels and the clopping of horses' hooves.

Sitting next to Pearlie, leaning against his shoulder, was Cal Woods, Pearlie's second in command at the ranch. His hat was also down and his eyes were closed.

Though he wasn't snoring, he was obviously asleep, too.

Monte chuckled. "Good thing those broncs know the way to town, Smoke, or them boys'd be in Denver by now."

Smoke nodded and reined Horse to a stop in front of the general store next to the jail. He stepped out of his saddle and tried the door, finding it still locked.

He shook his head. *Guess everyone but Monte and I are sleeping in this morning,* he thought. He climbed back up on Horse and called out, "Cal, Pearlie, wake your lazy butts up and I'll treat you to some breakfast over at Longmont's."

Pearlie opened one eye and peered out from under his Stetson. With a prodigious yawn, he nodded and nudged Cal awake. "C'mon boy. Food's callin' an' the boss is buyin'."

They left the buckboard in front of the store and ambled over to the Silver Dollar Saloon, following Smoke.

When they brushed through the batwings, the three men found Louis Longmont sitting at his usual table, drinking coffee and smoking a long, black cigar. The ex-gunfighter smiled and waved them over to his table. Even at this early hour, he was, as usual, dressed impeccably in a black suit and a starched white shirt with ruffles on the front, a black silk vest, and a red cravat around his neck.

Louis looked like a dandy, but he was in fact one of the fastest guns in the West. He was a lean, hawk-faced man, with strong, slender hands and long fingers, his nails carefully manicured, his hands clean. He had jet black hair and a black, pencil-thin mustache. He wore low-heeled boots. A pistol hung in tied-down leather on his right side; it was not for show alone. For Louis was snake-quick with a short gun. A feared, deadly gun hand when pushed. Just past forty years of age. He had come to the West as a young boy and made a name for himself first as a gunfighter, then as a skilled gambler. He was well educated and as smart as he was dangerous.

Smoke and Pearlie and Cal pulled up chairs across from Louis, who waved a hand at a young black waiter. "Tell Andre to scramble up some hen's eggs, burn three steaks, and make a fresh pot of coffee. These punchers look hungry."

Smoke's eyes flicked around the room in an unconscious search for danger, automatically noting three men sitting at a corner table on the far side of the room. Though it was barely dawn, two of the men had mugs of beer in front of them and the third a glass of whiskey.

The cowboy drinking whiskey sported a fancy double-rig of hand-tooled holsters containing pearl-handled Colts, and wore a black silk shirt and black pants tucked into knee-high stovepipe black boots. He had red hair and a red handlebar mustache. His hair was slicked down and glistened with pomade, and the corners of his mustache curled up, held in place with wax. His companions both wore pistols hung low and tied down on their thighs with rawhide thongs.

Smoke inclined his head toward the gunmen and said to Louis, "Trouble?"

Louis smiled and tipped cigar smoke from his nostrils. "They think they are. The one with the fancy rig calls himself the Arizona Kid." He paused to chuckle. "The big one on the left, the one with the shaved head, says his name is Otto, and the other one's name I didn't catch."

Louis paused while the waiter placed three mugs of dark, steaming coffee in front of them.

Pearlie built himself a cigarette and stuck it in the corner of his mouth, in unconscious imitation of his idol, the famous gunman Joey Wells, whom he had met and fought alongside the previous year.*

"They were here drinking all last night," Louis continued, glancing in the direction of the gunnies who were staring at Smoke and his men. "Said they heard Ned Buntline was in the area and they wanted to talk to him about writing a book about them."

At the mention of Buntline's name, Cal came fully awake, his eyes wide. "Mr. Buntline is in Big Rock?" he asked.

Louis smiled, knowing Cal's addiction to the penny dreadfuls Buntline penned. "He was. He came through here last week, said he was headed into the high lonesome to talk to some of the old mountain men before they all died off. He's planning on writing a story about how they opened the mountains up to the white man."

"Wow!" Cal said. "Maybe I can meet him and tell him how much I like his books."

Louis nodded. "You'll probably get the chance. He plans to stop by Sugarloaf and talk to Smoke on his way back from the mountains." He hesitated. "That's if Smoke will talk to him at all. Smoke isn't all that long-winded, especially when it comes to talking about himself. If Mr. Ned Buntline intends to get any

Honor of the Mountain Man

real information from Smoke Jensen, he'd better be real careful how he asks. Smoke has never been all that inclined to waggle his tongue when it comes to men who live in the high lonesome. There are some things that a man has to learn the hard way, not from some blown-up story in a book full of fancy language. Half of it isn't true to start with, a piece of some writer's imagination. I don't think Smoke will be all that excited about telling Buntline what he wants to know." He glanced at Smoke. "Am I right?"

Smoke seemed momentarily preoccupied with the three men in the corner, in particular the one Louis said called himself the Arizona Kid. "There's things ought not to be written up in some book," he said quietly. "A man who takes on high country all by himself learns a trick or two about how to survive. Learning it isn't easy, and I can show you more'n a handful of graves up in those mountains to prove my point."

"Like Puma's," Pearlie reminded. "That was one tough ol' hombre, only he put his life on the line an' his luck jus' plumb played out."

Smoke didn't want to be reminded of his dead friend. "Puma Buck was one of the best, like Preacher. But it wasn't Puma's luck that ran out . . . he went up against long odds, and sooner or later, as any gambler'll tell you, those odds catch up to a man who takes chances." He was still watching the Arizona Kid from the corner of his eye, strangely uneasy, feeling a heaviness in the air, the smell of danger.

Louis noticed Smoke's distraction "I don't think those boys are dumb enough to make a play," he said under his breath, his gun hand close to his pistol. "But if they do, I'll take down the gent who shaves his head. You can have the owlhoot with the double rig. If I'm any judge, he fancies himself as a quick draw, so I'll give you the pleasure of proving him wrong."

Smoke took a sip of coffee, using his left hand to handle his cup. "The one who calls himself the Arizona Kid will be the one to start trouble."

Louis chuckled mirthlessly. "Wonder just where in Arizona Territory he'd like to have his body shipped to? I don't suppose we'll have time to ask."

"I feel it coming," Smoke whispered, "just like a mountain man can feel a chinook wind before it starts to blow."

"I sure as hell hope you're wrong," Pearlie said, "on account I'm sure as hell hungry fer them eggs. . . ."

Two

Cal added his voice to Pearlie's concerns. "Y'all sure are makin' me nervous, all this talk about a shootin'. Maybe I ain't got so much appetite after all."

Pearlie looked at the boy. "Relax, son. If any two men can handle them three, it's Smoke an' Mr. Longmont. Truth is, either one could most likely handle all three, no matter how tough they claim to be."

Smoke wasn't really listening, pretending to watch a sunrise out the front windows when in fact he was keeping an eye on the three men at the corner table.

"It's my belly that ain't relaxed," Cal muttered.

Right at that moment the Arizona Kid signaled the bartender for another round of beers.

Louis seemed amused over Cal's uneasiness. "My money says when those eggs and steaks get here, you'll lick your plate clean as a whistle."

"Maybe," Cal replied, taking his own quick glance at the men in the corner "Those boys look like a bad case of indigestion to me."

Smoke still sensed the nearness of danger, a lifelong habit, learning to trust his instincts. There was something about the three gunmen, not merely the way they wore their guns tied down, but something more, an attitude of confidence, even arrogance, on their faces. He drank more coffee, hoping he was wrong about the prospects of trouble.

The bartender brought three beers to the table. Smoke heard one of the men ask who the newcomers were.

"That big feller's none other than Smoke Jensen," the barman replied. "He makes his home right close to Big Rock."

"He came struttin' in here like he thinks he's tough, them big shoulders thrown back."

The barkeep lowered his voice even more. "Make no mistake about it, stranger. He *is* tough. Plenty of men have tried him to see if he's as mean as his reputation. Some got away with a hole or two in their hides. Some went below ground to feed the worms."

The Arizona Kid was watching Smoke closely now. "You say his name is Smoke Jensen? Never heard of him. Maybe all he's got is that mean reputation."

The bartender glanced over his shoulder in Smoke's direction and quickly looked away. "I ain't no doctor, mister, but if I was you an' wanted to stay healthy, I wouldn't test Mr. Jensen to see if I'm tellin' you the truth." He turned on his heel and hurried away. The Arizona Kid and the gunman named Otto continued to stare at Smoke.

Like predicting winter weather in the high lonesome, Smoke knew what was coming. It was just a matter of time. The Kid wanted to draw attention to himself, perhaps to add to his self-importance if he got the chance to talk to Ned Buntline, to put another notch on his guns.

To keep young Cal and Pearlie out of the line of fire, he said, "Why don't you two go out and see to the buggy team and my Palouse. Won't take but a minute and you'll be done before the food gets here."

Pearlie nodded, like he understood. Cal needed no urging to push back his chair for a walk outside. As the pair was leaving, Smoke turned at the waist to look directly at the Arizona Kid and his partners, deciding there was no sense in wasting time when a confrontation was as sure as the snow in high country now. "You boys got a bad case of the goggle eyes," he said evenly. "Maybe I'm too particular about it, but it sticks in my craw like sand when some gent stares at me. Especially you, the carrot-topped hombre with the mustache, you just gotta learn some manners or somebody's liable to teach you some."

The Kid put down his beer mug and rose slowly to his feet, his back to the wall. "Is that so?" he asked, sneering, both hands near the butts of his guns. "Tell you the truth, mister, I don't see nobody in this room who's man enough to git that job done."

Smoke came to a crouch, then rising to his full height, lips drawn into a hard line. "Then look a little closer," he snarled, as every muscle in his body tensed. "I think it's time you boys cleared out of here. We'll take our little disagreement outside. A friend of mine owns this establishment and I'd hate like hell to be responsible for spilling blood all over his nice clean floor, or putting any bullet holes in his walls. Meet me out in the street and we'll settle this."

"Like hell!" the Kid bellowed, hands dipping for his pistols as Smoke had anticipated all along.

In the same instant, Otto and the other cowboy were clawing for their guns.

Lightning quick, employing reflexes that had kept

him alive in much tougher situations, Smoke came up with both hands filled with iron, Colt .44s, working his thumbs and trigger fingers in well-practiced movements, almost second nature to a man who kept himself alive by wits and weapons.

The Silver Dollar Saloon exploded in a thundering series of deafening blasts, becoming a symphony of noise when Louis Longmont added his gunshots to the concussions swelling inside the establishment's walls.

The Arizona Kid was driven back against wallpapered planks behind him, his mouth grotesquely distorted when balls of speeding lead shattered his front teeth. His hat went spinning into the air like a child's top as the back of his skull ruptured in flying masses of tissue, red hair, bone fragments, and brains.

At the same time Otto swirled, balancing on one booted foot while a spurt of blood erupted from the base of his neck above his shirt collar. Another slug entered his right eye, closing it upon impact amid a shower of crimson squirting from a hole below his right ear. Otto appeared to be dancing to an unheard melody for a moment, trying to remain upright on one foot, hopping up and down, dropping his gun to the floor to reach for his throat and eye socket.

The third gunman went backward through a shattering windowpane before his gun ever cleared leather, a .44 caliber bullet splintering his breastbone, puckering the front of his shirt as it sped through his body in the exact spot where Smoke placed it, with as much care as time afforded him.

Amid the roaring gunblasts, someone screamed outside the saloon, but it was the Arizona Kid who held Smoke's attention now as the gunman slid down the Silver Dollar's expensively decorated wall, leaving a red smear in his wake as he went to the floor in a heap, what was left of his mouth agape, dribbling blood down the front of his silk shirt, remnants of teeth still clinging to bleeding gums. A plug of his curly red hair was plastered to the wall above him, sticking there for a curiously long time before it dropped soundlessly to the floor beside him.

Otto teetered on one foot, making strangling sounds, blood pumping from his wounds as he somehow managed to remain standing, hopping for no apparent reason, since he had no leg wounds, merely unable to put his left foot down.

Smoke and Louis stopped firing, watching Otto perform his odd dance steps while gunsmoke rose slowly toward the ceiling.

"He'll fall down in a minute," Louis said, as though he was discussing the weather, or the felling of a tree. "Or should I put another slug in him and be done with it?"

"Hard to say," Smoke replied dryly, holstering his pistols, his eyes on Otto. "He does a right nice dance step. Too bad we ain't got a fiddler."

The thumping of Otto's boot and his choking sounds were the only noises inside the Silver Dollar for several seconds more as Smoke and Louis watched the dying man's struggle. Suddenly, Otto's knee gave way and he collapsed on the floorboards beside a brass spittoon with a soft gurgling coming from the hole in his neck. A dark stain began to spread across the crotch of his pants when his bladder emptied, a sure sign of the nearness of death.

Smoke sauntered over to the broken window, gazing out at the third gunman's limp body. "This one's dead," he told Louis in a quiet voice. "I reckon I owe you for a piece of glass."

"Nonsense," Louis replied. "Hardly a month passes that I don't buy a window or two, after some of my customers get a bit too rowdy. You don't owe me a thing."

Smoke turned to his old friend and grinned. "Yes I do, and you know it. The big guy, Otto, was a little faster than I had him sized up to be. I might have been picking lead out of my own hide if you hadn't been here to back me."

"Nobody is keeping score," Louis said. "We've been backing each other so long I lost count of who owes who a long time ago. I'm not keeping a tally book, but I'll wager it's heavily in your favor. You've stopped a lot of lead from flying in my direction over the years. Now sit down. I'll send someone for the undertaker and then I'll send out those steaks and eggs, if the cook didn't let 'em burn while all that shooting was going on."

Three

Sheriff Monte Carson came racing through the bat-wing doors with his gun drawn, followed closely by Pearlie and Cal. Carson stopped in mid stride when he saw the two bodies, and the broken window.

Carson looked at Smoke. "What the hell? I heard all the shootin' an' got here quick as I could."

"A little misunderstanding," Smoke replied, settling into his chair. "Two's dead and the other one's dying. They went for their guns first."

"You didn't need to explain that part," Carson said, putting his pistol away. "I've known you long enough to know you'd never draw on a man first. Should I send for the doctor to attend to that bald feller?"

"He's too far gone for that," Smoke answered, lifting his cup of cold coffee as a signal for a warm-up. "Two slugs, one through an eye and the other through his throat. He'll be dead before Doc can get here."

Carson looked around momentarily. "Louis told me about these three strangers, how they was askin' about Ned Buntline an' drinkin' a helluva lot of whiskey an' beer."

"They're done with their drinking now," Smoke

remarked with no trace of emotion, "unless you count the way that big one over yonder is drinking his own blood."

Carson took a deep breath. "I reckon I should be used to the fact that sometimes things start happenin' early in Big Rock now an' then. Before the last rooster stops crowin' at daybreak we got three dead men to bury. Maybe we oughta change the name of this town to Dead Man's Gulch. Damn, what a mess." He gave Louis a tight grin. "On top of bein' the undertaker's best friend, you've been mighty good for the glass windowpane business up in Denver."

Louis nodded, taking note of the fact that Cal was standing over Otto with a waxy look paling his cheeks. "It's a necessary expenditure in the whiskey trade, Monte. As a businessman, I have to be prepared for a certain amount of fixed overhead. Windows are a part of that figure."

Smoke heard Cal speak softly to Pearlie. "This feller ain't got but one eye. You can see plumb into his skullbone. I swear I'm gonna be sick. Lookee there, Pearlie . . . he's still breathin' once in a while. Jeez. I sure as hell ain't got no appetite now. You can have my steak an' eggs."

"A man dyin' ain't never a pretty sight," Pearlie replied, putting his arm around Cal's shoulder. "Go on outside fer a spell an' catch yer wind. You'll feel better in a little bit."

Cal turned and hurried past Smoke's table without looking at him, embarrassed by the way he felt sick to his stomach, Smoke guessed. Outside the Silver Dollar, curious citizens of Big Rock peered through front windows to see what all the ruckus was about so early in the morning . . . some were still dressed in nightshirts and long johns.

Louis spoke to the bartender as Sheriff Carson stepped over to the doors behind Cal, following him out to fetch the undertaker. "Tell Andre to hurry with that food," Louis said, as though he knew Smoke and Pearlie would be hungry despite what had just happened.

A nervous-eyed waiter refilled Smoke's coffee cup and gave a similar warm-up to Louis's, then Pearlie's.

"Helluva way to start the day," Smoke said under his breath as he brought the cup to his lips.

Louis chuckled and sat down. "I've had worse and so have you. Sometimes it comes with the territory if a man carries a gun."

Smoke thought of something. "I don't intend to talk to this Buntline. If he asks, tell him I'm not in the habit of talking about old friends, or even old enemies. He'll have to get his information someplace else."

Louis stared thoughtfully into his cup. "I doubt if any of the old-timers up high will talk to him either, if he can find any of them in the first place. I figure Mr. Buntline wasted a trip out here. As you know well, mountain men are a different breed, for the most part. I never knew one who could be called long-winded about what goes on up there."

Smoke recalled his introduction to mountain men and their habits. "Preacher wouldn't talk to other folks about it. Puma could be as talkative as a clam when somebody asked him about the mountains."

Louis glanced at him. "Preacher had a tremendous influence on you, didn't he?"

For a moment, Smoke closed his eyes, forgetting

the killings only minutes ago to think back to his upbringing. "More than anyone will ever know," he said. "I reckon it was the little things, not just how to survive in the wilds or how to use a gun or a knife or my fists. It was the way he took things in stride that I remember most. No matter how rough things got, no matter how bad any situation turned out to be, Preacher always kept his head. I never saw him scared. He never let his anger show when somebody crossed him. He was a man of damn few words, but when he talked it was a real good idea to listen. Never heard him say things twice, or ask a man but once to do what he wanted done. I learned real early to pay close attention to everything he told me, that there was a reason behind it. Nothing ever surprised him, either, no matter how bad it was. I used to think Preacher expected everything to go wrong. I was nearly grown by the time I understood that was his way of being ready for the worst."

Louis was studying Smoke's face. "I hear tell no one knows if Preacher is still alive. He'd be an old man by now. . . ."

Smoke remembered his conversation with Puma Buck, asking the same question one night before the battle with Sundance Morgan and his gang.* "I asked Puma what he thought one night. He said as long as there was beaver to be trapped up high, or grizzlies on the prowl, he didn't figure it was time for Preacher to cross over. I think that was his way of telling me something he was sworn not to tell, that Preacher is alive up yonder somewhere. Like you say, he'd be getting on up in years by now and maybe it's his pride

* *Vengeance of the Mountain Man*

that won't let him come down to show himself after age has robbed him of a few things, maybe some of his eyesight and hearing, some aching joints or an old wound that didn't heal. I respect him too much to go off looking for him even if he is alive in the emptiest parts of the high lonesome. Knowing Preacher like I do, I know if he wanted to see me or anybody else, he'd come looking for 'em, or send word. I've been thinking about it for years now, off and on. A prideful man is too proud to be humbled by old age in front of anyone else. I've got it figured he's still up there, hunting and fishing, exploring the last stretches of wild country. He's a mountain man all the way through, and his kind don't need people to enjoy what's around him."

"Maybe I shouldn't have brought the subject up," Louis observed, lighting another cigar with a sputtering lucifer. "I didn't mean to open pages in a closed book."

Smoke shrugged. "The book on Preacher isn't closed until I get word he's gone, or find his bones on some high mountain ridge someplace. As far as I'm concerned, he's still up there, having one hell of a good time living the way he wants."

Pearlie walked over, having overheard part of their conversation. "Puma said he'd lay money Preacher was still alive, that night me an' Cal got took to his cabin."

Louis gave Pearlie a stare. "I think the subject ought to be dropped right now, Pearlie." He looked toward a waiter with a tray laden with steaming plates. "Here comes your breakfast. If you want, I'll have someone tell Cal his food is ready."

"I don't think the young 'un is up to it just yet,"

Pearlie replied, "but I'll walk outside an' ask. The boy's seen a right smart share of killin' in his short years, but when he got a good look up close at some of them bullet holes, his belly went to doin' a flip-flop, which ain't the natural place to put no big passel of food. Like invitin' a schoolmarm to ride a pitchin' bronc."

Louis laughed, casting a sideways glance in Smoke's direction. "I know one schoolmarm who's up to the task. Sally can ride a bucking horse as well as any cowboy in this country."

Smoke's thoughts went to Sally. He'd promised her only this morning that they'd winter up in an old cabin high above Sugarloaf for a spell, so they could spend some time alone and perhaps encounter a few of the wandering mountain men still living in the Rockies northwest of the ranch. "She's a good hand with a horse," Smoke agreed. "She's a right decent hand when it comes to handling men, like her husband. I've never laid claim to being the smartest feller in Colorado Territory, but she can outsmart me damn near any time she takes the notion. When she's after something she wants, she can be deadlier than a two-headed rattler. Worst thing is, she lets me think I'm getting my way every time. A time or two I've actually believed it."

Pearlie shook his head in agreement. "Miz Jensen knows how to handle a man, all right. She'll come out the door smilin', like all she wants is to say howdy-do, when what she's really after is a cord of wood chopped or a load of hay pitchforked in the wagon fer the cows. Every time I see her smile at me I feel like I oughta take off runnin', 'cause there's sure as hell some work she wants done." He grinned when his plate of steak and eggs was put before him. "That's another thing 'bout Miz Jensen. She ain't above workin' a man to death with bribes. She'll bake up a real sweet peach pie, or fix a batch of them bearclaws with brown sugar, an' open every window in the house so a man goes plumb crazy over the smell. Sooner or later a hungry feller is jus' naturally gonna be drawn to the house on account of them wonderful smells, an' that's when she springs her trap. She'll git one of them pretty smiles on her face, and start tellin' me 'bout them delicious pies or whatever she's bakin', an' I know I'm caught, trapped like a bear in a shallow cave. Then she'll up an' invite me an' Cal to have a little taste of what she's been cookin', right after we git a load of wood piled up next to the kitchen door. What's a starvin' man supposed to do?"

It was Smoke's turn to chuckle over Pearlie's recollections when it came to Sally, as his own plate was set on the table in front of him. "Pearlie's right as rain. I'm married to a woman who knows how to get what she wants . . . one way or another."

As he was about to knife into his steak, Caleb Walz came into the saloon. Walz was Big Rock's part-time undertaker, when he wasn't in the act of cutting hair at his barber shop. Caleb tipped his derby hat to everyone, glancing at the bodies, a hint of a grin raising the corners of his mouth. "Looks like somebody drummed up a little business for me real early," he said in his perpetual monotone. "Whoever it was, I'm obliged."

Four

Ned Buntline had grown exceedingly frustrated over the past few weeks in his unsuccessful quest to interview some of the last of the old-time mountain men. Up on the Yellowstone he had finally been able to track down Major Frank North, leader of the famous Pawnee scouts. North had turned him down cold when he asked for an interview, stating flatly he believed dime novels were trash, a pack of lies, refusing to give Ned even a moment of his time other than to tell him to be on his way. A slap in the face, Ned thought, guiding his surefooted mule up a steep ridge roughly forty miles as the crow flies to the northwest of Big Rock in Colorado Territory. North had to know Ned had been responsible for Buffalo Bill Cody's rise to fame, along with other Wild West characters he'd glorified in his books. It hadn't been necessary for Major North to be so rude about it.

Now, in northwestern Colorado, Ned was trying to track down a few genuine mountain men for a series of stories that would set easterners on their ears. From a list given him by the old scout Alvah Dunning, Ned was searching for men with names like Puma Buck and Huggie Charles and Del Rovare, or the deadly gunfighter turned mountain man named Smoke Jensen. And there were others, a legendary figure known only as Preacher who many suspected to be dead of old age by now, one of the most elusive of all the early mountain pioneers, so that little was actually known about him or even what he looked like. Some claimed Preacher was only a figment of lesser men's imaginations, that he never existed at all except in stories told around mountain campfires, a dark hero of sorts with a penchant for killing anyone who intruded into his high country domain unless they crossed these stretches of the Rockies in peace, without disturbing it. But when it came to mountain men with a penchant for killing, all his sources were in agreement. Smoke Jensen was said to be a killing machine in this part of the West, a man not to be trifled with. If just half the stories Ned had heard about Jensen were true, he could be the man eastern readers would devour. Finding him, finding Jensen, was relatively easy, Ned was told. Jensen owned a high meadow ranch called Sugarloaf, having come down from the mountains a few years back to marry a woman from back east and live a quieter life, although as the stories went his existence was anything but quiet. Getting Jensen to talk to him was going to be the trick, according to those who knew about him or had made his acquaintance in the past. Jensen was a man of few words, and words were what Ned needed from him. The proposition promised to be touchy. Difficult.

Following a map given to him by an elderly Indian scout at a settlement named Glenwood Springs, Ned rode his brown mule slowly into higher altitudes, where it was rumored Puma Buck, Huggie Charles, and Del Rovare hunted and trapped. Perhaps with some sort of personal introduction from one of them to Smoke Jensen, he might just get what he came to Colorado to find . . . true stories of the exploits of mountain men. He hoped he might even be able to find out if this fellow they called Preacher actually existed, if he might still be alive and willing to talk.

Still, Ned was haunted by something Major North had told him in those few brief minutes they talked. North had said, "A man's got to *earn* his knowledge of the high lonesome, Mr. Buntline. No real mountain man is gonna hand it to you like a piece of cake. If you go lookin' for a man who knows the mountains, and if you find one, he ain't likely to tell you a damn thing."

Ned wondered if this would turn out to be the truth, making his ride to Colorado Territory a waste of time.

At the top of the ridge, Ned's mule stopped suddenly and snorted, pricking its ears forward. On a mountain slope across the valley, he saw a giant brown grizzly ambling slowly among tall ponderosa pines. Ned glanced down at the Henry rifle booted to his saddle . . . he was an expert marksman and this would be an easy shot . . . until he recalled what the old scout at Glenwood Springs told him.

"If you aim to find yourself a mountain man or two you'd best remember a couple of things."

"What's that?" Ned had asked.

"If they're close by, they'll be watchin' you, to see how you handle yourself. When you come across a wild critter, don't shoot it 'less you aim to eat it or wear its hide to stay warm. Those critters are as much a part of the high lonesome as them mountains themselves. Don't kill nothin' you ain't gotta kill to stay alive."

Ned had digested this bit of news. Hunting only for

sport was frowned upon by mountain men. "What's the other thing? You said there were a couple . . ."

The old man had almost laughed. "Learn to sleep with one eye open, son, or you'll be the one who gets a taste of lead. I done told you where to look for ol' Puma Buck an' Huggie Charles an' some of them others. Could be you won't be so happy if you was to find 'em. Depends on the mood they's in, an' how you go 'bout handlin' yourself whilst you're up there. An' watch yourself real close 'round Smoke Jensen. Be my advice you act real polite. If he don't care to talk about his high country days, or tell you 'bout Preacher, you'd be well advised to clear out of Sugarloaf as quick as that mule can carry you."

Ned watched the grizzly, discarding any notion of shooting it simply for the sake of proving he had good aim.

"No sense buying into trouble," he muttered, urging the mule forward with his heels.

Turning north, Ned had ridden only a quarter mile before he caught sight of a tiny log cabin nestled in a grove of pines that overlooked a ravine choked with brush. Even from a distance he could tell the cabin hadn't seen much use lately, or any repairs to its mud-chinked logs. But the cabin was a starting place, and he rode toward it. His mule still seemed uneasy even though he had left the grizzly moving in another direction.

A voice from a stand of pines to his left made his heart stop beating.

"Them's mighty fancy duds you's wearin' fer a man travelin' empty spaces!"

Ned jerked his mule to a halt, looking in the direction of the voice, finding nothing but tree trunks and shadows. He took a deep breath to calm himself. "You scared me. I wasn't expecting anyone else to be here."

"Coulda killed you if'n I took the notion."

Ned felt fear forming a ball in his belly. "I hope you're not a killer, whoever you are. My name's Ned Buntline and I'm looking for a couple of mountain men . . . men by the name of Puma Buck, Huggie Charles, or Preacher."

A dry laugh came from the trees. "Puma's dead. Got killed nigh onto a year ago. Huggie runs traps east of here. As to the feller you called Preacher, ain't but one man livin' who knows where he is, an' that's Preacher hisself."

"Then Preacher really does exist? He's not just a campfire tale?"

A silence followed. Ned was still nervous, wondering if he was in the man's gunsights now.

"Maybe he does an' maybe he don't," the voice replied. "You ain't said what you want with a mountain man."

"Just to talk to them. To hear tales about what it's like to live up here. I'm a writer. I write books for people back in the eastern states who'll never see this beautiful country. They love reading my stories about the West."

Another silence, shorter. "What makes you think Huggie'll talk to you anyways? He ain't inclined to use no oversupply of words."

"I was only hoping he would. I didn't think it would hurt to ask him. No one told me Puma Buck was dead. I'd also planned to talk to Smoke Jensen."

A laugh. "He's worse'n Huggie when it comes to waggin' his tongue. To say he's quiet would be like sayin' a beaver's got fur."

"I thought I'd try. I was warned he was dangerous."

"Fer a man who claims to make a livin' with words you sure as hell ain't been usin' the right ones. Smoke's a peaceable man when he ain't pushed, but he don't take kindly to gents who try an' ride rough-shod over nobody. There's men buried all over these here mountains who figured they could take what they wanted from gentler folks who knowed Smoke Jensen."

"I only wanted a chance to talk to him about some of his exploits so I could write about it. If I may be so bold as to ask, who might you be? I can't see you from here."

"If I'd wanted you to see me I'd have showed myself. You got a rifle, an' there's a pistol under that fancy coat. Till I knowed what you was after, I was stayin' right where I'm at. As to my name, there's some who call me Griz. That's short fer a grizzly bear, case you didn't know. I go by Grizzly Cole when I git asked my full handle. I'm acquainted with Huggie Charles an' Smoke Jensen, if it matters, an' I knowed ol' Puma Buck as well as I knowed my own name. But till I know more about who the hell you are an' what you're after, climb down off 'n that mule an' keep yer hands where I can see 'em. You reach fer that pistol an' I swear I'll kill you, mister. Now git down."

Ned was careful to keep both hands in plain sight as he swung down to the ground, holding the mule's reins. He wondered if this might be a piece of luck. Was he having his first encounter with a real mountain man?

Five

"I assure you, Mr. Cole, that I mean you no harm," Ned told him as he stood in front of his mule with his palms spread. "I only want to talk to a few mountaineers, the man who opened up this territory."

A shadow moved behind a pine trunk deep in the forest, and there was the brief glint of sunlight on a rifle barrel. A thin figure clad in buckskins came silently between the trees in Ned's direction.

"I kin assure you, mister, that I wasn't worried 'bout you doin' me no harm . . . not the way you rode up here in plain sight like a damn greenhorn. If a bunch of them Utes or Shoshoni was still huntin' white men's scalps, yer hair'd have been decoratin' some warrior's lodgepole tomorrow mornin'. It was the other way 'round when it comes to bein' in harm's way, Mr. Buntline. Any time I wanted, I coulda killed you quicker'n snuff makes spit."

Ned hadn't realized he'd made such a target of himself, yet neither had he expected to run across a mountain man so soon, figuring they'd be higher up in summertime, farther from the closest settlements. "I was told the Indian troubles were over in this part of the Rockies, so I felt I had nothing to fear if I rode out in the open."

The buckskin-clad outline of Grizzly Cole came to the edge of the forest. Ned could see a snowy beard surrounding his face and white hair falling below his shoulders. A rifle was balanced loosely in his right hand, and a huge pistol, probably a Walker Colt .44, was stuck in a belt fashioned from animal skin strips. While not one of his sources on the subject of mountain men had ever mentioned the name Grizzly Cole, Ned had a feeling Cole was one of the old-time mountaineers he'd been looking for.

"That's mostly true," Cole agreed, at last stepping out into slanted sunlight so Ned could see him clearly. "The Utes are at peace with the white man now, an' them Shoshoni don't range this far south no more. But a man had oughta practice bein' careful with his hide no matter how much he knows 'bout a stretch of the country. Things can change real sudden-like."

Ned felt somewhat more relaxed now. It did not appear Cole meant to harm him, not by the way he stood with his rifle lowered and his other hand empty. "Are you one of the early mountain men to come to this region?" he asked.

Cole's deeply wrinkled face twisted with a touch of humor, a grin of sorts. "Me? Hell no, I wasn't one of the first. Fact is, I come real late to this country, after Preacher an' Puma an' a whole bunch of others. I reckon you could say I'm a newcomer to these parts. Hardly been here more'n twenty years."

It was the mention of Preacher's name that caught Ned's full attention. "So there really is, or was, a mountain man by the name of Preacher?"

"He sure as hell weren't no ghost, if that's what you're thinkin'."

"Is he still alive? Would he talk to me?"

Now Cole wore a guarded look, shifting his weight to the other foot. Knee-high moccasins with beadwork and porcupine quills, badly worn in places, protected his feet. "I ain't in the business of answerin' questions. I trap beaver an' hunt a few griz now an' then fer their skins . . . that's where I got my handle, the one I go by. I done told you more'n I shoulda, how Puma was dead, an' where to look fer Huggie." He paused, and it seemed he was thinking. "I'll tell you this much, Mr. Buntline, so it'll save you some time. You ain't gonna find Preacher 'less he wants to be found, an' that's if he's still alive. He'd be close to ninety years old now, if he ain't crossed over the Big Divide up yonder in the sky. He never was a sociable feller, I hear tell."

"But have you actually met him?"

"Nope. Ain't many folks alive who kin say they did. One is Smoke Jensen, only Smoke ain't gonna tell you nothin' 'bout ol' Preacher. Preacher nearly raised Smoke, case you didn't know, an' I've heard it said even Smoke don't know if Preacher is still alive somewheres."

"Why would they cut off all communication between them if they were once so close?"

"Yer askin' the wrong feller, but I reckon it's what Preacher wanted . . . to live out the last of his years by hisself up in these here mountains."

Ned wanted more from Cole. "I've got a sack of Arbuckles in my packs. I'd be happy to build a fire and offer you a cup, just for the information you already gave me, a gesture of friendship or whatever you wish to call it."

Cole frowned, and it appeared he was sizing Ned up far more critically before he agreed to coffee.

"A cup of that Arbuckles do sound mighty nice, but I ain't gonna trade no more information 'bout my friends for it. You git that through yer head aforehand."

Ned nodded quickly. "I won't ask about your friends. You can tell me anything you want about yourself, if you wish to, or we can simply share a cup of coffee and I'll be on my way."

Cole glanced upslope at the old cabin Ned had seen earlier. "Bring yer mule. There's a firepit an' some seasoned wood up yonder. I use that ol' place from time to time, if'n I git caught in a snowstorm come winter. Ain't nobody lives there no more. Used to belong to a helluva mountain man . . ."

"Whose cabin was it?" Ned asked.

Cole gave him a stern look. "I done told you I ain't gonna talk 'bout none of my friends, them that's crossed over, an' them that ain't."

Ned blew steam away from the rim of his cup, all the while examining Grizzly Cole closely. Cole had to be near sixty, weathered skin and snowy hair, gnarled hands, rheumy eyes that had surely seen so many things he needed for his stories about the men who'd first explored these wild mountains. But Cole was not about to be tricked into telling him anything he wasn't willing to say, Ned judged.

"There ain't many beaver left in this part of the lonesome," he said. "Used to be beaver dams every quarter mile on these creeks. They got trapped real hard by men who didn't understand nature. You gotta take some an' leave some, so they'll multiply an' raise a new crop every spring."

"Experienced men like Preacher or Smoke Jensen and Puma Buck wouldn't have trapped them out, so it had to be others who did this to good beaver country."

Cole eyed him. "I done warned you I ain't gonna talk 'bout none of my friends. But you's right 'bout the three you mentioned. They knowed Mother Nature's ways, all right. If'n this high country never saw nobody but their kind, it'd still be plumb thick with beaver an' every breed o' critter there is. That's what put ol' Preacher an' Smoke on the warpath a long time back, when men come up here to change things. Some came with cattle to push other grazin' animals out. Some showed up with cross-cut saws to cut timber. There was a few who didn't bring nothin' but bad intentions. That's a part of what put Smoke Jensen into the gunfighter's trade."

Griz Cole was telling Ned far more than he meant to without realizing it, with a slip of the tongue now and then. "I'm going to ask Jensen if he'll talk to me about some of it. Readers back east would be fascinated."

"The only thing he's liable to tell you is to skedaddle if you ask him about the past. Huggie might talk to you a little, an' Del Rovare can git kinda windy at times, 'specially if his tongue got loosened with a dab o' whiskey. But there ain't none of 'em gonna tell you much, Mr. Buntline. These men ain't city folk with an inclination towards idle talk." He looked off at the mountain peaks around them, toying with his coffee cup for a time. "It takes a man who likes his own company to live up here, an' most of us don't have no hankerin' for outsiders who come nosin' around. Winters git long an' lonesome for some. Me, I like the sound of fallin' snowflakes on pine limbs, the howl of a north wind at night when the fire's warm inside a cabin."

"Do very many mountain men have a woman, a wife?"

"Some. Not many. Womenfolk ain't built for the loneliness or this rough life. There's a few. Smoke's got him a lady who takes to the high lonesome like a bear takes to honey. Sally's built different than most women. Puma used to have him a Ute squaw. Cute little thing. She died of the smallpox back in '59 I believe it was. Injuns ain't got much tolerance for a white man's diseases."

"Did Puma himself die of old age?"

Cole gave him a hard stare. "That ain't my story to tell, Mr. Buntline. You'll have to ask somebody else." He drained a big swallow of Arbuckles from his cup, squatting across the rock-lined firepit from Ned. "I've told you too much already. Much as I enjoyed this coffee, you an' me are done talkin'. If you ride north, maybe ten miles or so, you'll be in Huggie Charles's trappin' range. Now I'll warn you, he can be a real disagreeable feller at times, so don't go tryin' to push yer luck with him. You can say I told you where to look fer him. It'll be up to him if he decides to show hisself, or blow a tunnel plumb through yer head with his rifle. Depends."

"On what?"

"On the mood he's in, an' on how you handle yourself. If it was me, I wouldn't shoot no game or raise no ruckus. Just ride quiet an' mind yer own business. He'll look you up if he's curious 'bout why yer there." He drank the last of his coffee and stood up, wincing, as though he felt a pain somewhere in one of his legs. Then he bent down and lifted his Sharps .52 caliber rifle, holding it by the muzzle. "Good luck, Mr. Buntline. I'm grateful fer the Arbuckles. Don't figure on gittin' what you came here for. Them readers you've got is most likely to have to read somethin' else. Stories from a real mountain man are gonna be mighty hard to come by."

"I'm obliged for what you've been willing to tell me, Mr. Cole, and for the directions." He stood up and dusted off the seat of his pants. "Just one more thing. You said Smoke Jensen is running a ranch now, and I know it's close to Big Rock. That must mean he's given up his old ways, using a gun the way he did in the past."

Grizzly Cole wagged his head. "Yer dead wrong, son. Smoke ain't changed one bit when it comes to gunplay. He's every bit as dangerous as he ever was, a fact yer liable to find out if you press him any. Just last year, he put a feller by the name of Sundance Morgan into an early grave, along with a pack o' his hired guns, *pistoleros* from down around the Mexican border. He ain't given up nothin' fer the sake of ranchin' or anything else, an' if you happen to be in the wrong spot at the wrong time, you can git a firsthand look, if you live to tell about it."

"I'm not looking for trouble."

Cole smiled. "You said you was lookin' for Smoke Jensen. What you ain't understood just yet is them two are the same, if you ain't an acquaintance or a neighbor of his."

"But I'm not here to cause him any trouble . . ."

"Askin' him about the past is gonna put him on

the prod. If I was you, I'd find out 'bout mountain men some other way."

Cole turned away from the fire. Ned tossed out the grounds from his tiny coffeepot as Cole started toward a line of trees behind the abandoned cabin.

"Thanks again, Mr. Cole, for everything you've told me. I am in your debt. I'll be very careful while I'm up here."

Grizzly Cole ignored his remark, taking long quiet strides up a grassy slope with his rifle over his shoulder. Ned watched him until he went out of sight in shadows below the pines.

"At last," he muttered under his breath. He'd just had his first talk with a mountain man, and learned a number of things he could use. The heroes he would write about later on would be like Griz, hardened by an unbelievably brutal and lonely way of life into strong, silent types. This initial meeting with a true mountaineer had given him far more than he had hoped. Now it was time to look for more men of Cole's strange breed, until he had enough to make characters come to life on the pages of the series of books he planned to write about them.

Six

Smoke let Horse pick his own gait, an easy jog trot that was only a little faster than the buckboard loaded with supplies, to keep him well out in front of Pearlie and Cal and the flour, fatback, sugar, coffee beans, and other necessaries Sally put on her list, along with iron hinges for a sagging barn door, horseshoes and nails, saddle soap and axle grease, and a load of planking to fix a slant-roof cowshed. As the summer ended, all ranch chores needed to be attended to, despite not owning cows or bulls after selling off their herd to the Duggan sisters. This was a winter Smoke and Sally planned to spend alone, more or less, if you didn't count visits with some of Smoke's old friends in the mountains. Pearlie and Cal would be watching the ranch and saddle stock while Smoke and Sally enjoyed time together in a cabin that once was home to Puma Buck, a two-room affair with a dogrun and sod roof, plenty of shelter from the worst storms in a deep mountain valley where wintertime was both beautiful and bitterly cold. In the spring, Smoke planned to head down to New Mexico Territory, along with a handful of neighbors, to pick up a few prized Hereford bulls and a herd of Mexican longhorns in order to produce a hardier breed with more beef. It was an idea they'd talked about for some time, and after a telegram from John Chisum, called the Cattle King of New Mexico, offering them bulls at a good price, the decision was made. It would be a long and rugged drive, coming back north with spooky longhorn cows and the gentler, slower Hereford bulls, but well worth the increase in beef their offspring would produce. Smoke felt good about the notion. And about spending a winter with Sally where he could have her all to himself for a while, enjoying a few months without the responsibilities of ranch work and tending cattle.

Crossing a wooded switchback, Smoke heard a voice coming from a crossing over Aspen Creek down below, a high-pitched voice full of anger. He heeled the Palouse forward at a lope to find out what the shouting was all about, to see if a neighbor or a friend might be in trouble.

When he came to the caprock at the top of the switchback, he saw a sight he didn't fully understand at first. Two men were standing beside a team of mules at the crossing, mules hitched to a wagon loaded with wooden crates and barrels. He didn't recognize either one of them, for they were strangers to this part of the country—he was sure of it, and sometimes finding strangers close to Sugarloaf made him edgy.

Then he saw what was causing the disturbance. One of the men was whipping the mules' hindquarters with a blacksnake whip, and it was evident the mules had balked at the creek, refusing to cross, which was sometimes a trait in certain mules that hadn't been trained properly. The crack of the whip and the men shouting, one of them trying to force the off-side mule to take a step into the stream by way of striking it across the rump with a wood fence stave, got Smoke's dander up.

"Damn fools," he muttered, urging Horse down toward the creek at a full gallop. "Can't stand to see a man whip an animal when it don't understand what it's bein' whipped for. . . ."

It really wasn't his affair, and he knew it, but when a mule or a horse got a whipping it didn't deserve or understand, Smoke was likely to take a side with the animal even when it didn't belong to him. At times he wondered about the contradiction, the absence of feeling when men killed each other and the deep sorrow he experienced when an animal suffered needlessly. One mule could have easily been unharnessed and led across the stream so the other would follow on its own . . . but it was apparent these two men knew nothing about mules or their inclinations. If one mule balked at a stream, most often the other did. Smoke was about to offer his help whether it was wanted or not, since these weren't men he recognized as being from these parts.

The men saw him coming and one moved his right hand to the butt of a pistol belted around his waist, quite possibly a very deadly mistake if he'd pulled it out. Smoke pulled down on the big stud's reins when he got within earshot.

"Take it easy on those mules, boys. There's an easier way to get across."

"Who the hell asked you to interfere?" one bearded man asked in a low growl.

Smoke brought his Palouse to a halt. "Nobody," he said in a calm, even voice. "It's just my nature. Can't stand to watch a man whip a mule when the man's got less sense than the animal. I can show you how to get those mules and your wagon across."

"You're a smart-mouth son of a bitch, an' you god-damn sure are inclined to stick your nose in where it ain't wanted, whoever the hell you are."

Smoke gave both men a humorless grin. Then he spoke to the man who had spoken to him. "You're wrong on two counts, mister. I ain't no part of a son of a bitch, and I put my nose wherever I please when an animal's bein' injured. Now, get your hand off the butt of that pistol or I swear I'll make you eat it. If you give me a couple of minutes, I'll have those mules across the creek and you'll be on your way."

The cowboy touching his gun made no move to lift his hand away, and the gleam in his eye was a warning that Smoke had best be ready for trouble. He swung down, leaving the Palouse ground-hitched, his eyes fastened on the man resting his palm on his gun grips.

Smoke walked toward them, both hands dangling beside the brace of pistols he carried. "Get your hand off that gun or I'll make good on my promise," he said, approaching the cowboy whose hearing needed improvement.

"To hell with you, mister!" the man snapped, closing his fingers unconsciously for a quick pull, a signal to a man like Smoke that the time for talking had ended.

Smoke clawed one .44 free with the speed of a rattler's strike, thumbing back the hammer as he leveled it at the cowboy's belly. He halted a few feet away with his feet spread slightly apart as the cowboy's eyes became saucers, staring down the dark muzzle of

Smoke's Colt before he could clear leather. When Smoke spoke to him, it was in a hoarse voice.

"My mama used to say that when somebody don't listen, it can be on account of too much wax built up in their ears." He took a step closer. "She told me the best way to clean out somebody's ears is to jar some of that built-up wax loose." With the same lightning speed, Smoke struck the cowboy with the back of his free hand, a blow so powerful it sent the man reeling backward until he stumbled into the shallow stream and fell down on his rump in a foot of icy snowmelt gurgling down from the mountain peaks still capped by last year's snow.

"Shit!" the cowboy exclaimed, shaking his head to clear it, scrambling back to his feet with his denims soaked. Only now he had his gun hand held to his face, where an angry red welt was forming, after Smoke had knocked him into the water. He rubbed his sore cheek a moment while his companion merely stood there near the mules holding the fence stave. "You had no call to do that to me!"

"I never ask a man to do anything twice," Smoke replied, his gun still aimed in front of him. "I saw you whippin' these mules and it didn't sit well with me. When a man's dumber than the animal he's tryin' to use, giving it a blacksnake treatment it doesn't understand, I've got plenty of reason to slap the hell out of that kind of fool. I'm gonna get your team across this creek as soon as my ranch hands come over that ridge behind me, and after that's done, you can be on your way. But if I ever see you whip mules like that again, I'll take that same black-snake and work your ass over with it, same as you done to those poor dumb animals."

The other cowboy spoke for the first time. He was glowering at Smoke, holding the fence stave like a club. "You wouldn't be talkin' so big if it wasn't fer them guns, stranger."

"Is that so?" Smoke asked as he heard Pearlie and Cal in the buckboard rattle downslope toward him. "In that case, since you believe in what you say so strong, I'll take 'em off and we can test your idea." He examined the bearded gent with the club a little closer, making sure he wasn't carrying a gun, finding him to be thick-muscled, big-handed, probably the sort who thought he was tough with his fists.

Smoke turned to the cowboy standing shivering wet in the creek "Toss that pistol out with two fingers. Pitch it up here. Soon as my boys get here they'll make sure nobody goes for a gun while me and your pardner settle this."

"You ain't got the guts to fight Clyde bare-handed."

"We can fight with feather dusters or claw hammers, for all I care," Smoke replied, watching the cowboy lift his gun out very carefully to throw it near Smoke's feet. He picked it up, then holstered his .44 and removed his gunbelts, placing them in the back of the wagon. He spoke over his shoulder just as Pearlie drove up. "Boys, make sure that other feller stays right where he is while I teach this big fool a lesson."

Pearlie drew his pistol. "I reckon you'll explain after you're done beatin' this poor bastard half to death," Pearlie said matter-of-factly, like the outcome was certain.

Smoke turned to the man with the wood stave. "Not much to it, really," he answered back. "What we've got here is two of the dumbest assholes who ever tried to drive a team of mules. I watched 'em use a whip on this team, and that toothpick the big one is carryin' now. I can't hardly stand to watch men hurt an animal like that. I asked 'em real nice to stop, only they was not of the same mind on it. I'm gonna teach this one how it feels to have the hell knocked out of him with that very same club."

Clyde answered in a snarl. "You gotta come git it first, you cocky son of a bitch. Ain't gonna be easy."

It was Cal who said quietly, "I'm real sure you're gonna regret callin' Mr. Jensen a son of a bitch, mister, not to make mention of what you done to them mules."

"Are you Smoke Jensen?" the other cowboy asked, just as Smoke made a lunge toward Clyde before Clyde was ready for it. Swinging a powerful right hook at Clyde's jaw, Smoke felt his knuckles crack when they landed hard against bone just as Clyde drew back with his fence stave.

Clyde grunted when Smoke's fist struck him, and it seemed a mighty gust of wind lifted him off his feet, snapping his head around so that all he could see was mountains on the far side of the stream. Clyde staggered a few wobbly steps and then he knelt down as if he meant to pray, dropping the club beside him, his arms hanging limply at his sides.

Smoke walked up behind him and picked up the stave while Clyde blinked furiously, trying to clear his head. Smoke took a pair of short steps around the kneeling figure until he stood in front of him. "That's what it's like when a man hits another man in the head," Smoke explained, sounding calm. "And now I'm gonna show you how those mules felt when you were whippin' their asses with this stick."

He swung a vicious blow with the stave, striking

Clyde across the left cheek of his buttocks with a resounding whack.

"Yeeeow!" Clyde shrieked, tumbling forward until he landed on his chest with his palms covering the seat of his pants, his face twisted in agony.

Smoke took a deep breath, tossing the stick aside. "Now you know what the mules wanted to say. Remember how it feels to have the wood laid to your own ass. Me an' my cowboys will cross that team over the way it oughta be done. And I meant what I said. If I ever see or hear of either one of you whippin' a mule again when it ain't necessary, I'll come lookin' for you. Believe me, you don't want that to happen."

Pearlie was already climbing down from the buckboard. "I'll unharness the lop-eared mule an' lead it across," he said as if the remedy was all too clear. "Cal can drive the wagon across as soon as I git to the other side."

Smoke returned to buckle on his pistols as Pearlie went about the harness task, selecting what was obviously the gentler mule to lead it across.

Clyde came to his hands and knees shakily and shook his head again. "You broke one of my goddamn teeth when you slugged me," he complained, running his tongue over a chipped tooth.

Smoke almost ignored him, until he said, "Count yourself real lucky I'm not still breakin' 'em out one at a time. After that wagon gets across, I want you boys harnessed and headed on your way, wherever that is. But don't stay in this country too long or I might change my mind about leavin' the teeth in both of your mouths."

"I've heard of you, Smoke Jensen," the cowboy in

wet pants said. "I reckon me an' Clyde are real sorry we said what we did to you."

Smoke gave him a withering stare. "Save your goddamn apologies for those mules They've each got one coming after what you did to 'em with that club and whip."

He mounted Horse and watched Cal drive the loaded wagon easily across the shallow creek. Smoke waited until Cal and Pearlie waded back and climbed in the buckboard, then he glanced over to the men harnessing the mule.

"Let's head home, boys, so Sally won't be wondering why we're late."

Pearlie shook the reins over his buckboard team. He had a grin on his face. "I'll swear we had a loose hub on this here buckboard, so she won't have to be told the truth . . . that you killed two men early this mornin' an' just beat the hell out of two more over a pair of stubborn mules."

Smoke returned Pearlie's grin as he swung Horse toward the ranch. "Won't do any good to lie to Sally. It'd be a waste of good breath. She'll know there was a little trouble when she looks me in the eye. Damnedest thing I ever saw, how she knows before I ever open my mouth."

Seven

Jessie Evans, clear blue eyes shining below a mop of sandy hair under a flat brim hat, turned his stocky torso toward one of his men where they sat their horses hidden in a line of piñon pines above the Pecos River. Bill Pickett was watching a handful of John Chisum's cowboys in the valley driving a herd of market-ready steers upriver, beeves for a government contract with the Apache reservation west of Ruidoso, New Mexico Territory.

"This is gonna be too easy," Jessie said, grinning, some of his front teeth yellowed by tobacco stains. "Ain't but seven of them an' they're range cowboys who can't shoot straight. Let's make damn sure we kill 'em all so there won't be no witnesses who can identify us."

"It don't make a difference to me," Pickett replied, eyelids gone narrow. Killing was a passion with him, Jessie knew, after years of rustling cattle together. Pickett was a raw-boned man who had a preference for shotguns at close range, once stating that he liked to see his victims' faces when he blew them apart, the look of surprise they wore when shotgun pellets shredded their skin. He told Jessie he liked the smell of blood and gunpowder when it got mixed together.

Jessie looked past Pickett to Roy Cooper. Cooper had a big jaw, always jutted angrily, even when he was happy, which was rare unless he was with a woman and a bottle of tequila. "Ready down there, Roy?"

"Ready as I'm gonna be, boss," he said, his deep voice like a rasp across cold iron. He drew a .44 caliber Winchester from a boot tied to his saddle and worked the lever, sending a cartridge into the firing chamber. "I can kill one or two of 'em from here soon as you give the word."

Beyond Cooper, Ignacio Valdez showed off a gold tooth in the front of his mouth "Ready, Señor Jessie," he said, fisting a Mason Colt .44/.40 revolver. "I gon' shoot hell out plenty sons of bitches when you tell me is time."

Last in line was a reed-thin boy, Billy Barlow, a small-time rustler from the Texas panhandle. Jessie didn't fully trust the Barlow kid yet. There was something about him, the way he didn't look at you when you talked to him. But Jimmie Dolan said to hire shootists to get Chisum's cattle so the Murphy Store would get the beef contracts away from Chisum and John Tunstall, and Jessie had put word out all the way to the Mexican border that he was hiring guns to fight a range war. More and more experienced men were showing up at Lincoln to inquire about the job, and before this winter was out, Jessie could easily have fifty hired guns on Dolan's payroll by the time reservation contracts were up for renewal.

"Let's spill some blood," Jessie said savagely, putting a spur to his horse's ribs, freeing his Colt .44 from its holster in an iron grip. Jessie had long forgotten how many men he'd killed over the years, but it was something he knew he was good at. It had never mattered whether a man had his back turned or if he was facing him when he pulled a trigger. A killer for hire couldn't wait all day long to earn his money.

Five galloping horses charged down a rocky slope toward the Pecos, and toward a herd of eighty steers belonging to John Chisum, with seven cowboys pushing them toward Fort Sumner, and a butcher's block. The thunder of pounding hooves ended a silence in the serenity of the lower Pecos region.

Cooper was the first to fire, a booming shot from the back of a running horse that would be difficult for even the best of marksmen.

At the river's edge, a cowboy on a sorrel gelding yelled and barreled off the back of his horse, turning in midair, arms and legs askew, his cry of pain echoing off the bluffs that ran along both sides of the Pecos.

Valdez fired, more to spook the cattle than with any hope of hitting what he aimed at.

Longhorn steers began to run, a stampede that would only add to the confusion, charging along the grassy banks of the river at full tilt.

Jessie aimed his .44 carefully, knowing full well the action of the horse between his knees would worsen his aim. He waited until his gunsights rested on the chest of a terrified cowboy on a prancing pinto.

The pistol slammed into his palm, barking, spitting out a finger of orange flame. Jessie saw the cowhand jerk upright in his saddle. Runaway longhorns raced past the wounded man as he toppled to the ground, lost in a cloud of dust sent up by churning hooves boiling away from the stampede.

Barlow's rifle roared and a horse went down underneath a cowboy spurring frantically to cross the river. The chestnut collapsed, legs thrashing in shallow water, falling on the cowboy to pin him against a shoal of sand and rocks on the far side of the Pecos.

Nice work, Jessie thought, spurring his horse for more speed as he and his men thundered down the embankment. Maybe he'd been wrong about Barlow.

Pickett's shotgun bellowed, rocking him back against the cantle of his saddle, blue smoke erupting from one barrel. A steer bawled and fell on its chest in front of a cowboy trying to escape the melee aboard a goose-rumped bay. When the steer went down in the pathway of the galloping horse, it tripped the mount and sent its rider flying, as though he'd sprouted wings, into the river.

Valdez popped off three shots as quickly as he could pull the trigger, sweeping a hatless vaquero off the side of his running buckskin mare, sending him tumbling into tall prairie grasses near the riverbank.

"Ayii!" Valdez cried, turning his pistol in another direction.

Pickett's shotgun roared again, this time at much closer range to a cowboy whipping his gray pony with the ends of his reins to escape the hail of flying lead.

The man atop the gray did a curious thing . . . he turned to face the shotgun blast, and when he did his face seemed to come apart as pellets ripped away his cheeks. For a moment, there was no sound other than the banging of guns, until the cowboy slid off his charging horse into a stand of bulrushes growing along the edge of the water.

Fear-stricken cattle bounded in every direction, making a noise like honking geese. The herd split into three groups when trees blocked the longhorns' path. One bunch ran northeast, and a second charged across the Pecos, where a shallow spot kept them from having to swim. A third portion of the stampeding steers went straight ahead, crushing everything in its way.

Jessie took careful aim and fired at a cowboy abandoning the herd on a piebald gelding, shooting him in the back between his shoulder blades, driving him out of his saddle with the force of a sledgehammer blow before his horse could cross the river.

"Nice shot!" Cooper yelled, levering another round into his Winchester.

Valdez fired just as Jessie was about to rein south after a lone cowboy making his escape back down the trail running beside the Pecos. The cowboy slumped in his saddle, yet he somehow held onto the saddle horn and continued to rake his spurs into a black gelding's sides.

Jessie swung his horse south . . . there could be no survivors to tell Sheriff Brady about what happened here, or identify any of the attackers.

Behind him, he heard a gun crack. Pickett and Cooper would finish off any wounded men. Pickett would enjoy it. Of all the cold-blooded killers Jessie had known, Pickett had less feelings than any of them.

The cowboy on the black rounded a turn in the trail and for a moment he was out of sight. Jessie spurred harder, asking his big yellow dun for everything it had. The rhythm of its pounding hooves filled his ears. He stood in the stirrups for a better view of what lay ahead. A grove of cottonwoods lining the river prevented him from seeing the fleeing cowhand for a few moments, until his dun carried him past the trees.

A pistol barked suddenly. Jessie felt something tear the left sleeve of his shirt, followed by a burning sensation moving from his shoulder down his arm. In the same instant he saw the cowboy aboard the black horse sitting at the edge of the cottonwood grove.

"You bushwhackin' son of a bitch!" Jessie cried, aiming his pistol carefully before he triggered off a shot while bringing the dun to a bounding halt.

The cowhand rolled out of his saddle . . . his horse bolted away as he fell. He toppled to the ground clutching his belly with a groan.

Jessie stepped off his horse, walking slowly, gun pointed in front of him, to the spot where the Chisum cowboy lay. Jessie gritted his teeth, for the moment ignoring the stinging pain in his left arm until he stood over the fallen man, casting his shadow over a face twisted in agony, the face of a young cowboy hardly old enough to shave.

"You yellow bastard," Jessie hissed, "layin' for me behind those trees like that. You're gunshot, an' I oughta leave you here to die slow. But you pissed me off when you shot me in the arm, so I'm gonna do you a favor. I'm gonna scatter your brains all over this piece of ground. That way, when Big John Chisum or one of his boys finds you, he'll know we ain't just fuckin' around over this beef contract business. It'll be like a message to Chisum, only I ain't gonna sign my name to it."

He aimed down, cocked his single-action Colt, and pulled the trigger, the bang of his .44 like a sudden bolt of lightning striking nearby.

The young cowhand's head was slammed to the ground, blood shooting from a hole in his right temple. A thumb-sized plug of brain tissue dangled from the exit wound, dribbling blood on the caliche hardpan. A momentary twitching of the cowboy's left boot rattled his spur rowel, until his death throes ended abruptly as blood poured from his open mouth.

"I hope you get a good look at this, Chisum," Jessie said tonelessly. "Maybe you won't be so all-fired interested in the beef business."

He turned away to catch his horse, holstering his gun, examining a slight tear in the skin atop his left shoulder, finding it to be little more than a scratch.

He rode back to the scene of the attack just in time to see Bill Pickett standing over a motionless body, his shotgun pointed down. Pickett glanced over his shoulder when he heard Jessie ride up.

"This sumbitch is still breathin'," Pickett said, "only he ain't gonna be much longer." Pickett thumbed back one hammer on his ten-gauge Greener and calmly pulled the trigger, as if he was merely swatting a fly. The big gun roared, pulverizing the skull and neck of the wounded Chisum trail hand, splattering blood and hair and flinty pieces of bone across a six-foot circle of dry buffalo grass.

Pickett grinned. "Pretty sight, ain't it?" he asked, "like breakin' an egg, only it's got blood in it. Sumbitch hadn't oughta signed on with John Chisum in this war. Folks in Lincoln County better learn whose side to be on."

Another gunshot distracted Jessie before he could offer any comment. Upriver, Roy Cooper was down off his horse, his feet spread apart over another body. Jessie thought about how good it was to have men like Pickett and Cooper riding with him. He knew he could count on either one of them in a tight spot.

"Roy found him one," Pickett muttered, sounding as if he had wanted the job himself.

"Let's get those steers rounded up an' head 'em for Bosque Redondo so we can change them brands," Jessie said, reining his horse away from Pickett's bloody execution spot. Off in the distance he could see Valdez and Barlow trying to gather up one bunch of cattle.

"I ain't gettin' paid to handle no runnin' iron," Pickett said as he rode off.

"We've got Mexican vaqueros to do it," he answered back. "You're the same as me. . . . I'd rather have blood on my hands than cow dung. Don't stink near as bad."

Eight

The cow camp at Bosque Redondo was hidden in a piñon forest in an empty section of Lincoln County. Pole corrals held steers being branded, made ready for market, most often with a running iron changing brands belonging to previous owners. Jessie knew few questions were asked by the Territorial militia, since it was merely a police arm of the powerful Santa Fe Ring, as most men called it, a group of crooked politicians headed by Catron and L.G. Murphy. Jimmy Dolan was Murphy's ramrod in Lincoln County, and in this part of the territory, only John Chisum and a few of his followers were brazen enough to buck the Santa Fe Ring with bids on federal government contracts to feed reservation Apaches. But Chisum was bullheaded about it, refusing to knuckle under or sell to Murphy at a lower price. What was building here was a range war over beef. Folks were beginning to call it the Lincoln County War, and Jessie knew it had only just begun.

He sat in the shade of a thatched *ramada*, watching vaqueros work the branding irons, sipping tequila, chewing limes, thinking about yesterday's fight. Roy Cooper was in one of the huts with a Mexican whore. Bill Pickett, as he so often did, was cleaning his guns;

pistols and rifles, and his shotgun. Jessie was about to doze off when he heard someone shout, "Riders comin'!"

Jessie and Pickett scrambled to their feet, wondering if a party of Chisum riders had come for revenge. But what he saw in a ravine twisting into the camp was only a pair of horsemen, a little man in a battered top hat and a Mexican cowboy. However, both were carrying guns.

Jessie relaxed against a roof support of the *ramada* without worrying over the two riders. Two men wouldn't stand a chance against so many Dolan men, no matter how skillful they might be with pistols or rifles.

The pair rode up to him and halted sweat-caked horses in a patch of shade from a piñon limb. The man, only a boy by his appearance, spoke.

"We was told you were hirin' a few men," he said, his thin voice almost girlish, lilting.

"Men is what we're hirin'," Jessie replied, "not schoolboys who ain't old enough to need a razor."

"I'm eighteen," the rider said, his ears sticking out away from his head in an odd fashion. "The name's William Bonney an' this here's Jesus Silva."

"Like I said, we ain't hirin' no kids," Jessie replied in an offhanded way. "Come back in a couple of years."

"We can shoot," Bonney said. "I already killed a man over in Fort Grant, an' that ain't countin' Indians or Mexicans."

Jessie laughed. "You're full of lies, boy. Now ride on outa here before I lose my patience. If you're lookin' for work, you might try the Chisum outfit. Or there's this crazy Englishman by the name of John Tunstall

who's hirin' a few cowboys now an' then. Ask for Dick
Brewer. He's foreman for Tunstall an' he ain't much
older'n you. Appears Mr. Tunstall ain't opposed to
changin' diapers on some of his cowhands."

Bonney stared at him, and Jessie felt a strange sensation when he looked into the young man's green-
flecked eyes. He had buck teeth and looked downright
ridiculous in an old top hat, but there was something
about him. . . .

"You may be sorry you didn't offer us any work,"
Bonney said as he turned his horse. "We heard you
was needin' good men with guns."

Jessie gave him a one-sided grin. "Like I said before, come back in a couple of years, when you're
old enough to grow some chin whiskers."

Bonney and Silva rode off, back down the ravine.
Jessie watched them go, wondering.

Pickett had stopped cleaning his Winchester long
enough to listen to what was being said. "You might
regret that, like the boy said, Jessie," he remarked,
going back to his gun cleaning. "I've got a pretty
good nose for a man who ain't got no fear in him.
That Bonney boy ain't scared of nothin'."

"Maybe he's just too young to know to be scared,"
Jessie offered.

Pickett shook his head. "Age ain't got all that much
to do with it. It's what's in a man's backbone that
counts. He sure did look plumb silly in that ol' hat,
an' them's the worst-lookin' buck teeth I ever saw.
But there may come a time when you wish you'd have
let 'em hire on with us. I hope I'm dead wrong about
it, that we won't be wishin' we had Mr. William Bonney on our side of this fight."

Nine

Smoke's chest and arms glistened with sweat as he split the last of yet another cord of wood piled beside the cabin. It had been hard at first, to see Puma's old log dwelling where he and the Ute girl had lived so long ago, until smallpox took her. There were so many memories here for Smoke, and as colorful fall leaves swirled around him, with the coming of winter he couldn't help a recollection or two, of time he spent with Puma in this aspen forest back when they were younger men, and it saddened him some to think of Puma being gone forever. He told himself that wherever Puma was, there would be mountains and rivers and clear streams.

On the ride up to the cabin he and Sally talked about their plans for an improved cow herd, the Hereford bulls and what Sally said was sure to be a way to raise crossbred breeding stock for the future. Smoke even told her about another idea he'd been toying with . . . to buy a Morgan stallion to cross on their mustang and thoroughbred mares, adding strength and muscle and short-distance speed to the offspring. On the way down to New Mexico he planned to inquire about purchasing a Morgan stud. He grinned when he thought about their three-day trip up to Puma's cabin, how infectious Sally's enthusiasm was when she talked about the Hereford crosses. She was a rancher at heart, with a natural gift for handling livestock, better than most experienced men who made a living off raising cattle. But Smoke's grin was far more than amusement over her excitement when she talked about their future plans . . . it was an unconscious way of showing how much he loved her. He'd decided long ago that Sally had been the best thing that had ever happened to him. She had changed his life and he often wished for the words to tell her how much she truly meant to him.

Smoke rested the axe against the splitting stump and took a look northward. A line of dark clouds was building along the horizon. At these higher altitudes, a storm would mean snow, the first snowstorm announcing the coming of winter. They'd just barely had time to unpack the packhorses, clean out the abandoned cabin and stretch cured deer hides over the windows and rifle ports, repair rawhide hinges on crude plank doors, and clean out the rock chimney. Sally was inside now, fashioning hanging racks for their heavy winter clothing and other essentials, after putting their food staples away on what was left of the shelves Puma had made near the fireplace. They had plenty of warm blankets and a thick buffalo robe given to Smoke by a Shoshoni warrior years back. Last night, Smoke had held Sally in his arms atop that furry buffalo skin, watching her eyes sparkle in the firelight when he kissed her. He vowed to make this winter with her a special time, away from the day-to-day chores around the ranch which were now being done by Pearlie, Cal, and Johnny North . . .

what little there was to do with no beef cattle on the place, only the horse herd and old Rosie, their Jersey milk cow, to attend to. Smoke knew Sally needed the rest as much as he did, not only from ranch work but away from the troubles that seemed to follow Smoke Jensen no matter how peacefully he tried to live now. Trouble had a way of finding him, and he hoped it wouldn't track him down here, in a beautiful mountain valley near the headwaters of the White River, roughly eight thousand feet into the Rockies, where few white men had ever traveled, formerly the hunting ground of the Utes until a treaty with Washington moved them farther west. Here, Smoke could be at peace, spending time alone with his beloved Sally.

Falling aspen leaves showered to the forest floor, a mix of reds, bright yellows, and every shade of brown. Towering ponderosa pines grew thick on the slopes around them. The scent of pine was strong in the air, mingling with the smell of smoke coming from the chimney as Sally prepared their supper. They had plenty of foodstuffs and clothing, and enough firewood for even the most brutal winter, after almost a week of hard labor gathering dead limbs and fallen tree trunks. It had been a wonderful time, as was the ride up with Sally. If it were possible, he loved her more deeply with each passing day.

He heard light footfalls behind him.

"You must be getting old, darling," Sally said, smiling one of her memorable smiles. "I've never seen you needing a rest so often. You used to be able to chop wood all day without stopping to catch your breath every five minutes. I may have to look for a younger man, if this keeps up."

"A younger man would refuse to take all this punishment from a woman, no matter how pretty she was. I'm only slave labor, in your opinion. That would be just like you, to throw me away for a younger man as soon as I've chopped and split all this firewood to keep us warm."

"A younger man could have finished this job in half the time and still had something left for me."

He turned to her, hard muscles gleaming in the sunlight. "I may have a surprise for you tonight, Mrs. Jensen," he told her with mock seriousness. "I may be getting a little long in the tooth, but I can still chop wood all day and make love all night. I hope you feel up to it."

Her smile only widened. "I think I'm developing a headache just now. Maybe another time. Ask me in the spring."

He sauntered over and put his arms around her, staring down into her eyes. "Be careful, pretty lady, or you might force me to tear your clothes off right now and throw you down on a bed of pine needles. I'm not buying any headache stories."

She forced a frown, giving a halfhearted attempt to pull away from his embrace. "You're an animal. I've known it for years. You only brought me up here so you could use me, and I won't stand for it. I'll scream."

He chuckled. "No one will hear you, except for a few grizzlies or an elk or two. Scream your head off, for all I care. I'm taking what's mine."

"You think of me as a piece of property?"

"My property, and if any younger man lays a hand on you I swear I'll kill him. You can include older men in that same bunch." He scowled.

Sally tried to conceal the beginnings of a grin. "Not

only are you an animal, but you're violent, a savage beast. I should have listened to my mother. She warned me about you."

He maintained a stern expression "She did? Exactly what did she say?"

Now Sally was serious for a moment. "She told me that some men are loners, that they can't be tamed or tied to one woman or the same piece of ground for very long. She said it was bred in them, and that I'd never change you from being a solitary mountain man or a drifter."

"She was wrong," he whispered, bending down to kiss her gently on the lips. "She didn't give her daughter enough credit for knowing how to change a man's ways."

She stared deeply into his eyes. "Some things about you will never change, my darling," she told him softly. "You'll always be just a push or a shove away from another fight. You are two different people. One is the gentle man I love so dearly who can't seem to stop showing me or telling me how much he loves me. Then there's the other Smoke Jensen, the man almost everyone in Colorado Territory fears. It's hard to describe, how you can change so quickly. One wrong word, a wrong look, a wrong deed, and you become someone I scarcely recognize. It's not that you can't control your temper. . . . You always seem calm, in control of yourself. But when you get your mind set to go after another man, or a dozen men, for whatever reason, you can't be talked out of it. Not even by me, not even when you know how much it frightens me when I think about the possibility of losing you."

"You worry too much."

"What else can I do when the man I love is putting his life on the line?"

He thought about it for a time. "You can learn to trust me, to trust my instincts for staying alive. Over the years a hell of a lot of men have tried to kill me, for one reason or another. None of 'em got it done, although I've got a nick or two in my hide to show for it. Trust me when I promise you I'll always come home to you."

"It won't stop me from worrying. . . ."

He glanced up at the advancing clouds. "There's a storm coming. Probably means snow, this high, and maybe some rain we need for our pastures down at the ranch."

"You changed the subject, Smoke. We were talking about how much it scares me when you go off on one of your manhunts. Like what happened in Big Rock this summer when those three men came to town looking for Ned Buntline. Louis told me what happened. You could have ignored the way they were looking at you. Instead you prodded them into a gun-fight."

"They were looking for one anyway. I know I've got my share of faults, Sally, but when some gent challenges me, it's just my nature to answer back. Let's talk about something else, like what we're having for supper. Whatever it is, it sure does smell good."

"Venison and wild onions. I found some wild onions down at the creek when I went for a pail of water. And I've got another surprise. The Dutch oven is loaded. I've got it banked with a pile of hot coals, so it'll cook slowly."

"What's in it?" he asked, his mouth already watering.

"You'll have to wait and see, Mr. Jensen. I told you it was a surprise."

"Those tins of peaches. You made a peach cobbler, didn't you?"

Sally pushed away from him playfully. "I'll never tell, not unless I find a man who can chop wood without threatening to rip my clothes off."

"Don't tempt me, woman. I may just carry through with that threat."

"You're getting too old to catch me if I decide to run away. Which I just might do. Or I might take my clothes off and lie down naked under a pine tree, if the right man came along. But it would have to be for the right man. . . ."

He laughed, and came toward her.

Wind whistled through cracks in the logs. Outside, it was full dark. They sat side-by-side in the soft glow from the fireplace, listening to the wind and the whisper of the first falling snowflakes landing on the sod roof.

Smoke was so full of venison stew and peach cobbler he was sure he would burst. Sipping coffee, he stared thoughtfully at the flames. "We've got enough money in the bank to buy fifteen of those bulls at Chisum's price, and maybe two hundred head of good longhorn cows. We'll offer a few of the bulls to some of our neighbors. We'll need about ten to service that many cows."

"Everything I've been reading about Herefords makes this seem a sure way to breed cattle with more meat on them," Sally replied in the same thoughtful tone. "They are far better than shorthorns for the type of range we have, and I've read that they are resistant to most diseases, although they are susceptible to pinkeye in warm weather."

"Crossing 'em on longhorns will take some of that out of the calves. A longhorn don't hardly ever get sick, and they can take any kind of temperature extremes."

"I can't wait to get started next spring. Of course, I'll be worried until you get back."

"You're looking for reasons to worry. We talked about that before."

"I know you, Smoke. I don't see any way you can take men all the way down to New Mexico Territory without running into some kind of trouble. Sometimes, I think you look for it."

"That's not true," he complained, sipping more coffee. "I try to avoid it whenever I can."

"I want you to promise me that this spring, you won't let anything happen. Please?"

He felt her snuggle against his shoulder. "I'll promise you I won't let anything happen to me or our cattle. I'll swing wide of a fight whenever I can, even if some bastard is lookin' for one."

Sally touched his cheek, turning his face to hers. "I wish I could believe that," she said, then she kissed him hard before he could insist that he meant every word . . . just so long as nobody pushed too damn hard.

Ten

A layer of light snow blanketed the valley and slopes above the log cabin when dawn came gray and windy to this part of the Rockies. Tiny windblown snowflakes came across the higher ridges in sheets, spiraling downward where mountains protected the land from blustery gusts. Smoke came out before sunrise, when skies were brightening, to feed the horses. The temperature had fallen forty degrees overnight, hovering close to freezing, and as he put corn on the ground inside a pole corral protected from winds by a three-sided lean-to for their four horses, he shivered a bit in the cold and smiled inwardly. This was weather he understood, and he had a fondness for it. Surviving blizzards back when he was with Preacher had been difficult at first, until he'd learned how mountain men kept warm, no matter how cold it got, with layers of clothing and footgear made from tanned animal skins and fur, and how to prepare for weeks of hibernation like a bear when the elements in high country unleashed their fury. Glancing at snow-clad mountains around him now, he allowed himself to think about those times and Preacher, wondering if the old man might possibly be alive up there somewhere after so many years. Preacher would be against sentiment like this. However, Smoke found himself with a longing to hear that familiar deep voice, to see his grizzled face etched by hard times and adversity. Preacher wouldn't allow it, of course, if he were still alive in his declining years, a man with too much pride to let anyone, even Smoke, see him when age took its toll on him.

Spits of snow blew across a ridge to the northwest, flakes falling gently, almost soundlessly, around him. He inspected the horses; two pack animals, Sally's chestnut mare, and a bay and white Palouse three-year-old, sired by Horse, that he was breaking to mountain trails so it would be bridle-wise climbing narrow ledges, where surefootedness counted. When he was satisfied they were in good flesh and warm inside the shelter, he turned away from the pole corral to fetch pails of water from the slender stream at the foot of the slope where the cabin sat.

Carrying wooden buckets down to the creek, he was again reminded of Puma. This cabin and valley, the mountains, were full of old memories, and in some strange way it wasn't painful to remember them this morning. A part of him was comforted by those recollections of bygone days. The moments of sadness he felt when they first arrived here weren't with him now. He could remember Puma without feeling lonely for his company.

He came to the stream, brightened by a slow sunrise above thick storm clouds moving across the valley, his boots crunching softly in a few inches of newly fallen snow. There was a crispness to the air he didn't notice as often down at the ranch, a part of the experience in higher country, where most of his life he had felt at home. What had changed his feelings, his love for the high lonesome, was Sally. His whole life had changed because of her, and he'd never been so happy, so content. As he knelt beside the stream, he vowed to keep the promise he had made her last night, to steer clear of trouble whenever he could . . . not because he had any fear of it, of bad men. But because he loved her.

A small brook trout darted away from his shadow, moving downstream. Crystal clear water gurgled over multicolored rocks in the streambed, a sound so peaceful he couldn't help listening to it before he dipped his buckets full. To his right was a deep pool where, as the creek froze over, he would be chopping through ice to get their water, or using melted snow should temperatures drop and remain low for long periods of time.

Hoisting his buckets, Smoke thought about how different this was from his usual existence, or his more violent past. He gave a grin when he considered it, laughing at himself. His biggest worry now was chopping through ice, instead of chopping off the heads of his enemies. This was truly going to be a winter of contentment with Sally, not his usual fare of seemingly endless ranch work, always vigilant for the possibility of the return of old enemies, worrying about Sally while he was away.

When he entered the warm cabin, he found Sally building up a breakfast fire in the fireplace. Puma had installed two swinging iron cooking hooks, holding cast-iron cooking pots, that could be moved over the flames. A rusted iron frame for a skillet or a coffeepot sat to one side of the fire.

She smiled at him as he was closing the cabin door. "This is so nice," she said, adding split wood to a pile of glowing coals. "I thought I might miss my wood-stove, but I was wrong."

Smoke placed the buckets near the fireplace and took her in his arms. "The only thing I would have missed would've been you, if you hadn't come with me," he said gently.

"Nonsense," she replied, pretending to sound serious. "You would have found Huggie and Del. The three of you would have been so busy swapping yarns you wouldn't have noticed I wasn't there. I know why you wanted to come up here this winter. You get this yearning look in your eye when you've been away from your mountain men friends too long."

"That isn't true," he protested. "I'd much rather be with you."

She rested her cheek against his chest "I believe that too, and I've never doubted you loved me, but it's something else that brings you up here. You want to keep in touch with your past every now and then. I understand, darling. I know it's not just Huggie and Del and some of the others. It's this place, these mountains and valleys, the quiet, and the beauty of it drawing you back. It's okay. I love this high country as much as you do, in my own way. You don't have to make excuses."

"It wasn't an excuse," he mumbled near her ear. "Seems we never get any time alone."

"We're making up for that now," she whispered, tightening her embrace around his chest. "But I want you to know I will understand when you go off to look for your friends."

Once again, Sally was reading him like a book. He'd been thinking about Del and Huggie for a couple of days without any mention of it. "Maybe after

we get things squared away around here we'll go looking for Del. He'll get word to Huggie and a few of
the others . . . like Grizzly Cole and ol' Happy Jack
Cobb, if any of them are still around, or still alive."

Sally giggled, drawing away to look at him. "Who
is Happy Jack Cobb? I've never heard you mention
that name before. And why is he happy?"

"That's just it," Smoke told her. "Happy Jack
would have to be close to sixty now, an' nobody can
recollect ever seeing him smile in the last forty-odd
years. Puma named him that, best I remember. He
said Jack Cobb wouldn't crack a smile if he was to
discover the mother lode up here some day. He wears
this frown all the time, like he's mad at somethin',
only he isn't. It's just his natural expression."

She stood on her tiptoes to kiss him. "I'm happy,"
she said while searching his face. "I hope you are
too."

He swallowed when a strange dryness occurred in
his throat. "I've never been happier in my life, and
that's on account of you being with me."

They were Shoshoni by the way they wore their hair
and their dress, wrapped in buffalo robes, guiding
half-starved ponies into the far end of the narrow
valley, riding into the brunt of winds accompanying
the snowstorm. He pointed them out to Sally as she
was going inside with an armload of green limbs from
a pine tree for smoking trout he'd caught just before
noon. "Appears they're Shoshoni and they're way off
their range, this far south. Fetch me my rifle, just in
case these boys are renegades." It had been hard to
tell, due to increasing snowfall, until they came out
of the trees, a good sign in Smoke's experience.

Shoshoni warriors looking for a fight would have stayed hidden until they were very close to the cabin. "They smelled our smoke, being downwind."

"I see six of them," Sally said, her voice tight, changing pitch after she counted the warriors. "I thought all the Indian troubles were over up here."

"The Utes are gone. Shoshoni range north of here by more'n a hundred miles in Wyoming Territory. This isn't their usual hunting ground."

"I'll get your rifle. Maybe they're only looking for food and a place to get out of this storm."

"Maybe," Smoke agreed, thinking otherwise. There was no sense in worrying Sally until he found out what the Indians were up to. He put down the snowshoe he was repairing, watching the Indians ride toward him, wondering why they were so far south of their ancestral homeland.

Sally came out with his .44 Winchester and a box of shells, like she too expected the worst. She gave him the rifle and cartridges, shading her eyes from the snowfall with her hand.

"Those calico ponies look mighty hungry," he said, talking to himself more than for Sally's benefit. "Could be times have been hard up north. Buffalo hunters have damn near wiped out the big herds."

"Perhaps all they want is food. We have enough venison to give them—a hindquarter off that deer you shot. The meat's still good. I can roast it, if that's the reason they're here. Or we can give them all of it. You can go hunting again when this storm breaks."

"We'll give 'em a chance to explain," Smoke said, working a shell into the firing chamber, pocketing the extra shells. "You go back inside until I find out. It's real clear they're headed straight for the cabin."

Sally backed away, turning for the door. "I hope it's only food they want," she said again, her voice almost lost on a gust of howling winter wind.

Six mounted warriors crossed the stream and now Smoke was certain they weren't looking for trouble. Their bows and arrows and ancient muskets were tied to their ponies or balanced across their horses' withers in a manner that was clearly not meant as a threat.

The leader halted his black and white pinto twenty yards from Smoke and gave the sign for peace, and true words, closing his fist over his heart. Smoke returned the sign, then he held one palm open, inviting the Shoshoni to speak.

The Indian began a guttural string of words, a language not much different than the Ute tongue, asking if Smoke understood him.

Smoke replied, *"Nie habbe,"* meaning he spoke their tongue and understood.

The Shoshoni began a lengthy explanation of a tragic tale, how his people were starving because of white buffalo hunters on the prairies, leaving meat to rot in the sun this summer, only killing buffalo for their hides. Shoshoni children and older members of the tribe were dying of starvation. A dry spring and summer left little grazing for deer, elk, and antelope, and most of the wild game had drifted south into lands once controlled by the Utes.

"We have deer meat we can give you," Smoke told him in words he hadn't used for years. "You are welcome to make camp here until the snow ends."

"We would be grateful for the meat," the Indian said, his head and face partially hidden by the hood of his buffalo robe. "We have very little gunpowder and shot. Our arrows have been cursed by the Great Spirit and they do not find their mark on this hunt."

"I will have my wife cook the deer if you want."

The warrior shook his head "We must take it back to our village for the hungry children."

Smoke gave the sign for agreement, a twist of his right wrist with two fingers extended close together. He turned and walked to the dogrun between the cabin's two rooms, where the carcass of the deer hung from a length of rawhide.

Resting his rifle against a cabin wall, he cut down the deer and carried it out to the Indians. Another Shoshoni jumped off his pony to take it, cradling almost a hundred pounds of raw meat and bones in his arms.

The Shoshoni leader spoke, his voice softer to convey his gratitude. "You will be welcome in our village, White Giver of Meat. We leave you as friends in peace."

"*Suvate,*" Smoke replied, a single word to say the talk had ended and all was well, then he added a few clipped words.

With the deer slung over a pony's rump, the six Shoshoni reined their ponies away from the cabin, riding north up a very steep ridge that would take them into the worst of the winds and snow.

"Tough people," Smoke said under his breath, hearing Sally come out as the Indians rode off.

Sally came over to stand beside him, watching the buffalo-robed men disappear into a veil of snow-flakes. "Food was all they wanted," she said. "I'm glad you gave it to them. We have more than enough for ourselves."

"Their leader told me his people were starving up

in Wyoming country . . . that white buffalo hunters had killed off most of the herds and Shoshoni children were dying of hunger."

"We've both seen what buffalo hunters can do. It's a shame to see all that meat wasted," Sally said, "especially when Indian children are dying from starvation."

Smoke picked up the snowshoe, thinking out loud. "Our government doesn't seem to mind breaking its word to a few Indians," he replied to her remark. "Never had much use for politicians or the army in the first place. The more I hear about what they're doin' to most plains tribes, the less use I have for 'em."

Sally took his arm. "We've done all we can for them now. You can't change the world, Smoke. The government in Washington is going to continue its policy toward the Indians no matter how we feel about it."

He saw the Shoshoni as they crossed the high ridge in one brief letup in the storm. "I know you're right, Sally. I can't change the world, maybe, but when I see a wrong bein' committed it makes me wish I'd started shooting politicians and bureaucrats a long time ago. I've killed my share of men who carried guns, but there's times when it seems to make more sense to kill the bastards who run this country."

"I'd hoped we wouldn't have to talk about killing at all this winter."

Smoke squeezed her delicate hand. "We won't. If people will just leave us the hell alone."

"Maybe they will," she said hopefully. "Raising good cattle should be a peaceful enterprise. For so many years now I've been hoping your past would be forgotten, so we could get on with our lives together, as ranchers. You're not a gunfighter anymore, and I hope the word spreads."

He turned her toward the cabin, ducking his head into the wind and snow. Sally would never understand that for some men a gunfighter's reputation followed them all the way to the grave, in spite of their best intentions to change.

He had asked the Shoshoni to tell solitary white mountain men they encountered where he was, what part of the Rockies he was in, and that his name meant *smoke* in Shoshoni, hoping Del or Huggie or Griz would come down when one of them learned he was camped in Puma's summer cabin near the White River. Any one of his old friends would know who was staying here. Maybe when this storm let up, he and Sally would have some welcome company.

Eleven

He was wearing his old deerskin leggings, blood-stained in places from previous battles, one clear cold morning after the storm moved south, taking aim at a fat young doe to replenish their fresh meat supply. They had plenty of jerky and smoked fish, but every so often Smoke got a hankering for venison, the tender backstrap fried in a skillet or slow-roasted on a spit above a bed of coals. In a clearing half a mile from the cabin, he watched the doe paw through snow to find grass, unaware of his presence entirely. Sighting down his Winchester, he aimed for the deer's heart, hoping to make it a quick kill, when something to the east alerted the doe to danger, a distant noise or a scent on the wind. She bounded off into the ponderosa forest, leaving Smoke without a clear shot.

"Damn," he whispered, looking east to where the deer had sensed a threat seconds earlier.

Out of old habit, he didn't look at anything in particular, the way Preacher had taught him, waiting for something to move on a snowy mountainside dotted with pines and leafless aspen. Tiny hairs prickled on the back of his neck . . . something, or someone, was up there. Was someone watching him, he wondered, standing in the shadow of a pine, motionless, unwilling to make the first move, becoming a target, hunted rather than a hunter if the danger frightening the deer had two legs. Black bears and much larger grizzlies would be in hibernation by now. Mountain lions hunted all winter, and it could be a big cat up there somewhere, one of the most difficult wild animals to kill because it rarely came close to the smell of men.

He studied the slope, frosty breath curling away from his nostrils in below-freezing cold. Nothing moved.

"If it's a man, he's a careful son of a bitch," Smoke said softly. It could be more Shoshoni hunters, he guessed, another party ranging far to the south looking for meat. With that looming as a possibility he decided to creep backward and make for the cabin to make sure of Sally's safety. While she was more than capable of taking care of herself in most any situation, he couldn't let her face hungry Shoshoni alone. Sally was a hell of a shot with a pistol or a rifle, and she had his Spencer, along with one of his ivory-handled Colts.

When nothing showed itself on the mountain, he backed away to the shadow of another pine and inched from tree trunk to tree trunk on the balls of his feet, heading for the cabin by a route through stands of pine . . . longer, but far safer if he was being watched from the eastern slope, a sensation that lingered as he made his way among dense trees. He was certain now that someone was up there, a sixth sense telling him this was no mountain lion or late-feeding bear.

He was close to the cabin, less than a quarter mile,

when he heard a voice that sent him ducking behind a ponderosa trunk.

"You ain't near as cautious as you used to be, Smoke!" It came from a snow-covered ledge two hundred yards away, a shout. "If I'd took the notion, I coulda dropped you a couple of times. I ain't sayin' you ain't still one of the best, but that easy life yer livin' close to town has made you careless!"

He grinned, recognizing the voice now, swinging away from the tree to stand in plain sight, his rifle barrel lowered near the ground. "Show yourself, Del! You've got me cold! I'm a city slicker now!"

A shaggy mane of black hair peered above the ridge, with a beard to match. The man grinned a toothless grin and stood up with a long-barrel Sharps balanced in one hand. "It's damn sure good to see you, Smoke! Been a hell of a long time!"

Del Rovare began a gradual descent off the ledge, his odd bowlegged gait almost a swagger. He was a bull-like man who had learned to move his tremendous bulk across the mountains without making a sound, somehow. His moccasined feet barely made any noise through difficult snowdrifts where most men would have had trouble remaining quiet. Part French, he spoke Ute and Lakota and Shoshoni fluently. His fierce appearance often made outsiders fear him, when in fact he was most often a gentle giant who avoided difficulties whenever he could. But when he was challenged by man or beast, including rogue grizzly females protecting their cubs, he could be deadly, dangerous with a gun, a knife, or his bare hands.

Smoke walked toward him, and when they met in

a small open spot between trees, they embraced like the longtime friends they were.

Del grinned again. "I seen you was headed back to Puma's old cabin like you was worried. Don't fret over that woman of yours. She's fine, an' there ain't nobody else around."

"Did you talk to Sally?" he asked, noticing streaks of gray in Del's hair and beard, and a milky spot over the pupil of Del's left eye.

"Naw. Didn't want to scare her none. I jest watched fer a spell an' come looking fer you. She come outside once to gather a load of firewood. She's okay. I came down after I talked to Mo-pe an' his hunters. They told me you give 'em a deer fer them hungry kids they got up in Wyomin'. Damn nice of you. I give 'em six wild turkey hens I shot the other day. When Mo-pe said you was named after a cloud of smoke I knowed right away who it was stayin' here at Puma's summer lodge. I reckon you miss ol' Puma much as I do. Hell, all of us who live up here miss the ol' bastard, even cranky as he was sometimes. A man never had no better friend than Puma Buck if he took a likin' to you."

Smoke turned Del toward the cabin with a motion of his head as he tried to forget about the way Puma had died, in a fight that was Smoke's, not his. "Puma took a killin' that was meant for me," he said, trudging through snow, remembering in spite of himself. "If it had to happen, I wish it could have happened another way."

"You can't blame yerself, Smoke. Puma knowed what he was up against. An' there's another thing. Puma never was himself after his Ute woman passed away. Used to climb up high all by his lonesome an' sit fer days, starin' at the sky like he was thinkin' real hard 'bout her. He'd git kinda choked up if you was to mention her name."

Smoke thought about Sally. "Every man has his soft spots, Del. I've got the best woman on earth and she's changed me, to some degree. I get lonesome when I'm away from her too long, and I never figured that sort of thing would ever happen to me."

Del changed the subject quickly as they crossed over a low ridge. They could see the cabin down below. "I come to warn you 'bout somethin', Smoke. It ain't no kinda trouble, maybe just an aggravation. There's this long-winded feller ridin' a mule all over these mountains. Says his name's Ned Buntline, an' he says he's aimin' to talk to you. He writes books. A nosy son of a bitch too, askin' all sorts of dumb questions 'bout what it's like to live up here, askin' if Preacher is still alive, wantin' to talk to him if he is. I run the bastard off after he come up with too goddamn many questions. But he's lookin' fer you, so I figured I'd better warn you. He's already talked to Griz, an' ol' Griz wouldn't hardly tell him nothin'. He offered Huggie a jug of whiskey an' Huggie tol' him some things he hadn't oughta."

"Like what?"

Del needed a minute to form his reply. "Like where we all figure Preacher is, if'n he ain't dead by now. Nobody's seen him fer years, I reckon you know. But I was up at Willow Creek Pass this summer an' I found a footprint beside a stream. Ain't a livin' soul up there . . . never has been. Too damn high fer most anybody. Air's so damn thin a man can't breathe it right. I wouldn't have gone up there myself if it hadn't been I wounded a big elk bull an' followed his blood sign fer damn near five miles straight up, nearly to the tree line. That wounded bull wanted water, an' when I come to this creek, there it was, a print made by a man with a foot half a yard long. Ain't no such thing as a big-footed Injun, an' Preacher always had to make his own rawhide brush moccasins. Now, I ain't sayin' that footprint was his, but it was fresh, maybe a few hours old, an' it sure as hell reminded me of his tracks."

"He'd be close to ninety years old by now, Del, if it was him."

"Ain't claimin' it was him. Just sayin' how unusual it was to find that big footprint at Willow Creek Pass. I told Huggie 'bout findin' it. A few weeks back, Huggie told me he'd made some mention of it to that book-writin' feller whilst Huggie was dead drunk on that whiskey."

"I suppose Buntline headed for Willow Creek Pass to see if he could find Preacher."

"That's what Huggie claimed when I talked to him."

Smoke wagged his head as they neared the creek. "Preacher is just as liable to kill him as talk, if he's still alive. He won't have changed much in the disposition department. I've made up my mind not to talk to Ned Buntline either. He can find some other way to write his books. I'm spending the winter up here with Sally. Any son of a bitch who shows up who isn't an old friend of mine will get shown the trail out of here in one hell of a hurry."

"Griz told me the bastard was nice enough. I got tired of all the damn questions mighty quick, so I pointed to the way he rode up to my cabin an' said to clear out now. He got right back on his mule an'

I ain't seen him since. It was Huggie who told me Buntline was headed up to Willow Creek."

"If Preacher's alive, he'll handle it. Now let's see what Sally has got cooked up for lunch. She was makin' brown sugar bearclaws in the Dutch oven when I left."

"I'd claim them bearclaws was callin' to my sweet tooth, only I ain't got any teeth left."

Smoke chuckled as they crossed the stream, stepping ever so carefully on a walkway of flat, slippery rocks. "You won't need any teeth for Sally's bearclaws. Damn but it's good to see you, Del. It's been awhile."

"Good to see you too, Smoke. We had some good times, an' a few that was bad when lead was flyin'."

"We'll talk about some of them tonight. Sally cleaned that other room across the dogrun, and wc've got plenty of blankets to keep your old ass warm."

"My ass an' everything else is gettin' old," Del replied. "I get these powerful aches in my joints when it gits cold, and can't hardly see nothin' outa my left eye. Got this white stuff over it so it looks like it's snowin' all the time. Makes everythin' fuzzy as hell, too. One of these years I'm gonna have to come down outa the mountains, when I can't see to aim this rifle no more, or climb a mountain without it hurtin'. Till that day comes, I'm gonna enjoy every minute I've got left. I figure I'm goin' blind, Smoke, an' that's about the worst thing that can happen to a man who loves the looks of high country."

"I'd rather lose a leg than lose my eyes," Smoke said on their way to the cabin door. He noticed smoke curling from the chimney and something else, a delicious smell coming from inside that made his belly growl.

Del stopped a few feet away from the cabin. "You might be well advised to warn your woman I ain't had no bath fer a spell. She won't wanna stand downwind from me. If she'll offer me some of them bearclaws, I'll eat 'em out here."

Smoke laughed heartily. "Sally's used to the smell of a man who's been away from bathwater. C'mon inside. From what my nose just picked up now, I don't figure a skunk could get noticed over what that melted brown sugar smells like." He went to the door and pulled the latchstring.

Sally turned away from the crude, hand-hewn plank table Puma had built for his Ute bride years ago. "I see we've got company," she said. "It's good to see you, Del. You're just in time to try one of my little brown sugar pies. Smoke calls them bearclaws because of the way I shape them."

"I'd be plumb delighted," Del replied, showing off his gums before he leaned his rifle against the wall near the door. "I do git a real strong hankerin' fer somethin' sweet now an' then."

Smoke rested his Winchester on its pegs. For the rest of the day and most of the night, he'd be listening to Del's stories about recent happenings in the mountains. Some of them would evoke old feelings, good feelings, about the years he'd spent up here with Preacher. "How about some coffee?" he asked Sally, to get his mind off the story Del had just told him about finding that footprint at Willow Creek Pass.

Twelve

Ned Buntline was sure he was dying, slowly freezing to death sitting at the base of a rock ledge surrounded by snow and wind, unable to build a fire without the matches in his packs after his mule bolted away, breaking its tether rope for no apparent reason as though something had frightened it, perhaps a bear or a cougar Ned hadn't seen or expected to see at these high altitudes. The mule had trotted downslope, and now he was afoot, freezing, without any food or water, or a gun. Or those all-important matches he must have to get a fire going before he died of exposure. Shivering inside his checkered mackinaw, he knew he was only hours away from death. He'd gotten lost looking for Willow Creek, for his map showed nothing, no details of this region, only blank paper and the notation, *Unexplored.* Yet for days he'd felt he was close to the place Huggie Charles had described, even though the man had been half drunk at the time. Following the timberline west, he'd come to the rocky gorge Charles had mentioned, but somehow, after crossing it just as the snowstorm was letting up, the creek and high mountain pass were nowhere in sight. He'd tied his mule for a climb above the timberline to have a better view of what lay below. And that's when the mule had broken free. Ned had been following its tracks in the snow for hours, until his legs and lungs played out. The air up here was almost too thin to breathe, and the bitter cold only worsened his plight. Now, as the sun lowered behind towering peaks to the west, temperatures would plunge, and he would be lucky to survive the night without a fire to warm him.

He wondered now if it had been worth it, to try to find the legendary mountain man known only as Preacher. Looking was about to cost him his life, unless he found his mule. "Damn the luck," he stammered, teeth chattering, forcing himself to rise slowly on unsteady legs. Tracking the mule was his only hope.

Ned stumbled away from the ledge, feeling strangely sleepy, having trouble keeping his eyelids open. Staggering, almost falling in places, he made his way downslope, following hoofprints left by the mule. Lengthening shadows fell away from smaller pine trees below him, only the damn mule's tracks kept moving in the wrong direction, sometimes higher, continually westward, as if the dumb beast could have known its destination. Ned's feet were frozen numb, without any feeling, his boots and socks insufficient to warm them in a foot or more of snow.

Half an hour later, when Ned was certain he could go no further, the tracks suddenly turned down the mountain toward a snow-mantled line of much taller pines that seemed to wind back and forth aimlessly, winding around switchbacks, headed down to lower altitudes. Slowed to a snail's pace, truly staggering to keep his balance while maintaining some forward progress, he floundered toward the closest trees, gasping for breath.

Skies darkened as he entered the pines, however he could see a small trickle of partially frozen water, a stream coming from a spring hidden in a jumble of rocks. And there were the mule's prints, following the creek downhill.

For a moment, Ned allowed himself to hope, summoning all the strength he had. His mule could be around the next bend in the stream. Dreaming of a steaming cup of Arbuckles, flames to warm his hands, face, and frozen toes, he placed one foot in front of the other, now and then pausing long enough to use a pine trunk for support and to catch his breath.

Making his way down, wind whispered among snow-laden pine boughs, occasionally brushing a dusting of snow to the ground. Ned came to a sharp bend in the tiny trickle and pulled up short when he glimpsed a flickering light.

"A fire," he wheezed. He hadn't seen a living soul for days and couldn't fathom who could be up here. Would it be friend or foe? He had no gun, having hung his pistol belt around his saddle horn for his climb this morning.

"I have no choice," he said a moment later, taking short steps toward the distant flames. Whoever it was with a fire in this cold was about to have company . . . he would die anyway from these temperatures unless he warmed himself.

Getting closer, he saw his mule tied to a tree. A fire in a circle of stones near the creek bank revealed nothing else at the moment. A huge boulder covered with a mound of snow sat beyond the dancing flames, but as he drew closer he became puzzled by the white shape atop the giant rock. . . . It was too large and too irregular to be snow.

"I'm a friend!" he cried with all the voice he could muster in the thin air, even though he saw no one near the fire. "That's my mule! If you have a gun, please don't shoot me! I'm unarmed!"

No one answered his call. Had someone simply found his mule and built a fire for him before continuing on to their destination? It seemed unlikely. He struggled faster, eyes fastened on the strange white shape on top of the boulder, until at last he could see what it was when he was only twenty or thirty yards from the flames.

A figure in a white furry robe was perched on the rock, a hood made from the same material covering his head and any detail of his face. A long rifle lay across the man's lap. Ned was too cold and exhausted to care who it was just then, merely hoping the oddly dressed stranger wasn't planning to shoot him.

His knees wobbled the last few steps until he stood at the edge of the firepit. He looked closely at the dark hole in the hood where a face would have been revealed in better light.

"Who are you?" Ned asked, teeth rattling so loudly he was almost unable to hear his own voice, pulling off his gloves to warm his hands above the flickering flames. "I've never seen a robe that color. It looks like buffalo fur. Was the buffalo a rare albino?"

"You sure as hell ask a bunch of questions for a man who's damn near froze solid," a deep voice replied. "Any fool can see a man like you don't belong up here. Get warm. Boil some coffee if you've a mind to, then get on that mule an' clear out of here without askin' no more stupid questions."

"It isn't that I'm not grateful for what you've done," Ned replied, as some feeling returned to his fingers and feet. "I was only curious as to who you were, and why you'd help me."

"Felt sorry for you, Tenderfoot. I been watchin' you fer a couple of days. You ain't got the know-how to be up here, so take some advice afore your next fool mistake gets you froze till the spring thaw. Get back to the flatlands where you come from an' don't come back."

Ned wasn't quite sure what to say, or if he should say anything. "I'm a writer," he said, to explain. "I was looking for a mountain man they call Preacher. I intend to write a series of books about the real pioneer mountain men. Alvah Dunning told me about this Preacher fellow, and so did Major Frank North of the Pawnee scouts. Everyone seems to know about Preacher, only there are some who say he's dead now."

"Maybe he is."

"Did you know him?"

"Ain't none of your affair."

"Please don't be offended. My readers back east would love to know more about this famous mountain pioneer."

"You can write about some of the others."

"Not many of them will tell me anything. I found out one of the last of the early pioneers, Puma Buck, is dead. I was hoping he would tell me a few tales."

"He wouldn't, even if he was alive."

"You knew him?"

"Ain't none of your affair."

Ned looked down at his boots, wondering who the man was in the white robe. . . . He couldn't see his face. "My last hope, if I can't find this Preacher fellow, is a man named Smoke Jensen. I was told he used to be a mountain man before he took up ranching close to Big Rock, and that he knew Preacher better than any of the others."

A silence followed, long enough to be meaningful, but what did it mean and how could he find out? "Would you care for a cup of coffee? I have some Arbuckles in my pack."

"Nope. You ask too damn many questions to be good company over a cup of coffee." Now the white-robed stranger stirred, swinging off the rock. He stood for a moment looking at Ned, even though Ned couldn't see his eyes. He seemed bent as if with old age, stooped over, although it was hard to tell because his robe was bulky, touching the ground so even his feet and legs were hidden. "Boil your coffee an' head back where you come from quick as you can, mister, afore somebody, or these mountains, up an' kills you."

Before Ned could ask for his name again, the man whirled and walked away into the darkness beneath the pine canopy shadowing both sides of the stream.

"Thanks again, mister!" he called out.

There was nothing but silence and the soft crackle of flames for an answer. Ned knew he would always wonder who the benevolent stranger in the albino buffalo robe was. . . . He owed the man his life.

Thirteen

Jessie Evans liked all six of the Mexican *pistoleros*: Pedro Lopez, Jorge Diaz, Carlos and Victor Bustamante, a half-breed by the name of Raul Jones, and a fat Yaqui Indian simply called Tomo. All six were experienced gunmen and Jessie needed every good gun he could hire, since word had come that Big John Chisum was looking for men who could handle themselves. What was being called the Lincoln County War was now shaping up to be a deadly fight, if things continued the way they were. Cattle were being stolen on both sides. Jessie was ready to teach a few more Chisum riders a permanent lesson, while the territorial governor turned his head at the request of Catron and Murphy. Dolan said they might even burn down John Tunstall's store some night, to teach him to keep his nose out of the cattle contract business. Jimmy Dolan knew how to fight a war, how to win at any cost, and he had Murphy's money behind him to get the job done.

Jessie turned to Bill Pickett as sundown came to their camp at Bosque Redondo. "Let's test those new Mexican boys tonight. We'll ride over to Chisum's cow camp on the Ruidoso River. If we gather up about fifty head of steers, an' kill a few cowboys while we're at it, Dolan's liable to give us all a pay raise. We'll tell those *pistoleros* to shoot as many men as they can."

"Sounds good to me," Pickett replied, tipping a bottle of tequila into his mouth. "I was gettin' bored, sittin' 'round here, freezin' our asses off, waitin' fer somethin' to happen. I say we make somethin' happen ourselves. There's another thing I been thinkin' about. That goddamn high an' mighty Englishman, John Tunstall, has been hirin' more men. Mostly green kids, or so I hear tell. Wouldn't be nothin' wrong with shootin' that Englishman, if you ask me. He ain't connected to nobody important in this territory. Killin' him oughta throw a scare into Chisum an' everybody else in Lincoln County."

"I'll ask Dolan about it. All he said was, maybe we oughta burn down his store. Tell those Mexicans to saddle up. You an' me an' Cooper will ride with 'em."

Pickett eased his weight off a bull hide stool on the front porch of the cow camp bunkhouse. "Suits the hell outa me. We ain't spilled no blood since winter started. Time we turned some of this snow red. It gets tiresome, seein' everything white all the damn time."

The mighty roar of a shotgun from the darkness ended with a shrill scream. Loose horses and cattle bedded down for the night took off in every direction. A lantern brightened behind a cabin window as men in long johns carrying rifles raced out the door in the pale moonlight, shouting to each other.

Another withering blast of shotgun fire erupted from a spot behind a split rail fence, lifting a hatless cowboy off his feet in mid run, bending him at the waist with the force of speeding lead pellets entering his chest and belly.

A rifle cracked from the corner of a hay shed, dropping a Chisum ranch hand in his tracks, groaning, landing in fresh snow with his feet thrashing as though he meant to keep running while he lay on his back.

More guns roared from a loose circle around the cabin, and more men fell in the snow, yelling, crying out for help or lying still, dead before they went down.

Jessie leaned against the fence in the dark without firing a shot, watching Pickett, Cooper, and his Mexican gunmen in action, keeping a quick tally of the bodies. Eight men, then a ninth, collapsed in a hail of bullets. Terrified longhorns broke out of one corral, snapping rails like kindling wood, bolting toward freedom and an escape from the banging of guns. As the last of the Chisum riders fell, Jessie turned away from the fence to get his horse.

All gunfire stopped abruptly. Somewhere near the cabin a cowboy moaned. Pickett or Cooper would take care of his suffering in short order, along with any others who might still be alive.

"Let's round up those beeves," he shouted. "We'll gather as many as we can an' clear out. Somebody across the river is liable to have heard the noise."

He mounted a nervous sorrel gelding and held its reins in check until all his men were in their saddles . . . all but Pickett, his absence explained when a shotgun bellowed near one of the cowsheds.

Nine Dolan riders spread out to collect over a hundred head of longhorn steers. Jessie knew it was time to get the running irons hot again, changing brands before Sheriff William Brady went through the motions of investigating what would look like a massacre tomorrow morning. A serious escalation of the Lincoln County War had just taken place a few days before Christmas, a warning to John Chisum that the government beef contract business could be a little risky here in the southern part of New Mexico Territory.

Fourteen

It was very close to the beginning of April when Sally took a look at the sky one morning, then across the snow-filled valley with a slight frown on her face. She turned to Smoke as he was using a whetstone on his Bowie knife blade.

"It's time to go, my darling," she said. "This has been one of the most wonderful times of my life, but we can't hide up here forever. There's work to be done at Sugarloaf. By now the snow is melting down there. You've got to hire some extra men to help bring cattle up from New Mexico. Some of our neighbors who want Hereford bulls may ride along. I suppose I'm getting restless, but something tells me it's time. You've seen your friends, and we've had all these months of peace and solitude. Our staples are running low. As much as I'd love to stay here with you for the rest of my life, we can't. We have a ranch to run."

For weeks he'd been experiencing the same strange sensation, that it was time to leave, almost like an itching feeling, only it occurred inside, somewhere in his chest or in the back of his brain. He hadn't wanted to say anything to her. She seemed so happy here and happy with their closeness. "I agree," he said, sheathing his heavy knife. "I've really been thinkin' about the Herefords, and maybe finding a Morgan stud. We may still hit some bad weather if we start out early, but it'll be slow movin' those cattle so many miles. Some of that is still renegade Apache country, so we'll have to watch our herd real close in a few spots."

He stood up and cast a sweeping look at the snowy mountain peaks around them. "I'll hate to leave here. I reckon there'll always be a part of me wanting to stay in this high country from time to time." He smiled at her. "Especially with you. But like you said, we've got a ranch to run and miles to travel to make our plans for the future work out. We can start packing gear today and leave at first light tomorrow. It'll be slower, going down with all this snow on the ground. We should be back at Sugarloaf in four days."

"It'll be good to see Pearlie and Cal and Johnny," she said after a bit. "I didn't realize I'd miss them so much. I guess they're like a part of the family, almost. When I saw you with Huggie and Del, or Grizzly this winter it made me happy to hear you talk about what it was like to be one of them. You seemed to really be enjoying yourself."

"I was," he answered truthfully. "It was good to see them again, to talk about old times. I was sorry to hear Happy Jack got killed by that grizzly last spring, but a mother with cubs can be one of the most dangerous animals on earth. Griz Cole knows bears better'n anybody, and he said Happy Jack never did give 'em enough room. Carelessness caught up with him, I reckon. And none of 'em knew for sure what ever happened to Preacher."

She placed her hand in the crook of his arm. "Still, this was the most peaceful winter we ever spent together, and I'm so grateful for that. I'll always remember it, and how gentle you can be. The only time you used a gun was to hunt fresh meat, and I'm grateful for that too."

"Maybe I've changed," he told her. "Let's get started with that packing. Won't be as much to carry going down, so our pack animals will have an easier time of it."

She smiled and kissed him lightly. "I love you, Mr. Jensen."

"I love you too, Mrs. Jensen. Maybe I didn't realize just how much until we spent this peaceful winter together. It made me realize just how important you are to me."

She tilted her head, still smiling. "Maybe you have changed your ways, darling. Those are some mighty sweet words coming out of your mouth this morning. Maybe the old Smoke Jensen is gone for good, so I won't have to worry so much. . . ."

Pearlie and Cal and Johnny shook hands with Smoke and Cal gave Sally a hug, still being part boy despite a fast growing up riding alongside Smoke in a few tight spots.

"Everything's plumb satisfactory," Pearlie said. "Only had this one aggravation all winter long."

Smoke's expression clouded. "And what was that?"

"That feller Ned Buntline showed up, wearin' this derby hat like he belonged in Saint Louis or somewheres. Asked to talk to you. I told him you was gone fer the winter."

Cal's face brightened. "He told me all about how

he writes those dime novels. And you ain't gonna believe this! He wants to write one about you!"

Pearlie wagged his head before Smoke could disagree. "I went an' told him he'd be wastin' his time, that you wasn't gonna tell him a damn thing. He acted real disappointed. Then he told us this crazy story, 'bout some feller up near Willow Creek Pass who wore this albino buffalo robe. Buntline said he never saw his face or got his name, but he told us that feller saved his life when his mule run off. Built a fire so he wouldn't freeze to death, and tied his mule up fer him. Buntline said he was an ornery cuss. Wouldn't answer a single question 'bout who he was or how come him to be way up there. Downright unusual, fer a man to own an albino buffalo skin. Ain't seen but two my whole life, an' they was way off, wild as deer."

Smoke turned northwest, looking at the distant peaks outlined against a clear sky. Had Ned Buntline accidentally run into Preacher up there somewhere? He was reminded of the story Del had told him about the unusual footprint at Willow Creek Pass, not real proof of anything. Buntline's story might only be the product of a fertile imagination of the type he used to write his books.

He spoke to Pearlie. "Ride to the neighboring ranches, the Walker spread and Bob Williams's place. Ask them if they want to ride with us down to New Mexico Territory at the end of next week to pick up those Hereford bulls."

"We leavin' that soon?" Pearlie asked. "It's still a touch on the chilly side."

"It's a long trip, and comin' back with those gentle bulls will be slow," Smoke answered. "We'll leave next Friday, and anybody who wants to ride along with us is welcome company."

"I'll ride to the Williams place," Johnny offered, as Cal was helping unload the packhorses. "One thing, Mr. Jensen," he added, glancing over to Sally as she went in the house with an armload of winter clothes. "While I was in Big Rock the other day, Mr. Longmont said he read somethin' in the Denver newspaper, that there was big trouble down in New Mexico. Folks are callin' it the Lincoln County War, an' you said Lincoln County was where we had to go to meet Mr. John Chisum an' pick up them bulls. Mr. Longmont said there was dead bodies all over the place, an' it might not be a safe place to be."

While this wasn't particularly good news, Smoke said, "It isn't our war, Johnny. We'll stay out of it. If we can."

Pearlie chuckled. "I never did know you to avoid no kind of war. If there's any killin' goin' on wherever we's headed, I'm dead sure we'll get in on our share of it."

Smoke didn't want any danger discussed in front of Sally. "Don't say any more about it, Johnny, not when Sally's in hearing distance."

"Yessir. I mean, no sir, I won't."

"It's because she worries too much," he explained, unsaddling the bay Palouse colt.

Pearlie muttered, as he stripped the saddle off Sally's mare, "Maybe it's because she's got good reason to worry. This outfit ain't exactly famous fer ridin' the other way when lead's flyin'."

Fifteen

They made up quite a group riding south along the base of the Rockies, following a cattle trail that would take them to Durango before they crossed over the New Mexico line. Cal and Pearlie and Johnny, then Cletus Walker and Bob Williams, along with a seasoned cowboy from the Williams ranch by the name of Duke Smith. Smoke left Tinker Warren to help out at the ranch and watch over Sally while they were away. He trusted Tinker, and the old man could shoot straight if he had to, which was just as important as his cowboying skills when Smoke considered he was there to protect the most important thing in his life . . . Sally.

"Snow's already melted in this low country," Pearlie said, "an' here it is only the middle of April."

Cletus Walker offered his opinion on the subject. "Ain't near as pretty this far south, an' it sure as hell ain't as good grazin' land." Cletus was a stocky man in his fifties, a good neighbor and friend although he and Smoke rarely saw each other, his spread being over ten rugged miles east of Sugarloaf.

"It's warmer," Bob Williams remarked, a lanky bachelor who ran cattle in lowlands south of Smoke and Sally, "but I'll agree with Cletus that this is junk land compared to what we've got. There ain't hardly enough grass most places in this valley to keep a jackrabbit alive."

Duke Smith, not much older than Cal, said, "It's damn sure different all right. I never rode this trail afore, but I been up the Goodnight twice. Believe me, if you figure this part of Colorado ain't got much grass, wait'll you see the Goodnight down in the south part of New Mexico. You can count the blades of grass an' not run out of fingers in some of them stretches along the Pecos."

Cal had been unusually quiet for several days after they left the ranch. He rode silently beside Smoke as though his mind was on something else. "Down along the Pecos is where they's havin' that big fight, accordin' to Mr. Longmont. Lincoln County is where he said most of it was, an' that's right where we're headed. They's callin' it the Lincoln County War, if you'll remember."

"It isn't our fight," Smoke told him. "We're buyin' cattle and that's all. No sense getting yourself all worked up over it, Cal. I promised Sally we'd ride a hundred miles in the wrong direction to stay out of trouble."

"It'd be the first time," Pearlie observed dryly. "Seems we make a habit outa ridin' a hundred miles to look fer a fight on occasion."

Cal swallowed, seeming edgier than Smoke had ever seen him. "Just so nobody starts shootin' at us before they know we ain't on either side."

There were times when Cal reminded Smoke of himself as a boy growing up, when he was known by his given name, Kirby Jensen, in a bleak part of southeastern Missouri at the edge of the Ozark Mountain range. He remembered too how his Pa, Emmett, went off to war and how lonely he felt, trying to scratch a living out of thin soil to help support his Ma. It was after the war when he and his Pa rode west, running into the filthiest-looking old man he'd ever seen, dressed in greasy buckskins, calling himself Preacher and never anything else. It was another step toward manhood for Kirby Jensen, and a chance meeting where he earned the nickname Smoke early on, a meeting and a friendship that had changed Smoke Jensen's life forever. And now Cal was becoming a man, one step at a time as it must always be, learning lessons that would keep him alive, as well as making him a man who could be a trusted friend and perhaps, later on, a deadly adversary. Cal had the basics, the things it took inside—courage and true loyalty to those who stood by him. His uneasiness now over the trouble in Lincoln County was just his way of preparing himself to stand and fight beside Smoke and the others if the need arose.

Smoke recalled his frontier education with Preacher, his own early fears, until Preacher taught him how to stay alive . . . and how to kill when necessary. With those skills came confidence, along with experience. While Preacher had been a hard taskmaster at times, he explained that it was necessary, that life-and-death struggles are unforgiving, usually allowing no mistakes. It had been hard to live up to Preacher's expectations, without understanding it was a rite of passage into manhood in a land filled with sudden violence and harsh conditions. More than any other single thing, Preacher had taught him to rely on himself.

Smoke wondered if these memories were coming

back because of the footprint Del had found at Willow Creek Pass, and the story Ned Buntline had told of encountering a solitary mountain man up there who handed Buntline his life. That would be just like Preacher, to help a tenderfoot in trouble and then abandon him as quickly as he'd arrived. Or was Smoke merely trying to comfort himself with the thought that Preacher was still alive up in the high lonesome, living out his final years?

Leading a string of spare horses, Duke pointed to a distant line of trees wandering back and forth to the south, stretching across the far horizon. "That looks like a river way off yonder," he said.

"It's the San Juan," Cletus told him, before Smoke could say it. "Means we're gettin' mighty close to the New Mexico Territory line. Durango oughta be off to the west a few miles."

Smoke settled back against the cantle of his saddle, hearing the bay Palouse colt's hooves squish through melting snow and mud with some satisfaction. The young horse was proving itself to be like its sire, Horse, a solid trail pony with endurance and an easy gait, with enough stamina to outlast most other breeds in this part of the country. Crossing their mares on a good Morgan stud, he and Sally could raise tough cow horses with early speed at shorter distances.

"We'll also be ridin' into Apache country," Bob warned as they neared the river. "Time we loaded our rifles an' the rest of our guns."

It was wasted advice for Smoke Jensen. He couldn't remember a time when his guns weren't fully loaded, or being reloaded for another round of gunplay. An empty gun was about as useless as a three-legged horse.

He noticed neither Cal nor Pearlie were checking their weapons, and Johnny North did not so much as look down at his pistol or rifle. Sugarloaf riders learned to be prepared for most anything at any time. Otherwise, they didn't stay on the payroll.

Smoke smiled when he thought about Sally. If she happened to be wearing a dress, underneath it, strapped to her leg, she kept a short-barreled Colt .44. And if she rode the ranch in a pair of denims, she wore a gunbelt just like the rest of the cowboys, with a Winchester booted to her saddle. For a gentle-natured schoolteacher, she could damn sure shoot straight with a handgun or a rifle.

Above the river, on a twisting road that would take them to Santa Fe, then farther south, they were climbing into the San Pedro Mountains toward El Vado Pass two days later when Smoke sensed danger, a feeling he would be hard-pressed to describe, a tingling down his back resembling a chill. Although for now he saw nothing to arouse his concerns, the sensation was there just the same.

"Keep your eyes open," he said over his shoulder. "Maybe it's nothing, but my nose smells trouble up ahead."

"That's enough fer me," Pearlie remarked, pulling out his Winchester, resting it across the pommel of his saddle. "I never have knowed how you could smell it comin', but I'll take an oath you've done it more times than I care to remember. Jerk that smoke stick, boy," he said to Cal, "an' git yerself ready to use it. Johnny, if you like the sweet smell of this air, you'd best git ready to fight fer your next breath of it."

"I don't see a damn thing," Cletus said, squinting into the sun's glare off melting snow on slopes leading toward the pass.

"Neither do I," Smoke told him. "I just figure it'll be a good idea to stay watchful."

Bob and Duke drew their rifles, levering shells into the firing chamber, resting the buttplates against their thighs as their horses carried them higher. Cletus remained unconvinced for the present, leaving his rifle booted.

"Could be all you smell is a skunk," Cletus argued, when nothing moved on either side of the pass.

"Maybe," Smoke said softly, his experienced eye roaming back and forth across steep slopes dotted with smaller piñon pine trees and still barren aspen, it being too early in the spring for new leaves. "Skunks come in several shapes. I'm lookin' for the two-legged variety. They've got a different smell."

The sounds of hooves filled a silence. Smoke left his rifle in its boot, opening his coat to be able to reach for both Colts in case he needed them in a hurry.

Then he saw the source of his concerns, five or six Apache warriors by the cut of their hair, brandishing rifles, rounding a cutbank near the top of the pass. They rode to the crest of the trail and halted their multicolored ponies, fanning out, blocking the pathway of Smoke and his neighbors.

"Son of a bitch!" Cletus exclaimed, pulling his Winchester free. "How the hell did you know, Smoke?"

Smoke halted his horse without answering Cletus, judging the distance, measuring how much drop a slug would take reaching an Indian more than three hundred yards away. A .44 caliber rifle cartridge held a considerable amount of gunpowder, properly loaded with the maximum number of grains, but unlike a Sharps, its range was far more limited and the bullet had a tendency to fall at shorter distances, requiring a higher aim and a piece of luck.

Only now, Smoke unbooted his Winchester, when it became all too clear the Apaches were after their horses and money, blocking the roadway through El Vado Pass. He chambered a shell. "I'll aim over their heads once," he told the others, "a warning shot to convince 'em we're willin' to fight our way through if we have to. Maybe we can scare 'em off. We've got 'em outnumbered. I'd be willing to bet these are young renegades, not older warriors with a lot of fighting experience. Let's hope they back off."

Aiming well above the warriors' heads, he triggered off a booming shot that echoed off the slopes. The result was not what he expected.

All five Apaches jumped their ponies forward, shouldering rifles, racing down the trail to engage the enemy. Smoke took it in stride, levering another round. "Start droppin' as many as you can, soon as they're in range," he said, placing his rifle sights on a warrior's blanketed chest. He heard war cries and the thunder of unshod hooves.

Smoke fired, feeling the Winchester slam into his shoulder. The Apache disappeared from his sights almost instantly, performing a backflip off the rump of his galloping pinto.

Cal fired before Smoke could aim again, and to Smoke's surprise a squat Apache warrior toppled to the ground, rolling in snowmelt slush and mud, arms and legs like the limbs of a limp rag doll, until he tumbled to a halt at the base of a piñon pine.

"Nice shot," Smoke told the boy, when only three Indians remained in the reckless charge.

"I allowed fer the drop like you showed me," Cal said as he worked another cartridge into place, his horse prancing underneath him following the explosion so near its ears.

A fierce war cry ended the instant Smoke pulled the trigger and an Apache tossed his rifle in the air to reach for his throat while he was falling backward. Before anyone could fire another shot, the last two Indians swerved their ponies around, drumming heels into the little horses' sides to race back up to the top of the pass.

Without a word, Smoke urged his Palouse forward, keeping one eye on the fallen warriors and the other on the pass. When he came to the first downed Indian, he saw a pulpy round hole in the Apache's neck and a circle of blood growing around his head. He would be dead in a matter of minutes.

The Apache Cal had shot had a mortal wound near his heart, and while he was still breathing slowly, his life would end soon. Cal rode up just then, peering down at what he'd done.

"Jesus," the boy whispered, losing some of the pink in his cheeks. "Looks like I killed him."

The others rode up to inspect Cal's handiwork.

"You done yerself proud, boy," Pearlie said. "Couldn't have done no better myself at half that distance."

"You sure as hell can shoot, son," Bob said. "I had you figured to be a little bit on the young side to have any nerve, but I was damn sure wrong."

Smoke gave Cal a nod, all that was needed to praise him for the time being. Later, he would tell the boy how steady his aim and nerves had to be to make that kind of shot at a moving target from two hundred yards away.

Riding further up the trail, Smoke gazed down at his first victim briefly. A bullet hole ran through the warrior's side, exiting near his backbone. "This one's gonna die slow. Maybe, if his friends come back for him after we're across this pass, it'll be a lesson to them."

Pearlie was grinning, looking at Cal. "I'm right proud of this young 'un. His color ain't all come back just yet, but fer that kind of shootin', I'm gonna overlook a little bit of change in his face. Damn nice work, son."

Sixteen

Jessie Evans had promised he would put a stop to that damn Englishman's interference. John Tunstall was complaining to the sheriff, the territorial governor, and almost everyone else about cattle rustling in Lincoln County, and the killings, even though there was no real evidence as to who was responsible. Witnesses were hard to come by. But when Jimmy Dolan said he wanted the Englishman taken care of right then, after another complaint had reached Sheriff Brady this morning, there wasn't anything to do but get the job done immediately.

Today, riding with two new gunmen he'd recently hired, Tom Hill and Billy Morton, they were headed to Tunstall's ranch to scare him out of the country or silence him. Jessie would have been more comfortable bringing extra men with him, however, word had it that Tunstall had only five or six green kids working for him and with Dolan screaming his head off to put the Englishman in his place, either headed back to England or in a six-foot hole in the ground, Jessie decided the three of them could handle it rather than ride all the way out to Bosque Redondo to pick up a few more shooters. On the road to Tunstall's ranch, Jessie told Billy and Tom what he wanted done.

"Look for any excuse to kill him," Jessie said, "an' if any of them wet-noses reach for a shootin' iron, blow 'em away. We gotta get this done right. Jimmy's madder'n hell about all them letters Tunstall's been writin'."

"Why do we need an excuse?" asked Billy, a narrow-eyed man who had a reputation in West Texas as a backshooter. "Let's just ride up to the house an' kill the son of a bitch. Mr. Dolan don't have to know. We can say he went for a gun."

"There may be too many witnesses," Jessie replied. "If we have to, we'll take him off somewheres at gunpoint an' do the job where nobody's watchin'."

"It don't make a damn bit of difference to me," said Tom Hill, another Texan who made his living in the gunfighter's trade. "Unless he's got himself surrounded by some good men with a gun, I say we just shoot the sumbitch an' be done with it, so we can earn our money."

Jessie saw no need in planning it until they saw what they were up against at Tunstall's place. "We'll wait till we get there to make up our minds. Don't worry none 'bout his cowboys. I've seen a few of 'em. Hardly more'n school boys. John Chisum is another matter. He's payin' top wages for men who can shoot. He aims to turn this into a killin' contest. Dolan told me Buck Andrews is on Chisum's payroll now, an' so is Curly Tully. Them two boys is dangerous as snakes. I've knowed Buck for years, an' when he sets out after a man, he'd best be real careful. Curly can be worse'n Buck, if the money's right. Curly ain't scared of no man on earth, an' he ain't opposed to killin' a man in his sleep if he gets the chance. Chisum's got plenty of money behind him, an' that's what's gonna make this dangerous as hell. Soon as Chisum gets an army of shooters behind him like he's doin' now, all hell's gonna break loose."

Billy looked behind them, resting his palms on his saddle horn while his horse trotted down the two-rut lane leading to Tunstall's place. "Don't none of them names scare me," he said in an offhanded way. "A man's just a man when the shootin' starts."

Tom grunted and nodded once, sighting along the horizon as he spoke. "Billy's right. Just show us the bastards you want killed, an' we'll do the rest. Couldn't help but notice you got Bill Pickett on your payroll. Now there's what I call a crazy mean son of a bitch. I was with him on a little job up in Fort Worth a few years ago. Didn't know who he was back then. We was hired to help clear some hard cases out of a saloon in Hell's Half Acre, when the law wouldn't do it on account of they was scared of 'em. Pickett come in the back way with that scattergun, an' when he started shootin', wasn't much left but blood and shredded meat all over the floor. Hell, I was half scared he was gonna shoot me, the way he was blastin' lead all over the place. Buck Andrews an' Curly Tully are bad men with a gun, but they ain't never run into the likes of Bill Pickett."

Jessie knew all too well how dangerous Pickett could be, and along with Roy Cooper, Ignacio Valdez, and the *pistoleros* he'd hired from below the Mexican border, Chisum would be up against so many killers, he wouldn't have time to bid on any beef contracts. And while he never said so publicly, Jessie knew he was a match for any of them, including Pickett. . . .

He'd tested his guns against some of the best in El Paso and Juarez, Laredo, and other tough border towns.

Crossing a gentle rise in the prairie, Jessie signaled a halt when he saw a buggy and five mounted men coming toward them. The cowboys were pushing a herd of loose horses. He recognized John Tunstall at once, even from a distance.

"Yonder he is, the feller drivin' the buggy. This is as good a place as any, boys. Fill your fists with iron an' we'll charge straight toward 'em, throwin' lead. That'll scare off his young cowboys, an' we'll shoot Tunstall right here."

Tom and Billy drew pistols. Jessie pulled his .44 and dug spurs into his horse's sides. Firing a few rounds in the air long before they were in range, Jessie led his men toward John Tunstall and five riders. . . . Even from here Jessie could see three of them weren't carrying guns.

Two cowboys swung off, spurring for the top of a rock ridge to the east. The others milled back and forth for a moment near the buggy, then they rode off to the south as hard as they could ride, leaving Tunstall alone in the middle of the road.

Jessie grinned as he bore down on the buggy. This was going to be even easier than he'd thought. Tunstall's men deserted him without firing a shot, proving they were the young cowards he had known they would be.

The Englishman reined his buggy to a halt. He carried no gun Jessie could see. He watched Jessie and his men gallop up without showing any sign of fear. Tunstall wore a brown suit and a bowler hat, his usual attire. Jessie pulled his mount to a stop a few yards from the carriage.

"What was all the shooting about, Mr. Evans?" Tunstall asked as he looked at their drawn pistols. "You have frightened my men and scattered our horses. Please explain your actions."

Jessie found it hard to believe Tunstall could be so calm in the face of three armed men who were his enemies. "Your boys did scatter like quail, Tunstall. Don't appear they've got much in the way of backbone."

"I ordered them to leave, to keep them from being injured if this were a robbery."

"Ain't no robbery," Jessie told him. "You've been complainin' to Sheriff Brady an' to Governor Wallace an' the soldiers at Fort Stanton about cattle rustlin'. You've wrote a bunch of damn letters accusin' Mr. Murphy and Jimmy Dolan of bein' behind it all. Somebody's gotta stop you from writin' all them goddamn letters, Tunstall, accusin' the wrong people, makin' 'em look bad when they ain't done nothin' to you. You took the wrong side in this here cattle war, Tunstall. John Chisum is a goddamn thief an' a liar."

Tom was looking at the rocky ridge. "Two of them yellow-bellied bastards are watchin' us from up yonder. Me an' Billy could ride up there an' run 'em off."

"Ain't gonna be necessary," Jessie replied, thumbing back the hammer on his Colt. "Mr. Tunstall just pulled a gun on me. Got no choice but to defend myself." He aimed for Tunstall's chest and pulled the trigger.

The sharp report startled Tunstall's buggy horse—

it lunged forward as a small hole puckered in his suit coat a few inches above his heart, the bullet's force pinning him to his buggy seat for a few seconds. Billy grabbed the buggy horse's bridle to keep it from running off.

Tunstall slumped forward clutching his chest, blood pumping from his wound. He mouthed a few silent words, hands tightening around his reins in a trembling grip.

"That oughta be the end of them letters," Jessie said as he swung down to the ground. "Hold my horse," he told Tom. "Let's see if Mr. Tunstall is packin' a gun."

He found a small-caliber revolver hidden inside the Englishman's coat. "Lookee here, boys. Mr. Tunstall was armed. Even though he's the same as dead right now, he's gonna fire a couple of shots at us."

Jessie aimed the pistol at the ground, firing twice, again spooking the horses. Then he placed the revolver in Tunstall's right hand and pushed him back against the buggy seat.

"Now then," Jessie said, grinning a one-sided grin with no humor in it. "What we got here is a case of self-defense, an' you boys can testify Mr. Tunstall's gun fired two times."

"I seen it with my own two eyes," Tom replied casually.

"I was lookin' right at him when he tried to kill you," Billy said. "Plain and simple, Jessie. You didn't have no choice but to defend yourself. I'll swear to it on a stack of Bibles as high as your head."

"Only thing to worry 'bout," Tom said, glancing back to the ridge, "is them two. They seen what happened."

Jessie climbed back on his horse. "Too far away. Nobody can be sure who they saw, or exactly what happened from so far off."

"We can ride up there an' kill 'em," Tom suggested. "I see one wearin' an old top hat looking down at us now."

Jessie looked at the ridge again. "I remember him. He came to Bosque Redondo lookin' for a job with us. I ran him off 'cause he was too young. Seems like he said his name was William Bonney."

"If we ain't gonna kill 'em, let's clear out," Billy said. "No tellin' who else might come along."

Jessie gazed down at John Tunstall. Tunstall was still able to breathe, although now blood was coming from his mouth and nose in rivulets. "We did what we set out to do. Jimmy's gonna be real glad to hear Mr. Tunstall won't be writin' no more of his damn letters."

Tom and Billy swung their horses away from the buggy, but they waited when Jessie sat his horse. Jessie stayed a moment longer, watching blood pool on the floorboards of the buggy.

"What's wrong, boss?" Tom asked.

"Just thinkin'. I say it's time we quit messin' around. I say we kill every son of a bitch who does business with Mr. John Chisum, no matter who it is."

"Suits me," Billy remarked. "I thought that's what we was gettin' paid to do anyways."

"Murphy ain't got enough starch in him," Jessie said. "If he wants to end this war real quick, he'll just turn us loose to burn a little gunpowder."

"One of us oughta keep an eye on John Chisum's ranch," Tom suggested. "Anybody who shows up to buy cattle, we kill 'em. Won't be long till word spreads that it's dangerous, buyin' beef from Chisum."

Jessie thought about it. "That's one hell of a good idea, Tom. I'll ask Jimmy. The first sumbitch who comes to Chisum's spread buyin' cattle, we kill 'em soon as they get out of earshot of the ranch."

Billy was watching the ridge. "I still claim we'd be a lot smarter to ride up there an' kill them two."

Jessie wagged his head. "Leave 'em be. Sheriff Brady ain't gonna believe 'em anyways."

"Whatever you say, Jessie. You're the boss."

Jessie led his men away from the buggy at a trot, in no real hurry to leave the scene. Down deep, he knew he had just put out one of the major fires causing trouble in Lincoln County, and when word of it reached Chisum and some of his friends, this cow war would soon be over.

At the top of the rise, he looked backward. The two cowboys who rode for Tunstall were riding their horses carefully down to the buggy. "That oughta teach 'em a lesson," he said under his breath, kicking his horse to a short lope.

Seventeen

Smoke took Cal aside while the others sat around their fire eating beans and fatback. Cal had been behaving strangely since he'd shot the Apache, riding along in what appeared to be a moody silence. As soon as Smoke got the boy off in the dark, he gave him a questioning look.

"What's eatin' on you, Cal?"

Cal couldn't look Smoke in the eye, gazing up at the stars for a time. "I reckon it's rememberin' that Indian I shot back yonder, Mr. Jensen, remembering what he looked like with that big hole in him . . . knowin' I done it."

"Killin' a man is never easy," Smoke said gently. "Sometimes it's necessary. Those Apaches were coming after us, and if one of 'em had gotten off a lucky shot, one of us might have been killed. You did what you had to do in order to save your friends and that's part of accepting the responsibility of being a man."

Cal shoved his hands in the front pockets of his denims. "I wasn't scared or nothin' like that. I reckon I hadn't oughta admit it, but it sorta made me sick when I seen what I done. I wish I could be more like you, Mr. Jensen. I've seen what you done to bad men, like them boys who rode with Sundance Morgan. I seen how you stay calm, like it don't rattle you none when you kill somebody."

"It comes with time, Cal. You have to make up your mind that it's them or you, or your friends. Some men seem to have a natural gift for fightin', like some others have a gift with breaking horses."

"It never did bother you right at first when you killed a man?"

He thought about it a moment. "I suppose I'd already made up my mind that it had to be done, that there wasn't any other way. There's some men who need killin'. They break the law and bring harm to other folks who can't defend themselves. I never went out lookin' for a man to kill. Seems like they always found me, one way or another, and I've been willing to oblige 'em when it was a fight they wanted."

"You're the best at it I ever saw, Mr. Jensen, but to tell the truth I don't think it's my natural callin'. You taught me how to shoot, an' how to look out for myself. I'm real grateful for that. When I looked down at that dyin' Indian, somethin' in my head said maybe it was wrong, even though he had a rifle an' he was shootin' at us. I can't explain it proper. . . ."

"Some men ain't cut out for killing, Cal. You know how to do it when it's necessary, and that can be a good thing, so you can defend what's yours if somebody tries to take it. I think you realized for the first time how final death is, after you took another man's life. Understandable, to feel that way. It may keep you from becoming a killer yourself, unless you've got a good reason to kill."

"But you've killed plenty of men and it don't seem to bother you none. Leastways, you don't show it."

Smoke turned back toward the fire. Cal would understand the incident today, given time. "I never killed a man who didn't ask for the opportunity. The Apache you shot knew it could turn out either way . . . he'd lose his life, or you'd lose yours. He took a gamble, a calculated risk, and he lost. You did yourself proud, and you may have saved a friend's life because of it . . . even mine if the Indian had gotten lucky."

"I hadn't thought of it quite like that," Cal said. "Maybe it wasn't so bad after all, what I did today."

Lincoln Township was a little place, two stores and a blacksmith's shop and a few smaller businesses, a two-story courthouse near the Rio Hondo, surrounded by the Capitan Mountains. When Smoke and his cowboys rode into town on an April afternoon, the village was in an uproar, and it wasn't long until Smoke learned from a blacksmith that two funerals were about to commence.

"Billy Bonney an' some of his friends gunned down Sheriff Brady an' his deputy, George Hindeman. It was retaliation for the murder of John Tunstall, pure an' simple. Billy the Kid, as they call him, led the attack. The governor is puttin' out a warrant for his arrest, along with them others. We's fixin' to have two funerals today, the sheriff's and his deputy's."

Smoke didn't care to hear all the details. "Can you give us directions to John Chisum's ranch?" he asked.

"East of here. It's called South Springs ranch an' that's where you'll find him. It's a day's ride. Can't miss it. It's on the west bank of the Pecos River."

Smoke gave the town a final look. People were standing in groups talking among themselves as two funeral wagons waited at the end of the street near the courthouse and a tiny church. "Thanks," was all Smoke said, wheeling his horse eastward to ride out of Lincoln. The shootings weren't any of his affair.

Pearlie had a twinkle in his eye when he looked at Smoke, then he spoke to Cal. "Like I said not too long ago, young 'un, where there's trouble, you'll usually find Smoke Jensen. Either it comes lookin' fer him, or we ride smack into it. First thing a man learns when he rides for the Sugarloaf brand is to keep his guns cleaned an' loaded. I knowed things was too quiet this past winter. Ain't hardly spring yet an' here we are, square in the middle of a range war."

John Chisum was a towering figure at six-foot-four in boots, with a square jaw and slitted eyes, with suspicion in them when Smoke and his riders arrived at South Springs ranch. There were men wearing guns near the barns and corrals, a seedy-looking lot for the most part, paid shootists if ever Smoke laid eyes on one. It seemed every one of them was watching Smoke and his men ride in to the ranch.

Smoke swung down and walked up to Chisum, offering his hand. "Name's Smoke Jensen, from Big Rock, Colorado Territory. I wrote you awhile back and you sent me prices on some Hereford bulls."

Chisum's expression changed to friendliness. "Of course, Mr. Jensen. I remember now. You were interested in a dozen to fifteen young bulls, as I recall. I quoted you a price of two hundred dollars each and the offer still stands." He turned to a pockmarked gunman leaning against a porch post. "It's okay, Buck. Tell the boys they can relax an' go back to work. These men are invited guests." He looked back at Smoke. "Tell your men to turn their horses into an empty corral an' then come to the house. I'll offer you coffee or whiskey or both, an' a bite to eat as soon as Maria can get the stove going."

"We're grateful. It's been a long ride," Smoke said as he gave his horse's reins to Pearlie.

Chisum frowned a bit. "Did you run into any difficulties on the way down?"

"A handful of renegade Apaches gave us a try a few days ago, but we handled it."

As Smoke was climbing the porch steps, Chisum gave the hills a sweeping glance. "In case you haven't heard, we're having our share of problems in Lincoln County, only it isn't Indians who are causing it. Cattle rustling has gotten so bad I've had to hire guards to watch my herds. There've been a number of killings, and I've lost almost a dozen men. A rancher friend of mine was murdered in cold blood, and just yesterday our sheriff and one of his deputies were gunned down. The army post over at Fort Stanton won't do anything to stop all this killing, and I fear it will only get worse. The territorial governor, Lew Wallace, may be our only hope of ending what amounts to all-out war."

"We've heard a little bit about it," Smoke said, following Chisum into a big log house decorated inside with mounted cattle horns and colorful Indian blankets nailed to the walls. Leather chairs sat around a massive fireplace and Chisum pointed to one as he went to a cabinet for a bottle of whiskey and glasses.

"You were lucky you didn't ride into a cross fire," Chisum said, pouring Smoke a shot of whiskey, "and I'll warn you to be careful heading back with any cattle you buy from me. We've got rustlers and gunmen riding all over the county stealing cows and killin' folks." He glanced down at Smoke's pair of pistols. "I can see you and your men are well armed, but you'd better know how to use the iron you're packing."

"We can handle ourselves, I think," Smoke replied before he tasted his drink, finding it to be good sour mash, not the cheap watered stuff.

"Glad to hear it," Chisum said, settling into a chair. "If you're lucky, you won't run into any trouble-makers."

"Never was real lucky in that regard," Smoke told him, "but if trouble comes our way, I know what to do with it."

Chisum chuckled, reading Smoke's face closely now. "I'm a pretty good judge of men, Mr. Jensen, and I don't figure that's any exaggeration. Some gents send out a warning to other men by the way they carry themselves. While we don't know each other, I'm pretty sure I'd hate to tangle with you if you got on a mad."

Smoke grinned. He took an immediate liking to Chisum. "I'm looking forward to seeing those bulls. And if the price is right, I'd like to buy about two hundred young longhorn cows to cross 'em on."

Chisum nodded. "I'll give you your pick of my longhorn heifers for twenty-five bucks apiece."

"That's a fair price if they're in good flesh. We've got to drive 'em a long way, so they'll need to be in good trail condition."

"You'll be well satisfied," Chisum assured him, downing his drink in a single gulp. "A Hereford is a good cross on a longhorn. More meat, and the calves are almost disease free. The Hereford breed is the thing of the future in the cattle market, as far as I'm concerned."

"My wife's been reading up on 'em and she says the same thing," Smoke said. "We're just hoping they take well to colder country."

"They do, and they can handle the heat in summer. If they have faults, it's that they're short-legged creatures, so they don't trail as well as a longhorn, and a purebred Hereford is subject to pinkeye in hot weather sometimes."

These were some of the same things Sally had told him about Herefords. Smoke was glad to find that Chisum was being honest about his bulls. He decided Chisum would make a good neighbor and friend, if they lived closer. Chisum would be a good man to ride the trails with . . . he had character. "Soon as the boys get a drink in 'em, I'd like to see those bulls," he said.

Chisum stood up and poured another round. "I'll tell Maria to get the stove hot and fix something for everybody to eat. We can go down to the barns and look at those bulls anytime you're ready."

Eighteen

Billy Barlow came galloping up to the log cabin at Bosque Redondo on a lathered, winded horse. He jumped to the ground, seemingly out of breath himself even though his horse had done all the traveling.

"Could be trouble, Jessie," he said to Jessie Evans. Billy had been assigned to watch the Chisum ranch for cattle buyers, and to see if Chisum was hiring any more gunmen.

"How's that?" Jessie asked.

"Seven riders leadin' spare horses just showed up at Chisum's. I had my field glasses on 'em when they come along the road from Lincoln. They was all carryin' guns, plenty of 'em, an' I'm pretty sure I know who one of 'em is."

"Who is he?" Jessie asked, not really interested since he didn't trust Barlow's judgment in these matters.

"A feller from up in Colorado Territory by the name of Smoke Jensen."

"The name don't mean nothin' to me."

"Maybe it oughta. I spent a little time up there workin' on a ranch. Smoke Jensen is one bad hombre with a six-gun. Up in them parts damn near everybody knows him. He's a killer, Jessie, an honest to goodness killer. He's got about the meanest reputation a man can have, an' there was six more rode in with him."

Jessie leaned forward on the bench where he sat watching men change cattle brands in the corrals. He didn't figure Barlow was good enough with a gun to know much about gunmen. Since William Bonney and some of his friends had ambushed Sheriff Brady and Deputy Hindeman, he'd been thinking of a way to strike back. It was a cowardly way to kill two men, hiding behind a fence until they came into range, gunning them down without warning. Bonney and his young friends were calling themselves Regulators now and someone said they were wearing badges authorized by an old justice of the peace, Judge Wilson. Their badges didn't mean a damn thing, and Bonney and his green companions were nothing to worry about, but if Chisum was importing more professional gunmen like Curly Tully and Buck Andrews, this was another matter. "I'll send Roy Cooper an' six of them Mexican *pistoleros* back with you. You show Roy who this Jensen feller is. If Jensen an' his pardners leave the Chisum ranch for any reason, Roy'll know what to do. Saddle a fresh horse an' tell Roy I want to see him. Before this Smoke Jensen causes us any trouble, we'll kill him. It's as simple as that."

Barlow seemed uncertain. "I wasn't jokin', boss, when I said this feller is dangerous. Maybe you oughta send some more men with Roy."

"I'm runnin' this outfit," Jessie declared angrily. "You tell Roy I want him, an' tell them Mexicans to saddle horses up as quick as they can. Show Roy who this Jensen feller is . . . point him out through them field glasses when you get a chance. That makes eight of us an' seven of them, and as far as I'm concerned,

Roy is better'n any three men with a gun. Maybe Jensen's just passin' through. No need to get yourself so worked up over one man's reputation."

Barlow backed away in the face of Jessie's anger, leading his horse toward the corrals. Jessie leaned back against the cabin wall, pulling a cork from the neck of a tequila bottle.

Bill Pickett appeared to have been dozing at the other end of the porch with his hat over his face. But as Jessie took a swallow of tequila, Pickett sat up straight, watching Barlow as he went looking for Cooper.

"Barlow may be right," Pickett said. "Maybe you oughta send more men. I'll go. Hell, I ain't shot nobody in so long I plumb forgot what it's like to see a man die. All we're doin' is sittin' around this stinkin' cow camp waitin' for somethin' to happen."

"I don't put much stock in what Barlow said about this Jensen bein' a real shooter. Maybe Jensen just stopped by the ranch to say howdy. Either way, if he leaves Chisum's, Roy'll make sure he don't go no place else. Barlow ain't all that good with a gun himself, so ain't no reason why he'd know if a man was one of the best. You stay here. We'll go lookin' for that Billy Bonney an' his friends in a day or two. If we kill 'bout a half dozen of them so-called Regulators, it'll help square things for what they did to Sheriff Brady an' Hindeman. We can't let a thing like that go unpunished, or afore you know it every son of a bitch in Lincoln County will be wearin' a badge."

"Well, damn," Pickett muttered, leaning back against the wall with his hat over his face. "I was tryin' to remember if I'd ever killed anybody named Jensen before, which I ain't. Not that I recall anyways. There ain't always time to ask a feller's name before you blow him to pieces."

"Be patient, Bill," Jessie said. "You can kill that Bonney kid instead."

Down at the corrals, men were running back and forth leading horses to the saddle shed. Roy Cooper came ambling up to the cabin with his rifle balanced in his palm.

"Barlow said we's supposed to head fer Chisum's an' blow hell outa some owlhoot named Smoke Jensen," he said.

"Barlow claims he's a shooter," Jessie said, "from up in Colorado Territory. Him an' six more just rode in at Chisum's place. Take those five Mexicans ridin' with Pedro an' see if you can kill this Jensen an' his pardners, if they leave the ranch. If they stay, keep an eye on 'em. Find out what Chisum's up to. If he's hirin' more guns, we need to know."

Cooper frowned. "This ain't no way to fight a war, Jessie. Hell, we've got damn near thirty men as it is. How come we don't ride over to Chisum's an' kill him an' every last one of them sons of bitches?"

"Orders from Dolan. We kill 'em off a few at a time an' it don't make so much ruckus. Just take care of Jensen an' his men till we get word from Dolan that things have changed. I figure them kids killin' Brady and Hindeman will touch off the boys up in Santa Fe. They've got the purse strings, so we do what they say. After all, Roy, you ain't no different from me. We're only in this for the money. . . ."

"This Jensen's as good as dead," Roy promised, wheeling away from the porch.

Jessie felt better about things now.

Nineteen

Smoke rested his elbows on a corral pole admiring a group of curious, stocky young bulls with sorrel bodies and white heads, a pair of short, curved horns, and more meat than he had ever seen on a cow.

"They're more than I expected," he told John Chisum, wishing Sally could see these impressive specimens of beef cattle for herself right now. "They carry more muscle across the hindquarter all the way up their backs to their chests. If the crosses are even half this good, it'll mean a bigger profit for every calf we sell."

"I'll show you some of the crosses when we ride out in the pastures," Chisum said. "You won't be disappointed. You're looking at the future of the cattle business."

"I'd like to see those crosses," Smoke said, pulling away from the fence. His men were lounging on Chisum's front porch after a delicious meal of beefsteak, tortillas, beans, and rice. "My boys and neighbors look damn near foundered after all that food. You and me can ride out to look at the crossbreds while my bunch recovers from Maria's good cooking."

Chisum grinned. "Let's saddle a couple of horses," he said as they turned for the barns. "I've got a bunch of crossbred steers close to the house in a pasture north of here. It's less than a half hour ride."

"Sounds good to me," Smoke replied, thinking of pastures at Sugarloaf filled with white-faced cattle in a few years. "Just so you'll know, I'll take fifteen of those bulls. A few are for my neighbors, who aim to start the same breeding program. If you got no objections, we'll pick the bulls and roughly two hundred longhorn heifers tomorrow morning. I brought cash, so you'll be paid on the spot."

"Then we've got a deal," Chisum said, offering Smoke his hand as a way of sealing their bargain.

The crossbreds all had white faces. Some were brindle in body color, while others were spotted like many longhorns, or a solid black or brown. The steers they saw were long yearlings, born last year, and they carried more beef than Smoke had imagined. Riding across a narrow, tree-studded valley turning green with spring grass, they rode among the gentle cattle without disturbing them. At the far end of the valley, a pair of Chisum cowboys kept watch over the herd. Smoke noted they were carrying rifles and pistols as if they expected trouble.

"Your cowhands go heavily armed," he said. "Too bad you're havin' all these problems with rustling. Seems to me like the law would step in."

Chisum's jaw went tight. "The law 'round here is mostly a bunch of crooks wearing badges, taking bribes from powerful men up in the territorial capitol at Santa Fe. They look the other way when I got robbed, for the most part. Now and then they go through the motions, investigating any rustling. That leaves it up to me to protect my own interests if I want to stay in business.''

"So you've hired your own gunmen," Smoke observed. "I guess it makes sense if it's the only way."

"I feel I've got no choice, unless our new governor takes some action. Things have gotten so far out of hand it isn't safe to ride my own land any longer. These rustlers get more brazen as time passes, when nothing official is done about them. I'm hoping all that will change this summer. But if it doesn't, I intend to fight fire with fire. I've hired two experienced manhunters . . . Buck Andrews and Curly Tully. If I lose one more cow or one more ranch hand, I'm sending them after whoever is responsible. I'm through sitting on the fence waiting for the law to come to my rescue. I'm taking things into my own hands.''

"That'd be my way of handlin' it," Smoke agreed as they rode to a pine-covered ridge at the north end of the valley. "I'm a real firm believer in takin' an eye for an eye."

"You'll need to watch the cattle you purchase from me very closely until you get out of this area," Chisum warned. "They won't spare your herd if they think they can take it."

Now it was Smoke's jaw tightening a little. "Let 'em try," he said quietly as they neared the trees where the last groups of crossbred steers grazed peacefully.

It was a sudden glint of sunlight on metal up on the ridge that made Smoke twist in the saddle, one hand reflexively going for a holstered Colt. "Watch out!" he snapped, eyes glued to the spot. "Somebody's up there with a gun."

Chisum wheeled his horse for the closest tree. "Get

to some cover!" he yelled, wasted breath since Smoke was already heeling his borrowed horse in the same direction.

Almost at the same instant, a rifle cracked somewhere above them. A piñon branch snapped above Smoke's head just as they rode into the pines.

"Stay here an' draw their fire!" Smoke bellowed, jerking his other pistol free, caught up in a rush of white-hot rage over the attempt to drygulch them.

He drove his spurs into the ribs of Chisum's bay gelding, beginning a full-tilt charge toward the top of the ridge without knowing how many men he faced. . . . At the moment he didn't give a damn. Smoke was hell-bent on teaching a bushwhacker some manners as he reined his galloping horse among the trees upslope. He heard a pistol bark behind him. . . . Chisum was drawing their fire with his big Walker Colt .44.

Smoke saw a man kneeling with a rifle to his shoulder, hiding behind the trunk of a piñon. Steadying his pistol, despite the gait of a running horse underneath him, Smoke snapped off a quick shot at fifty yards.

A splash of crimson flew from the rifleman's left ear as he was turning toward the sound of a speeding horse. The bushwhacker's rifle discharged harmlessly in the air as he spun away from the tree with blood squirting from his skull.

Another movement caught Smoke's attention, a stocky Mexican in a drooping sombrero turning a rifle in Smoke's direction. As the Mexican readied for a shot, Smoke fired a roaring pistol shot aimed at his chest.

The Mexican staggered backward, dropping his

Winchester to clutch his breastbone, where a dark red hole suddenly appeared in his soiled white shirt-front. Drumming his spurs into the bay's sides, Smoke raced toward another shadowy shape in the dense pine forest, bending low over his horse's neck, aiming as best he could with the bounding strides of the bay throwing his gunsights off a fraction.

The outline of another Mexican gunman became clear enough for a tricky shot and Smoke took it, hearing the roar of his .44 fill his ears, a wisp of blue gunsmoke curling past his face.

A sombrero-clad figure jerked upright next to a thick pine trunk, reaching for his shoulder, moving into plain sight just long enough for Smoke to fire again. A cry of pain filled the forest around them as Smoke pulled his bay to a sliding stop at the edge of a piñon thicket, leaping to the ground before the horse came to a complete halt. . . . He had no way of knowing how many more men were hidden along this ridge, and now it was time to hunt them down individually, stalking them until he was certain no one else was there.

The third man he'd shot slumped to the ground, groaning. Off in the distance, maybe a hundred yards further down the ridge, he heard voices, men yelling to each other in rapid Spanish, at least two more gunmen who would pay dearly for trying to ambush him and Chisum.

Smoke crept forward, both pistols at the ready, his anger slowly cooling to a more calculated revenge. Moving on the balls of his feet, he advanced toward the sound of voices. His horse trotted back downhill to escape the noise of guns. Darting from tree to tree, never knowing where another attacker might be, he heard the drum of pounding hoofbeats coming from the back side of the ridge, a lone horseman escaping the battle, apparently running out of nerve.

Soundlessly, he stepped across beds of fallen pine needles, keeping to the shadows wherever he could. Now all was quiet along the ridge. . . . The voices had stopped.

A moment later, he heard another horse take off at a gallop, and he wondered if the last bushwhacker had pulled out, until he caught a glimpse of a running man, a Mexican wearing a sombrero, carrying a rifle.

It was a difficult target, requiring Smoke to steady his Colt against a tree trunk. When he fired, the report echoed back and forth throughout the pines, accompanied by a yell as the potbellied Mexican went facedown, legs still pumping, trying to crawl.

Staying behind trees, Smoke hurried over to the wounded man, who left a blood trail over dry pine needles and yellowed winter grass beginning to turn green near its roots. The Mexican had a flesh wound across his ribs. Before Smoke knelt beside him, he gave the forest a close examination, until he was satisfied they were alone.

He put the muzzle of a Colt against the Mexican's right temple and spat out a question. "Who sent you? You've got just one chance to answer before I scatter your brains all over this ridge."

"Jessie," the Mexican hissed, clenching his teeth against the pain. "Jessie . . . Evans."

Smoke didn't recognize the name, although it wouldn't have mattered anyway. "You ain't hurt all that bad, Pancho, or whatever your name is. Get on your horse an' ride back to this Jessie Evans. Tell him if he ever messes with Smoke Jensen or any of my friends again, I'll come lookin' for him and I'll kill him. I want you to make that real clear. My friends and me are ridin' back to Colorado with a herd of cattle in a couple of days. If I lose so much as one cow or one bull, I'm gonna come lookin' for Jessie. There won't be no place in New Mexico Territory that's safe from me if anything happens to my cows or my friends. I've got no stake in this range war, but I'll goddamn sure take a hand in it if one more shot gets fired in my direction, or if I lose a single head of livestock. Understand, Pancho?"

The Mexican nodded, glancing sideways to the gun Smoke held to his head. *"Sí,* señor. I will tell Jessie."

Smoke wasn't quite satisfied yet. "I killed three of your partners just now, an' put a little gash across your ribs 'cause you were lucky. Don't count on bein' lucky the next time. Tell Jessie Evans what I said."

"Sí, señor. I swear I will tell him."

"I imagine Evans figures he's pretty tough, pretty good with a gun. He can go on believin' that if he wants, only be sure an' tell him he's never crossed paths with Smoke Jensen before. If he does it again, I'll fill him so goddamn full of bullet holes he won't have to take his pecker out to piss, 'cause he's gonna be leakin' all the time."

"I will tell him you are one bad hombre, señor. I have seen this . . . for myself."

Smoke lowered his Colt, lifted the Mexican's pistol out of his gunbelt, and took his rifle before he stood up cautiously to check his surroundings. Then he spoke to the Mexican again in a voice like ice. "I don't really figure it'll do any good to give Jessie that warning, but I'm doin' it anyway, just in case he's got more sense than most. Men who think they're tough usually have to be proven wrong. You can tell him Smoke Jensen is just the man who can get that job done. If it's a fight he wants, I'm the man he's lookin' for."

John Chisum lowered his pistol when he saw Smoke riding down to the cattle pasture. He waited until Smoke rode up to him to speak. Both Chisum cowboys guarding the herd had ridden up to the north end of the pasture with guns drawn.

"I heard all the shooting," Chisum said. "You must have scared them off. I stayed put, not knowing whether I'd be in your line of fire. When these boys rode up, we were about to head up this slope, when all of a sudden, the shooting ended."

"You'll find three dead Mexicans up there in those trees," Smoke said. "I reckon somebody oughta bury 'em an' notify their next of kin. I wounded another bushwacker and we had a little talk before I let him go. He told me he works for a man by the name of Jessie Evans. . . ."

"He's the ramrod of Jimmy Dolan's gang of rustlers," Chisum said bitterly, "only I can't prove a thing and nobody in official circles will look into it. Evans is a paid killer from down in Texas some place." Chisum stared at Smoke a moment. "You said you killed three of them all by your lonesome?"

Smoke began reloading his pair of Colts. "Mexican *pistoleros*, by the look of 'em. I've tangled with their kind before."

"You must be one hell of a gunman yourself, Mr. Jensen. I'd like to offer you a job, if you're interested."

"My guns ain't for hire," he replied, closing the loading gate on an ivory-handled .44 before he holstered it. "But I did send Jessie Evans a little message, by way of his wounded sidekick. I told him if one more bullet came at me or my men, or if I lost a single cow on my way back to Colorado, I'd come lookin' for him, and that I'd kill him."

"Evans won't scare easy," Chisum declared.

Smoke gave the crossbred steers another look as he said, "I wasn't meanin' to scare him, Mr. Chisum. I meant every goddamn word. Whoever this Jessie Evans is, he'll be a dead son of a bitch if he tests me on it. Now, if you're ready, let's take a look at those young longhorn cows you're offering for sale."

Twenty

Billy Barlow glanced over his shoulder as his horse ran up a steep incline. Another horseman was gaining ground on him. Was it the broad-shouldered crazy man with two pistols, he wondered. He relaxed some when he recognized Pedro Lopez racing away from the scene of the shooting, the same as Billy had when it became clear the man who rode with Chisum had no fear, no sense, like a locoed bronc, the way he'd charged up that mountain with both guns blazing.

Billy slowed his horse to a walk at the top of the climb to scan the trail behind Pedro. The lunatic with two guns was not following them. He waited for Pedro to catch up.

Pedro's horse was floundering under the punishment of spurs when Pedro rode up beside Billy.

"He ain't followin' you?" Billy asked, looking again at their backtrail, finding it empty.

"No," Pedro gasped, looking back himself. *"El hombre loco* is too busy killing Jorge and Carlos and Raul. This son of a bitch be *muy loco,* to come at us like that."

"He ain't just loco," Billy said. "He can goddamn sure shoot."

"Verdad, it is the truth," Pedro wheezed. "He come

straight at us like *un idiota.* I never see a man so fool-ish as him before today."

"It's like he wasn't afraid of our guns at all."

Pedro mopped his brow with a bandanna, glancing back again to look for dust or any sign of the stranger. "I see Roy Cooper ride off very fast when this *idiota* come up the hill. He ride to the east. I don't under-stand. Cooper is *loco* himself, but he is also mean with a gun. But he don't stay when this stranger come shooting. He run away, like he know this hombre don't be right in his head."

"I didn't see which way Cooper went," Billy said. "I was too busy lookin' out for my own ass. That guy, whoever he is, can't have a lick of sense to charge us like that all by himself with just two pistols. He's either dumb as a rock, or nearly the meanest bastard who ever stood in a pair of boots."

"Maybeso Cooper go back to get him when he think we all go away," Pedro suggested.

"I ain't so damn sure," Billy replied. "Maybe Mr. Roy Cooper ain't as tough as we think he is. He lit out of there like his tailfeathers was afire."

Pedro shrugged. "Who can say? I see Cooper shoot those cowboys in the night like he enjoy it."

"Maybe he don't enjoy it so much when some-body's shootin' back at him."

"Señor Jessie be plenty mad when he hear this," Pedro said, as though he was speaking to himself.

"Then let *him* face this crazy son of a bitch. We'll tell him he'd better bring Pickett an' every spare gun he's got if he aims to kill that big bastard. I got a feelin' this guy ain't gonna be easy to kill."

"Is the truth," Pedro muttered, looking over his

shoulder yet another time. "I don't see Victor. Maybeso this hombre kill him too."

"You're right about one thing," Billy added as he urged his horse to a lope. "Jessie sure as hell ain't gonna like this when we give him the news."

Roy Cooper lay on his belly in tall grass near the mouth of the valley, putting his rifle sights on the square-shouldered cowboy who came at them earlier. He was riding beside Chisum and his ranch hands like a man who didn't have a care in the world. Roy knew the others were either dead or they'd deserted him, which was typical of Mexican gunmen—short on courage when things got tight.

The range for his Winchester .44 was still too great to be sure of the shot, and thus Roy waited, holding his rifle against his shoulder, doing his best to keep the barrel from catching sunlight that might warn the riders below of his presence. He was sure he could take down the newcomer when the distance was right.

The stranger's head turned toward the grassy hilltop where Roy lay, but only for a moment. "He didn't see me," Roy whispered. Then the stranger did an odd thing. . . . He got down off his horse and walked into a line of trees while the others halted to wait for him.

"He needed to piss," Roy told himself. "He's too bashful to pull his pecker out while everybody's watchin'. Maybe I can get him when he walks out of them pines. . . ."

Time seemed frozen, although it did seem to be taking the stranger a hell of a long time to let his water down. Roy was motionless, his rifle aimed for the spot where the stranger went into the trees, judging his chances of a quick kill with just one slug.

Minutes passed. "Maybe he's takin' a shit," Roy wondered softly. The others, including Chisum, sat their horses in clear view as though nothing was wrong, never once looking up at Roy's hiding place.

A sound behind him, something brushing against the grasses, made him turn. Then a towering figure blocked out the sun. The glint of a huge knife blade flashed.

"Son of a . . ."

A blinding pain entered Roy's rib cage, along with a noise like snapping willow limbs. Cartilage was torn from his sternum by a single slash of a razor-sharp knifepoint. He heard himself scream, staring into a face twisted with hatred above him, and just as quickly, the scream died in his throat when a second swipe of the blade went across his windpipe, slicing through cords of muscle, ligaments, and skin.

"Die slow, you backshootin' bastard," a grating voice said quietly.

Roy's backbone arched, and he struggled to bring his gun up at the same time until a heavy boot landed on his wrist, knocking the rifle from his hand.

"You've got no balls, pilgrim. You're just another yellow son of a bitch who can't face the man he aims to kill. I've known half a hundred like you. I don't know your name, but it don't matter who you are. *What* you are is dead, only not yet, not till the ants feed on you for a spell, until your blood runs all over this hill."

Pain shot through Roy's body from head to toe and for a moment he was sure he would lose consciousness. He made a second attempt to sit up, choking on his own blood, strangling when it entered his windpipe.

"Wish you could live long enough to tell this Jessie Evans he's messin' with the wrong man. But you won't. You'll be dead in half an hour, maybe less."

Roy saw winking stars before his eyes, but he could still see the twisted face looming over him.

"Bleedin' to death is a helluva slow way to die, mister. I hope it don't hurt too awful bad. But if it does, think about all the cows you stole that wasn't yours, or the men you killed who never had a chance. Think about those things while you're dyin'. You ain't got long."

Roy fell back on the grass, unable to breathe at all now.

"Adios, cowboy, whoever you are," the same voice said as Roy slipped slowly into a black void.

Jessie watched two men ride in at a hard gallop with a vague sense of apprehension. He recognized Barlow and Lopez by their horses. "Somethin's wrong," he told Pickett.

Pickett came up from his bull hide chair, squinting in the sun's glare, cradling a shotgun in the crook of his arm. "It's that Barlow boy an' Pedro Lopez. They's after their horses with a spur mighty hard."

"Wonder where Roy is?" Jessie asked. "It ain't like Roy to let 'em split up . . . 'less there's been trouble."

Billy and Pedro galloped their winded mounts up to the cabin, and Barlow was the first to speak.

"We got real problems," Barlow said, dropping to the ground in more of a hurry than Jessie felt was warranted. "This stranger showed up at Chisum's. We had it all laid out to kill him, only he come at us like a nest of hornets. He rode right up the ridge where we was hidin' an' started shootin' like a bullet was never gonna hit him. Roy Cooper took off in the other direction soon as it happened."

"Is true, Señor Jessie," Pedro agreed, climbing down from his lathered horse. "This stranger, he don't be afraid of nothing. He ride his horse toward us while we be shooting, and he don't act afraid."

Jessie stood up. "Where the hell is Roy?" he asked with a note of impatience. Roy Cooper had never run away from any man that Jessie knew of.

"He run away, just like Billy say," Pedro said. "He ride off like he be scared of this hombre."

"Nonsense. Roy ain't afraid of nobody."

Billy shrugged. "Can't explain what he did no other way, boss. He jumped on his horse an' rode east as fast as that brown gelding could travel."

"What happened to the others?" Jessie demanded.

"Maybeso all are dead," Pedro answered. "This big hombre, he come up shooting with two *pistolas,* one in each hand. He no be afraid of our guns."

Jessie's attention was distracted by another rider coming in at Bosque Redondo, a man slumped over his saddle like he was in a great deal of pain.

"Who's that?" Jessie asked.

Pedro looked over his shoulder. "It is Victor Bustamante, and there is blood on his shirt."

"Ain't nobody gonna convince me Roy Cooper took off when it was time for a killin'," Jessie stated. "See what the hell that Mexican has to say. . . ."

Victor Bustamante rode his grullo gelding up to the cabin with obvious pain twisting his face. He stopped his horse in front of the porch. Blood was leaking from a wound across his right side, covering his right pants leg.

"I have . . . this message for you . . . Señor Jessie," he said in clipped, breathless words.

"What kind of goddamn message?" Jessie wanted to know, as he grew impatient with this latest bit of news.

"This hombre . . . he call himself Smoke Jensen. He say he gone kill you. . . . He say he come looking for you if we don't stop shoot at him."

Jessie's sun-etched face crinkled. "Who the hell is Smoke Jensen? I never heard of him."

"He be one *malo hombre,*" Victor replied, still holding his side, wincing. "He kill Raul and Jorge real quick. Then he kill Carlos and he shoot this hole in me."

Jessie stiffened. "The son of a bitch said he was gonna kill me?" he asked in a voice that boomed all over the clearing where the cow camp was hidden. "You mean that arrogant son of a bitch had the nerve to say that?"

"*Si,* Señor Jessie. He say he want me tell you how he kill you if anybody shoot at him or his *compadres* again. This be what he say to tell you."

Jessie glanced over at Pickett. "Who the hell is Smoke Jensen?"

"Never heard of the bastard," Pickett replied. "I'll go saddle a horse an' we'll see if he's as tough as he says he is."

"Where did this happen?" Jessie asked Billy.

"North of the Chisum ranch by maybe ten miles."

"An' you claim Roy took off runnin' when it happened?"

"Yessir. That's sure the way it looked. Roy jumped

on his horse and rode east as fast as that pony could travel. Last we saw of him, he was headed for the Pecos River."

"That ain't like Roy. Maybe he was gonna ride a circle around 'em."

"It sure as hell didn't look that way, boss. Soon as Raul an' Jorge got killed, Roy took off. He never fired a shot at this Jensen feller."

"Roy ain't no coward."

Billy shrugged. "Maybe he just knowed it when he was outgunned. That Jensen never wasted a bullet. He killed Raul so quick it was like they was standin' two feet apart. Then he shot Carlos an' Jorge, all of 'em from the back of a runnin' horse. I took off right after that, when I seen there wasn't no stoppin' this Jensen. He ain't no ordinary man."

Jessie scowled. "You ain't nothin' but a yellow son of a bitch, Barlow. Get your gear an' clear out of here. I'll have your wages ready."

Pickett lifted his shotgun and started down the porch steps two at a time. "I'll saddle a horse an' round up Ignacio, Billy, an' Tom. Let's see if this Jensen is as tough as he claims to be."

Jessie gazed across the corrals. "Tell those boys from up in Arkansas to ride along with us. Chisum may have hired himself a fancy shooter, only we'll see how good he is when the odds are against him. That one-eyed feller from Arkansas says he can hit a sparrow on the fly with a Sharps rifle. We'll let him show us how good he is."

Pickett ambled off toward the corrals, in no apparent hurry to get things started. Jessie looked at Billy. "Get your gear out of the bunkhouse, Barlow. You're finished with this outfit, an' if I ever lay eyes on you again, I'll kill you myself." He turned his attention to Victor. "Have somebody fix you a bandage for that scratch. Then get mounted on a fresh horse so you can show us where all this happened. Jensen could be dead by now, if Roy caught up with him. One thing you can bet on—Roy Cooper didn't run from no kind of fight."

Twenty-one

Smoke heard horses coming up the hill as he wiped blood off his Bowie knife on the dying man's pants leg. Standing out in plain view, he knew Chisum and his cowboys could see him now, and they were riding up to see what had brought him here. . . . He'd only said to wait for him until he took care of a little unfinished business, without telling them a man was lying in ambush for them on this hilltop, just out of rifle range. Again, he'd seen a flash of polished metal in the sun as they were riding out of the valley, and he knew what it meant. There wasn't time to explain.

"What happened, Mr. Jensen?" Chisum asked just before his horse snorted, scenting blood as it trotted toward Smoke.

"We had another surprise waiting for us," Smoke replied as he sheathed his Bowie, "another gent who thought we'd ride right past his hiding place so he could shoot us down."

Now Chisum saw the body lying in a patch of tall, bloody grass near Smoke's feet. "Damn," he said, swinging off his red sorrel to get a better look.

One of Chisum's cowboys said, "That's Roy Cooper, another one of Dolan's hired guns. A feller told me Cooper had a real bad disposition, that he was a sure enough professional killer."

Smoke took a last look at Cooper. "He should have chosen another line of work. It's just one man's opinion, but it don't seem he was all that good at it."

Chisum was staring at Smoke with a bit of slack in his jaw. "You killed him with a knife. How come you didn't use a gun?" he asked. "You must have slipped up behind him."

Smoke walked over to the bay a Chisum cowboy brought up the hill, taking its reins. "He was real busy watchin' what was in front of him. It's a mistake a lot of men make before they wind up on Boot Hill."

Chisum watched Smoke mount his horse, still not quite ready to believe what he'd seen or heard. "For a big man, you sure as hell get around mighty quiet. It's hard to slip up on a man from behind like that. And all you had to do was shoot him. You'd have been within your rights, seeing as he was trying to kill us with a rifle."

Smoke was far more interested in the beefy carcasses of Chisum's crossbred Hereford steers right then, the incident with Cooper already pushed from his mind, even though the gunman was still alive, still breathing shallowly. Smoke gazed across the valley, thinking of cattle like these carrying a Sugarloaf brand. "I've got no choice but to agree with you, Mr. Chisum. Herefords represent the future of the cattle business out west. A longhorn's tough, and they can get by on poor pastures, but they don't carry the meat these crosses do. In a couple of years, I hope to have steers like those yonder ready for market."

Chisum shook his head and mounted his horse. "You're quite a puzzlement, Mr. Jensen. On the one hand you seem like a very knowledgeable cattleman, but when the shooting starts, you behave like a seasoned Indian fighter, or a trained soldier."

Smoke turned his horse toward the valley floor. "Sometimes a man has got to be a little of both," he said, "if he aims to hold on to what's his."

The night was clear and chilly, near forty degrees, as Smoke and Pearlie and Johnny and Bob Williams stood at the corral fence examining Chisum's Hereford bulls in the light of the moon. Cal and Cletus and Duke were inside the house enjoying another piece of Maria's chocolate pie.

Bob seemed a bit doubtful. "They look too short-legged to suit me," he said, "but they've damn sure got the meat on 'em. I reckon it's the crosses that count. Until a railhead comes close to Big Rock, we've still got to drive our cattle to market a hell of a long way. A short-legged cow ain't gonna cover much ground in a day. But I'm ready to try a couple of bulls. That pretty little wife of yours done a lot of convincin' when we talked about Herefords last fall. Put me down for two of them young bulls." He glanced over to Smoke. "I sure hope we make it all the way home with 'em, Smoke. After what them two cowboys of Chisum's told us this evenin' about all the shootin' you did up north of here, I'm wonderin' if us or these cattle will ever see Big Rock country."

"There's always a risk, Bob," Smoke told him. "I never once got up in the mornin' with any guarantee I'd see the end of the day."

"I like our chances," Pearlie said, chewing on a piece of straw. "I ain't sayin' it's gonna be easy, but I still like our chances of gettin' home with these here stumpy bulls. One thing they ain't gonna do is outrun no horse."

Johnny North offered his opinion. "It's outrunnin' lead we have to worry about, with all these hired guns on the prowl."

Smoke heard a noise near the bunkhouse. Four of Chisum's men were unloading dead bodies wrapped in canvas tarps from the back of a wagon, arranging four corpses in a neat row near the front porch. "We'll make it," Smoke said tonelessly. "Let's get some shut-eye. Tomorrow I'll pick out two hundred head of young cows for me and Sally's new herd. Then we'll be on our way."

Pearlie turned away from the fence, yawning. "It's been a spell since we had a roof over our heads. I'm gonna sleep like a baby tonight in one of them rawhide cots."

"I'm ready to turn in," Johnny agreed. "Cal's gonna have a bellyache if he ain't careful. I never saw a boy his size eat so much in one sittin'."

Pearlie nodded as the four men ambled toward the bunkhouse. "I done told that boy he's got worms. Can't nobody eat that much without a bellyful of worms helpin' him."

Smoke gave the outlying black hills a passing inspection as they headed for bed. He wondered if the gunman named Jessie Evans had gotten word of what had happened to his crew of killers today. While he didn't know anything about Evans, he was certain a shootist with a reputation on the line wouldn't take any advice from a stranger . . . not until someone convinced him otherwise.

Twenty-two

Boyd, Jack, and Lee Johnson were tobacco-chewing brothers from northwestern Arkansas, on the run from the law and Hanging Judge Isaac Parker's unyielding rope justice in his judicial district. Judge Parker had been known to hang three men at the same time, a fate the Johnson brothers had hoped to escape by coming to New Mexico Territory. Boyd, eldest of the three, had but one eye, having lost the other to an Arkansas Toothpick knife similar in size to a Bowie. Along with the Johnsons came two cousins with similar reputations. Dewey Hyde was wanted for murder, in both Arkansas and Mississippi. Marvin Hyde had warrants out for him in Missouri charging him with murdering a Methodist minister for what was in the collection plates on a Sunday morning. As a gang, they were considered a blight on the citizens of Arkansas by Judge Parker, who ordered a squad of United States deputy marshals to chase them halfway across Indian Territory. But individually, none was more dangerous than one-eyed Boyd Johnson, a burly man with a thick red beard and deadly aim with a rifle. When Boyd and his followers answered Jessie's call for experienced men who knew how to use a gun, it was a natural place for the Johnson brothers and the Hydes to show up.

As the hour approached midnight, Jessie led fourteen mounted men into the hills west of John Chisum's South Springs ranch, all heavily armed. Jessie was still puzzled by the disappearance of Roy Cooper. . . . It just wasn't Cooper's nature to turn tail and run. Roy was utterly fearless in any kind of fight, whether it be with guns or knives or fists. Cooper wouldn't have left the scene of a shoot-out without good reason, a plan of some sort to exact his brand of vengeance against this owlhoot named Smoke Jensen for taking the lives of Carlos, Jorge, and Raul. What Victor described, with Jensen charging recklessly into their guns, had to be nothing more than blind luck. Or stupidity. No man with all his faculties charged single-handedly into the teeth of seven riflemen behind cover. Those were the actions of a madman.

When they could see the ranch down below, Jessie held up his hand for a halt. A light was burning behind the windows of Chisum's main house. The bunkhouse was dark.

"We'll throw a circle around 'em," Jessie explained, making a motion with his hand. "Catch 'em in a cross fire. Get as close as you can to that bunkhouse, 'cause that's where his paid guns are more likely to be. Pour lead into them windows an' kill every son of a bitch who comes out them doors. . . . There's one at the back leadin' to the outhouse. I'll take four men an' make a circle 'round the main house. Soon as the shootin' starts, Chisum will come runnin' out. One of us will get him an' that'll be the end of this cattle war for good."

"What'll Dolan say?" Tom asked. "He told us all we was supposed to do was rustle a few cattle an' kill a few cowboys if they put up a fight. He never said nothin' 'bout killin' Chisum outright."

"I'll tell him it was an accident, that Chisum got in the line of fire. Main thing is to be sure we get this feller Smoke Jensen. It's payback time for him. Victor said he was a real big feller, like Chisum, only he was wearing buckskins. Just be damn sure you kill him, whoever the hell he is. All that tough talk about him comin' gunnin' for me is gonna cost him. I'll cut off his goddamn head an' stick it on a fencepost at Bosque. Be a reminder to any son of a bitch who threatens me."

Boyd Johnson urged his horse alongside Jessie's, a Sharps rifle resting against his leg. "I'll git him fer you, boss. All I gotta do is git him in my sights jest once."

Jessie gave Boyd a sideways glance. "We're about to find out if you're as good as you claim to be. Kill Jensen, an' I'll talk to Dolan 'bout givin' you a little bonus money." He looked over his shoulder. "Take Victor with you so he can point him out in the dark. Just make damn sure you kill the son of a bitch, no matter what it takes." Now Jessie spoke softly to the rest of his men. "Spread out. Billy, you an' Tom an' Bill Pickett come with me. Everybody else covers that bunkhouse. I'll fire the first shot into one of them lighted windows at the big house. As soon as you hear it, start pourin' lead into the place."

Silent riders spread out in twos and threes, beginning a circle around the Chisum ranch headquarters. Jessie led his handpicked men down a grassy embankment, toward a stand of oak where they could tie their horses.

"I'm gonna enjoy this," Pickett said. "Wish it was daylight so we could see 'em bleed better."

Tom Hill spoke up again. "I sure hope Jimmy don't get mad over this. He said he was glad we killed Tunstall, so he didn't write no more complainin' letters. Hope he feels the same way if we kill John Chisum."

Jessie had some private doubts. Dolan wanted a controlled war that wouldn't draw too much attention in the newspapers up in Santa Fe or over in Silver City. But when Victor brought back that message from Jensen, it got Jessie's back up. "Ain't no son of a bitch gonna threaten me like Jensen did," he said. "I'll tell Jimmy that Chisum was hirin' too damn many gunslicks, an' we had to do somethin' about it."

Bill Pickett offered his opinion. "You worry too much, Tom. Dolan ain't payin' us to sit an' whittle on a stick."

They came to the trees and dismounted, taking rifles and a few extra boxes of cartridges along. Pickett carried a Winchester and his shotgun, one in each hand, as they began a slow walk through the darkness toward Chisum's house, hunkered down to keep from being outlined against a night sky full of stars, in case Chisum had posted any guards.

"No dogs," Pickett said as they neared the house. "Means I can get close enough to use ol' Ten-Gauge Betsy."

Jessie felt his pulse begin to race. Like Pickett, he was looking forward to a killing spree. His men had been idle too long, and until today, when this Jensen started killing a few of his *pistoleros*, things had been too damn quiet to suit everybody at Bosque Redondo. It was hard to keep men who killed for a living content unless they were doing what they were being paid to do.

Twenty-three

Smoke lay asleep beside an open bunkhouse window when something he couldn't identify disturbed his slumber. Several men across the room were snoring and for a moment he wondered what it was that had awakened him. Cletus Walker and Bob Williams were at the main house talking with Chisum over drinks, talking about the cattle market and some of Chisum's troubles with the Santa Fe Ring and L.G. Murphy and Jimmy Dolan. Smoke had retired early, preferring sleep to conversation after so many days on the trail. But now something had interrupted his sleep, something beyond the window above his bunk.

He sat up slowly, peering out at a moonlit ranch yard and the hills beyond. A vague uneasy sensation warned him something was amiss, yet he was unable to see or hear anything out of the ordinary.

Swinging his legs off the bed, he put on his boots and took his gunbelts from a bedpost, and as an added precaution, he picked up his Winchester, after strapping both cartridge belts around his waist.

He crept to the back door and opened it softly, waiting for his eyes to adjust to the darkness. He was startled when he heard a soft whisper behind him.

"What is it?" Pearlie asked, sitting up.

The pockmarked gunfighter named Buck Andrews said, "I heard somethin' too, like horses." He swung his legs off the bunk beside Pearlie's to nudge a gunman named Curly Tully, who was in a deep sleep, snoring in the next bunk. "Wake up, Curly. I'd take an' oath I heard somethin' outside. Git up and fetch yer guns."

Tully raised his head off the pillow and shook it. "Maybe you was only dreamin'," he said sleepily.

"Wasn't no dream," Andrews told him. "It was horses."

Smoke let his gaze roam back and forth looking for a shape that didn't belong. It was too dark to be sure of anything at a distance. "Might be a good idea if you woke everybody up," he said a moment later, when it appeared something scurried across the crest of a hill behind the bunkhouse, perhaps only a wolf or a coyote. "If this is part of that bunch we tangled with today, they'll be lookin' for revenge. Get these men out of the bunkhouse and have 'em spread out around the corrals and barns. I'll go warn Mr. Chisum that something ain't right out yonder. First of all, it's too damn quiet. That's damn near always a bad sign in my experience. Make sure nobody shoots unless we get shot at first. I'll see if I can find out who it is, or if it's anything at all."

Andrews got up while Pearlie pulled on his boots. He woke Cal up and whispered, "Git dressed, young 'un. Smoke says he thinks we may have us some company."

Andrews went down the rows of cots, awakening cowboys, while Smoke edged out the rear doorway, his senses keened. He could almost smell trouble coming on a soft night wind blowing across the ranch.

Moving quietly in the shadow of the eaves, where the bunkhouse roof ended, he made his way to a corner and waited, hidden by the shadow until he crossed the ranch yard to a windmill tower and a water trough, crouching down, unable to shake the feeling that someone was out there in the hills. He could hear sleepy men stirring in the bunkhouse.

He stepped lightly along the front porch and tapped on the door, watching the moonlit hills.

"Who is it?" a deep voice belonging to Chisum inquired, a note of concern in his question.

"Smoke Jensen. I think we've got some night visitors off to the west. Maybe north of us too."

Chisum swung the door open. "I'll get my rifle and wake up the men."

"Buck Andrews is already gettin' 'em up. I told 'em to spread out around the corrals and barns. I'll slip out there to see if it's just my imagination. I told everybody to hold their fire unless someone shoots at us first. And it'd be a good idea to douse that lantern."

Cletus appeared behind Chisum and Smoke was about to leave the porch to scout around.

"What is it, Smoke?" Cletus asked.

"I ain't sure it's anything yet. Just grab a rifle in case we got company."

The lantern inside went out as Smoke crept off the porch to make his way to a split rail fence around ranch headquarters, an open stretch of ground that could be dangerous to cross, yet he was without choices. Hunkered down, he raced across the yard in the bright moonlight, knowing an experienced gunman would see the gleam of metal from his rifle.

A booming shot from a large-bore gun thundered from a grassy hilltop, the wink of a muzzle flash pinpointing the shooter's location. A split pine log on the top rail of the fence in front of Smoke most certainly saved his life from a heavy rifle slug, probably a .52 caliber, as the bullet splintered wood only a few inches from Smoke's face, splitting the dry log almost in half.

He dove to the ground, crawling beneath the bottom rail as fast as he could toward clumps of foot-high prairie grass that would hide him.

"Mr. Evans got my message, no doubt," Smoke hissed between gritted teeth, feeling his mind-set change suddenly, back to the savagery that had been a part of his nature in years past. Now, with a single-mindedness he could never fully explain to Sally, he would become a manhunter on a killing rampage. Something even he wasn't able to comprehend took control of him, his thoughts, his actions, a lust for killing in any way possible, after someone made an attempt to take his life. Until it was over, his mind was a blank, his conscience without a voice, focused only on finding and killing his enemies. Afterward, he sometimes pondered on what it was that overtook him at times like this, when all reason and concern for his personal safety were discarded. All that mattered now was killing, silencing the gun on the hilltop . . . and he was sure there would be more guns out there, waiting for their opportunity to arrive.

Boyd Johnson knew he'd missed. "It was that damn fence," he whispered to his brother Lee. "I'll git the sumbitch next time, soon as he shows hisself."

A rifle cracked from a hilltop north of the ranch, and then a chorus of gunfire erupted from every direction Answering guns thundered from barns and hay sheds and deep shadows all across the ranch headquarters.

"They was expectin' us!" Lee shouted above the roar of so many guns.

"Shut up, little brother!" Boyd snapped. "You's gonna tell that bastard right where we is!"

Boyd waited, aiming down at the fence where he'd last seen the big fellow, bare-chested, wearing buckskin leggings. "That was him," he muttered angrily. "I had the sumbitch dead in my sights till he come to that goddamn fence. I know one thing fer sure 'bout this Jensen feller—he's damn sure lucky, or he'd be dead as a pig right now."

The crackle of exploding rifles filled the night with sound, making Boyd uneasy. It helped to have keen hearing when a man was stalking about in the dark with a gun, but gunfire was drowning out every other noise, making it impossible to hear footsteps, the snap of a twig, or the brush of grasses against a man's boots.

"How come you ain't shootin', Boyd?" Lee asked, as minutes dragged by without Boyd firing a shot, which caused Lee to keep his gun silent too.

"Nothin' to shoot at yet," Boyd answered. "No sense in lettin' 'em know where we are till we got us a target we know we can hit. Let them others waste ammunition. Remember what Pa told us when we was kids huntin' squirrels—Make every shot count, 'cause gunpowder an' shot is expensive." Scanning the spot where he'd last seen the gent he believed to be Jensen, it was hard to figure where such a big feller could be hiding.

Something tapped him on the sole of his right boot, and Boyd whirled around, focusing his lone functioning eye on the outline of a bare-chested man holding a pair of pistols. "How the hell did you . . . ?" he exclaimed, as both six-guns belched stabbing fingers of yellow flame.

Something cracked against Boyd's forehead, slamming his head to the ground with the force of a mule's kick. He heard Lee let out a scream as lightning bolts of pain shot through his skull in great waves. His vision blurred as he caught a glimpse of the man who had shot him and his brother, and damned if he could explain why the bastard seemed to be grinning just seconds before everything went black. He felt his body floating off the ground and he could not explain the sensation. . . . Bodies didn't float. But he was thankful that now, his terrible pain was fading away.

Dewey Hyde pumped seven slugs through his Winchester in a fit of rage, knowing he'd hit nothing with any of his bullets. Spittle dribbled down into his beard when he forgot to spit with a wad of chewing tobacco in his left cheek, thus he spat and took seven more shells from his pocket, pushing them into the loading gate to fill its cartridge chamber. As the roar of gunfire came from all directions, he wondered idly if Marvin was having any better luck in the ravine below, to the west. This kind of a fight didn't suit Dewey, not when he couldn't see who he was shooting at so far away in the dark.

"Turn around, creep," someone said behind him. "I want to see your ugly face before I blow it off your skull."

Dewey made a quick half turn, swallowing tobacco juice in his haste and fear, bringing his rifle around for a shot at the owner of the strangely calm voice in the middle of a deadly gun battle like this. He saw a squatting figure, muscles bunched in his bare chest, aiming two pistols at him from only a few yards away.

Before Dewey could aim, he heard a noise, an explosion, and in the same instant something akin to a red-hot poker entered the soft flesh beneath his chin—he was sure he could feel fire as it traveled upward, through his mouth and tongue, jarring him the way an iron-rimmed wagon wheel did when it struck a rock. He was scooted backward by the flaming poker entering his brain, and he could feel it tearing through the top of his head. Without truly understanding what was happening, he puzzled over the hot sensation, like fire. How could fire get inside his skull like this?

He lay back as the figure stepped over him, heading down to the ravine where Marvin was shooting. Dewey tried to yell, to warn Marvin, only his mouth was full of blood and tobacco juice and he could feel only the stump of his tongue moving when he tried to speak. He coughed and closed his eyes. Marvin would be able to take care of himself until Dewey could figure out what was wrong. For some reason, in spite of what had just happened to his head, he felt sleepy, and it was sure as hell the wrong time to be needing to take a nap.

Marvin Hyde decided it was time to pull back. Some of the bullets fired from the ranch were coming too close, whizzing over his head by no more than a foot or two. He didn't want somebody to get off a lucky shot that would turn out to be unlucky for him and in all this noise and confusion, Jessie Evans would never know he'd moved to a safer place.

Marvin came slowly to his hands and knees, pulling his rifle along in the grass, its barrel still hot from so much shooting. A few feet more and he was behind the lip of the shallow ravine, where he could stand up.

As he turned around, he came face-to-face with a half-naked man holding two pistols. "Who the hell are you?" Marvin asked, unable to recall this fellow's face as being a member of Jessie's gang.

"Your executioner, plowboy. I'm gonna put a hole through your overalls while you're wearin' 'em."

"The hell you say!" Marvin cried, bringing his Winchester up for a shot.

The roar of a Colt .44 caught Marvin in mid swing, before he could get his rifle muzzle lifted. He was torn off his planted feet by what felt like a whistling gust of wind striking his chest. His rifle flew from his hands as he fell backward from the force of it, and when he fell on his back it was as if an anvil had been dropped on his rib cage. He couldn't breathe at all, not a single breath, and when he touched his chest he felt something wet on the front of his bib overalls, then the hole this sneaky stranger had promised.

He saw the stranger hurry off into the darkness, and thought how he needed to warn Dewey. But try as he might, he could not raise his head or suck in enough wind to shout to his brother.

He noticed his legs were trembling uncontrollably, feet twitching as though they had minds of their own. It occurred to Marvin that joining up with Jessie Evans and his gang hadn't turned out to be such a good idea after all. Maybe he and Dewey should have stayed in Indian Territory, or headed north for the Kansas line.

Off in the distance, he could hear the pop of rifles, and it sounded like they were moving away, growing fainter. With all his strength, he tried to draw in a breath of badly needed air, and found again he couldn't. Marvin had always feared drowning in a river someplace, running out of air. How could a man drown out in the middle of a cow pasture?

Twenty-four

Smoke crept forward, toward the shape of a man lying prone at the crest of a rocky knob, firing down at the ranch in regular bursts, as fast as he could reload a Winchester .44. Smoke had a decided advantage tonight that he couldn't always count on—the noise made by so many rifles firing at once. This made it far easier to slip up behind his quarry, not having to be so careful where he placed each foot.

The rifleman fired seven shells and then paused to load his gun, giving Smoke just the opportunity he needed.

"Turn around. I've got a message for you from Jessie," he said quietly, just loud enough to be heard above the din of guns banging.

A Mexican with a thin mustache looked over his shoulder as he continued thumbing shells into his rifle. He opened his mouth to speak, until he realized he did not recognize Smoke's face in the dark. Then he saw Smoke's pistols.

"Dios!" the man cried. "You are not with us!"

"No, I ain't."

"But you say you have a message from Señor Jessie . . ."

"I suppose I should have said I have a message *for*

Jessie," Smoke said. "Trouble is, I can't leave you alive to give it to him."

The Mexican seemed to understand at once that he stood no chance of turning his gun on Smoke in time. *"Por favor,* please do not kill me, señor."

Smoke answered softly, in case other members of Jessie's gang were close enough to hear him despite the constant rattle of rifle fire back and forth. "Funny you'd beg for your life when you came here to kill us. If the tables were turned, would you give me a chance to ride off?"

"Of course, señor. It would be the honorable thing to do in this situation, when you have the drop on me."

"You think I oughta give you a chance to aim that rifle at me first?"

The Mexican hesitated, thinking. "I do not believe you would do that, señor."

"Then you're callin' me a liar."

"No, señor. I only say I do not *think* you would be so foolish."

Smoke lowered his pistols to his sides. "Aim it at me. Go ahead. I'll give you plenty of time."

Another hesitation, then suddenly the Mexican squirmed around, sweeping his rifle barrel toward Smoke.

"Long enough," Smoke whispered, whipping his left pistol up, and gently squeezing the trigger so the motion wouldn't ruin his aim.

His Colt barked, jumping in his fist, its echo lost in a wall of noise coming from the surrounding hills and the ranch down below. The Mexican's body jerked as though he'd been startled, jolted by the bullet passing through him at close range. He threw back his head and shrieked in pain, letting his rifle fall between his knees. He sat there a moment, staring at Smoke, then he looked down at his belly, where a dark stain was spreading over the front of his shirt.

"Madre," he groaned, touching the bullet hole in his stomach with a fingertip.

"Your mother can't help you now," Smoke said. "It'll take you awhile to die, bein' gutshot."

"Take me to the doctor in Mesilla!" the Mexican begged in a high-pitched voice. "Can't you see that I am badly wounded and without a doctor, I will surely die?"

Smoke turned away from the knob. "I might have considered it, if it wasn't for the fact you came here to kill me an' my friends. *Adios, bastardo."* He strolled away into the deep night shadows, looking for another victim, another paid assassin who came to South Springs ranch seeking a murderer's payday.

A rifle spat flame to his left, behind a thick piñon pine trunk. Smoke crept toward the light on the balls of his feet.

Jack Johnson knelt in matted grass at the base of the tree, with brass cartridge casings scattered all around him. Now and then he saw a muzzle flash wink near one of the barns or a corner post of a corral. He wondered why Jessie Evans would order an attack on such a well-defended ranch. Jack guessed a dozen men were shooting back at them.

"Evans is a fool," Jack mumbled. "Nobody in his right mind would challenge an outfit armed to the teeth like this bunch, if he knew it ahead of time. This could go on all night. . . ." He took aim at a flickering flash of light and fired, knowing he stood no chance whatsoever of hitting anything at this range. A banging series of gunshots answered his bullet, all high or wide of the mark, whining through tree branches above his head.

He wondered about Boyd and Lee, guessing they were as frustrated with this standoff as he was. At least the three of them had found work in New Mexico Territory, no easy task for men with warrants out on them.

Jack doubted anyone on either side had been wounded or killed, what with everyone shooting in the dark at uncertain targets.

A short pause came in the endless gunfire, long enough for Jack to hear someone behind him, figuring it was probably Boyd or Lee. He glanced over his shoulder while he levered another shell into the firing chamber. "Ain't this the worst?" he said to a man coming toward him from the rear, from friendly territory. "Can't see a goddamn thing down there. Looks like somebody oughta decide this ain't worth it, an' call it off."

"Somebody should have," a voice replied, a voice Jack didn't recognize.

Jack offered a simple solution. "Why don't you go tell Mr. Evans this is a waste of time?"

"I'm looking for him now. Where is he?"

"Him an' Bill Pickett an' two more is near the big house down yonder. They was gonna try an' get Chisum if they could."

"Shoot him down in the dark?"

"Hell yes." Jack began to wonder about all the strange questions, and he looked over his shoulder again. "Who the hell are you anyways, an' how come you're askin' so goddamn many dumb questions?"

"My name doesn't matter. What *does* matter is that you've got only a few seconds to live."

A chilling tingle went down Jack's spine when he realized he'd been talking to an enemy, one of the shooters from down below. With his rifle aimed in the wrong direction, it would take luck and perfect timing to get out of this alive. "I didn't quite hear what you said, mister," he replied, just as he made a springing dive forward toward a smaller tree trunk a few feet in front of him.

A gun roared while Jack was in mid flight. Something snapped between his shoulder blades . . . it felt like his backbone had been broken. He landed on his face and chest without feeling any pain, and when he tried to move his arms and legs to crawl to the tree, his limbs refused to obey his commands. He lay there a moment, wondering what was wrong.

"I'll tell Evans what you said, that he oughta call this off," the voice behind him said.

Tiny tremors began in Jack's hands and feet. He saw a circle of light and he began moving toward it despite the fact that his legs were motionless. Somewhere in the night a cricket chirped, the last sound he heard before he was surrounded by an eerie blanket of silence.

Smoke began working his way toward a dark grove of trees to the west of Chisum's house, the logical place for men to take up firing positions if they were bent on killing whoever was inside.

Twenty-five

Jessie whispered softly to Bill Pickett, "Wonder what the hell is keepin' Billy?" He'd sent Billy Morton to find out what fool was shooting a pistol from hills north of the ranch, when all his men had brought rifles. Nobody with good sense would shoot a pistol from that distance, yet the distinctive sounds of a .44 had come fairly often . . . not always from the same spot.

"I told you somethin' was wrong," Pickett replied, keeping his rifle trained on a shattered window of the house where rifle fire exploded now and then. "They was ready for us. Some son of a bitch warned 'em we was comin'. I figure it was that little coward Barlow, after you ran him off. He probably rode over here an' offered to throw in with 'em, tellin' Chisum we was on the way." Pickett glanced north. "The way I got it figured, one of 'em slipped around behind them Arkansas boys an' now he's takin' potshots at 'em with a pistol. If they're as good as they claim to be, one of 'em will kill whoever it is. That last pistol shot was five or ten minutes ago. Maybe the bastard is already dead if one of them farmers got him. Come to think of it, there ain't been no shootin' at all comin' from them hills lately."

Jessie felt his anger rising. "If I find out that little bastard Barlow warned 'em, I'll kill him myself. I still can't figure what's takin' Billy so long to get back here." As he said it, he saw Billy coming up a draw behind them, moving in a crouch to avoid flying lead. "Yonder he is. . . ."

Morton hurried up to Jessie as best he could, keeping down like he was. He sounded out of breath when he spoke quietly to Jessie. "Big trouble, boss. Somebody's sneakin' 'round up in them hills, killin' off them pig farmers from Arkansas. The one-eyed Johnson brother is dead, an' so is the young skinny one. I found that big redheaded guy with the top of his head blowed off, an' it damn near made me sick to my stomach. His brains was all over the place, only the big bastard was still breathin'. I left him layin' there. I got the hell outa there quick as I could, to bring word down to you. At least one of 'em got behind us, maybe more."

"This has to be Barlow's doin'," Jessie growled. "They was ready for us. Hell, they was already spread out all over creation soon as the first shot was fired. I swear I'm gonna kill Barlow. It ain't my way of doin' things to pull away from a fight, but if some of 'em got behind us, we're caught in a cross fire. Spread the word to pull out. Tell Tom to warn the boys over to the south to clear out now."

Pickett turned away from the tree with a disgusted look on his face. "Far as I can tell, we ain't shot nobody tonight. It was them who done all the killin'."

"We rode into a trap," Jessie said, heading for the draw as exchanges of gunfire lessened even more. Keeping his head down, he ground his teeth together while they made for their horses. A double-crossing son of a bitch had done them in tonight . . . he was sure of it.

Pickett seemed reluctant to leave, glancing over his shoulder, scowling in the moonlight. "Wish I'd had the chance to kill at least one of 'em," he whispered. "Don't seem like it's askin' too much to be able to kill just one. I ain't smelled no blood in so long I plumb forgot what it smells like."

"We'll get another chance," Jessie promised. "Lopez told me there's at least a dozen more *pistoleros* headed up from Juarez to hire on with us. Said they'd be here by the end of the week. If Chisum thinks he's heard the last of us, he's goddamn sure in for a helluva surprise."

They reached their tethered mounts just as Pickett said, "I reckon that Jensen feller was all talk. Every one of them yellow bastards kept their heads down so damn low there wasn't nothin' to shoot at. The only thing they did smart was puttin' a few men behind us, an' they couldn't have done that 'less Barlow warned 'em we was comin'."

Jessie mounted, thinking about the warning Victor had brought them from Smoke Jensen, whoever the hell he was, about how if one more bullet flew, he was planning to kill them all, including Jessie. "Like you said, just big talk is all it was. Maybe he got lucky killin' those *pistoleros* like he done. If it hadn't been for Barlow, we'd have killed Chisum an' every one of his shooters tonight. That Buck Andrews an' Curly Tully was supposed to be bad men. Killers. Only, when the shootin' started, they stayed down just like the rest of 'em, includin' that big-winded Jensen feller." He reined his horse around. Shooting in the distance had all but ended. "Tomorrow I'll ride up to the Mescalero reservation . . . see if some of them red-skinned bastards who know how to shoot are interested in makin' a little money. There's always a few renegades lookin' for some excitement." He urged his horse to a short lope, back in the direction of Bosque Redondo. "One way or another, I'm gonna have John Chisum's ass."

They were a few miles from the Chisum ranch when Tom Hill, Billy Morton, Ignacio Valdez, Pedro Lopez, and three more riders caught up with them at a hard gallop. Pedro was the first to speak, after jerking his horse to a halt.

"I see this hombre, Señor Jessie. I only see him one time. Then I hear gun, *una pistola.* I go see where he is, only nobody is there, only Juanito Gonzales, and he is dying. He say this *loco hombre* come from behind where he was shooting and he shoot him. Juanito tell me this hombre ask where to find *you,* that he have this message for you. It no make sense, Señor Jessie, how this hombre know your name and want to give you a message."

"Jensen," Jessie snarled, curling his lips when he said the name. "It had to be Jensen." Rage welled in Jessie's chest, and he gripped his saddle horn fiercely, trying to control an outburst of unreasoning anger. "That's who got behind us. It was that bastard Smoke Jensen. I never laid eyes on the son of a bitch yet, but I'm swearin' an oath I'm gonna kill him. He's as good as dead. All I gotta do is find him. . . ."

Twenty-six

Smoke alerted the anxious men spread out across South Springs ranch before he crossed the fence in the dark, fearing a bullet might come flying his way from a nervous Chisum cowboy after a pitched battle like the one they'd just been through.

"It's me, Smoke Jensen! Don't anybody shoot! Looks like they cleared out!"

He heard Pearlie's distinctive voice from a cowshed off to his right. "That's Smoke all right, men. Lower them guns so you don't shoot him accidental."

Smoke went over the fence, his pistols holstered, as Pearlie and Cal hurried up to him.

"How many was out there?" Pearlie asked. "Sounded like a whole damned army."

"Twelve or fourteen," Smoke replied, continuing on his way to Chisum's house. "I scouted around after they left, just to make sure all of 'em hightailed it out of here."

John Chisum met him at the porch steps. He gave Smoke a half grin. "Never heard so much lead flying in my life," he said with obvious relief. "They had us surrounded. Must've been at least twenty riflemen out there . . ."

"More like a dozen or so," Smoke replied. "A few

more than that, maybe. I got six of 'em by circling around behind some of their positions. No sense goin' after the bodies till daylight comes."

"You killed six of them?" Chisum asked, relief turning to disbelief when he heard the number. "How in the hell did you do that without getting your ass shot to pieces?"

"They didn't expect nobody to come at 'em from the rear, I reckon."

"You're an amazing man, Mr. Jensen, talking about knocking off half a dozen men like you'd been out picking peaches. Those boys were hired gunmen, not amateurs. Evans and Dolan have sent word all the way to Mexico that they're hiring top shootists to fight on their side of this war."

Smoke shrugged, climbing to the porch. "They didn't appear to be all that experienced, not to me. Maybe I didn't get the cream of the crop this time. But if they come back again, or if they try to stop me and my friends from drivin' our herd up to Colorado, I'll test the rest of 'em. I don't pay much attention to what a man's reputation is supposed to be. Just because some fool hires out to kill other men don't make him good at it."

Chisum wagged his head. "You sure as hell know your business. I wish you'd consider a proposition from me to stay on until this range war is over."

Smoke discarded the notion with a wave of his hand. "I'm in the cattle business, Mr. Chisum. Like I told you before, my guns ain't for hire at any price."

The rancher rubbed his chin thoughtfully. "But you can't deny you know the profession, the gunman's trade. I've seen you in action."

"I've had a little experience with it."

"What made you change? It must have been something of great importance to you."

"A woman," he replied. "My wife broke me of a lot of bad habits, and I don't figure she's done with it yet."

Chisum laughed. "She is certainly an influential lady, even if I haven't met her."

Smoke found himself yearning for a shot of whiskey right at the moment, although he answered the statement. "It isn't so much just influence. When she gets her mind set on doin' things her way, it's mighty hard to change it." He glanced into the house through a broken windowpane. "If all your whiskey bottles didn't get busted, I could use a swallow or two of that good stuff from Kentucky, before I go back to bed."

"I'll have one with you," Chisum said, "and I'll send a bottle out to the men. They've earned it." He turned around and led Smoke inside, lighting a lantern that revealed shattered glass all over the floor. "We were lucky tonight," Chisum added as he went to the cabinet for the whiskey.

"How's that?" Smoke asked, not quite sure what seemed so all-fired lucky about being attacked from all sides.

"Lucky to have you here," he replied. "Maybe this will serve to discourage Evans and Dolan from making any further attempts like this one."

Smoke settled into a stuffed bull hide chair near the fireplace. "I wouldn't count on it," he said quietly, glancing out a window. "Men like those who visited us just now ain't so easily discouraged. They'll be looking for a payday. I'm not much of a gamblin' man, but I'll bet we see 'em again before too awful long. Could be as early as tomorrow."

Chisum handed Smoke a shot glass brimming with golden whiskey as he said, "I sure as hell hope you're wrong."

Smoke tasted his drink, finding it delicious, even though it burned all the way down his throat. "I'm seldom ever wrong when it comes to men with bad intentions," he told Chisum. "I've had more'n my share of experience with their breed."

Riders for Chisum acted as herd-holders while Smoke and John Chisum rode through hundreds of two- and three-year-old longhorn heifers. When Smoke pointed to a good long-backed cow, Pearlie and Cal and Duke cut it away from the main herd to a lower meadow, where Smoke's selections were being held in a bunch by Bob Williams and Cletus Walker, along with a pair of Chisum cowboys. These young cows were in good trail flesh, making it easier for them to be driven to Sugarloaf without long grazing delays to keep the longhorns from getting hungry.

"You've got a good eye for a mother cow," Chisum told him as they rode through the herd. "You're picking my choice from the bunch damn near every time."

"We've got a long drive ahead of us," Smoke replied, with a nod toward a brindle heifer which Cal immediately cut away from the others, "and I figure picking a longer back will make the crosses better suited for our type of range."

"I've done the same thing myself. We've got no

railheads within two hundred miles, so I have to make damn sure what I raise can be driven to market."

"We're in the same boat. Denver is the closest railyard for us, an' that's a considerable drive through mountain country most of the way."

A cowboy from ranch headquarters came riding up as they were picking the last of the heifers. He pulled his horse to a stop and spoke to Chisum.

"We found six bodies in them hills, Mr. Chisum. With the four we got already, makes ten. Them first four is already startin' to stink. It'll take two wagons to carry 'em all the way to Roswell so they can be buried proper. Trouble is, they wasn't carryin' no papers sayin' who they was, so I reckon the undertaker'll have to bury 'em without no name on the marker."

"Take two wagons," Chisum said. "Tell Sheriff Romero they came gunning for us, and that I'll ride in tomorrow and give him a full report."

"Yessir," the young cowboy replied, wheeling his horse for a ride back to the ranch.

Chisum was staring at Smoke now. "Ten men," he said. "You killed ten of Dolan's gunmen without a lick of help from us, in a manner of speaking. I still have trouble believing it . . . how just one man could do all of that."

Smoke didn't care to talk about it, how easy it had been to send ten careless gunmen to early graves. "That oughta be about two hundred head, give or take. Let's drive 'em back to the ranch and I'll pay you for 'em, and for the bulls. We can get a final count while we're drivin' 'em to the corrals."

"After all you've done for me, I'm tossing in ten extra head to help account for losses on the trail.

You've been a good man to have backing me during all this trouble, and it's my way of showing gratitude."

"No need for that," Smoke argued. "I did what I did because my friends and neighbors were in the line of fire. This ain't our fight, but when it spilled over, an' bullets started flyin' in our direction, those boys had me to reckon with. We rode all this way to conduct an honest business transaction, an' I damn sure won't stand for nobody gettin' in the way of it, not for no reason."

"I understand," Chisum told him. "All the same, I benefited from it, and I'm giving you ten extra heifers. No reason to talk about it anymore. It's done."

Smoke found he was liking Chisum and his honesty more and more. Chisum would make a good neighbor, and a solid friend a man could count on when the going got tough. "It's your decision, Mr. Chisum," he said, "only I want it understood I never expected payment for what I did."

Chisum didn't answer, swinging off to beckon to one of his men riding herd with Smoke's heifers. "Go back and pick out ten good long-backed heifers to add to this bunch," he said. "Tell Shorty to help you. Bring them up along with this bunch as quick as you can, only make damn sure none of them are cripples. They'll be headed to Colorado Territory in the morning."

Twenty-seven

Pearlie shoveled refried beans and salsa into his mouth with a tin spoon, until his cheeks were bulging. They sat at a long oak table in John Chisum's dining room eating Maria's spicy hot Mexican food, their faces outlined by coal oil lamps overhead.

"I'm gonna miss this cookin'," Cal said around a mouthful of flank steak seasoned with hot sauce, folding a tortilla over a piece of meat heavily coated with *salsa picante*. "We'll be eatin' beans an' jerky plumb to Big Rock, an' I'll be rememberin' what this tastes like."

Bob Williams was sweating from the chili peppers in his food, and he sleeved perspiration from his brow. "This is sure fine eatin', if a man's stomach is made of iron. I'm gonna eat it even if it kills me."

"It'll put hair on your chest," Cletus promised.

"Already got enough hair there the way things is. What I need is another glass of water."

Duke Smith nodded. "Can't put enough water in a man's belly to put this fire out. If it was snowin' outside, I'd run out an' eat a fistful, just to cool my tongue."

Chisum grinned. "Mexican food is supposed to be hot. It isn't any good otherwise."

Pearlie eyed his plate. "If hot's got anythin' to do

with it bein' good, this has gotta be the best I ever tasted."

Cal was too busy chewing to offer an opinion at the moment, and he merely nodded, beads of sweat on his forehead, cheeks, and neck.

Cletus lifted the bandanna tied around his neck and wiped away a trickle of perspiration coming from his hatband while he chewed methodically on a bite of steak. "I've never seen fire on a plate, afore tonight," he said. "Come mornin' there'll be a line at the outhouse half a mile long. That Maria can make fire taste mighty delicious."

"She fixed flan custard to cool everybody off," Chisum said. "That's for dessert."

Smoke listened to all the banter, but his mind was on the ride they would undertake at dawn. He was almost sure Jessie Evans and his gang hadn't had enough of a lesson last night to convince them of their folly. "I want two men riding point on this herd," he said. "I'll be scouting what lies ahead, but in case there's trouble, I want Pearlie and Duke guiding this bunch of cattle until we're well north of Lincoln County."

"You expect trouble," Chisum observed.

"I always expect it. That way, I'm pleasantly surprised if it don't show up."

"It usually does," Pearlie muttered, again filling his mouth with Maria's cooking. "But if any outfit between here'n Big Rock can handle it, it'll be the Sugarloaf crew. Hell-fire, I wouldn't know what to do if somebody wasn't shootin' at us half the time. I'd figure I was with the wrong bunch if we wasn't duckin' lead."

Chisum seemed puzzled. He looked over at Smoke.

"You said you were in the ranching business now, however, your men act like they expect problems."

Smoke thought about it a while as he was chewing. "I guess I've got too many old enemies who won't leave things alone. Now and then a batch of 'em shows up to try an' settle old scores."

The rancher appeared to be mildly amused. "Looks like after awhile word would spread that you're the wrong man to be trifled with."

Pearlie chuckled. "There's been times when dead bodies did sorta stack up 'round the place. It's been quieter lately, so maybe like you say, word got out that Sugarloaf is the wrong spot to come lookin' for a little bit of excitement."

Smoke finished cleaning his plate. "That egg custard does sound nice," he said, changing the subject. Down deep he felt sure there would be excitement enough driving their cattle back up the trails to Big Rock country.

"One more thing," Chisum said as he got up to tell Maria to bring the flan, "I asked one of my hands to send a telegram to Fort Stanton while he was in Roswell delivering those bodies to Sheriff Romero. I told him to ask Colonel Dudley to meet you along the trail up to Fort Sumner somewhere with a squad of his soldiers, as an escort just in case Evans and Dolan try to rustle any of your cattle. I doubt if Dudley will agree. He's hand in glove with Tom Catron and his Santa Fe Ring when it comes to this beef contract business. I find I'm not only pitted against a gang of paid guns in this range war, but I'm also at odds with the most powerful politicians in the territory. They'll do all they can to put me out of business." He looked down at Smoke. "That's one reason

I wish you'd reconsider staying on here for a while, Mr. Jensen. I have a feeling I'll need all the help I can get . . . men who know their way around a gun."

"Sorry, but I'm not interested. I've got a wife waitin' for me up in Colorado an' a ranch to run. If things were different, I'd stay. As to those soldiers from Fort Stanton, I don't reckon we'll need 'em. I try to make a habit out of handlin' my own affairs."

Chisum nodded and disappeared into the kitchen. Smoke saw a frown on Bob's face.

"After what happened last night, I sure wouldn't mind havin' a soldier escort," Bob said.

"Me either," Cletus added, toying with a spoon. "Wouldn't be no disgrace to have a company of soldiers ridin' with us part of the way."

"If they show up, we won't send 'em back," Smoke said, more to comfort his friends than anything else. "But you heard Mr. Chisum say it ain't likely they'll show. Apparently the army is backing the other side in this conflict. I never had much high regard for soldiers or politicians."

Johnny hadn't said a word during supper, but he spoke up now, after mention was made of the soldiers. "Don't know 'bout the rest of you, but I was plenty scared last night . . . bullets flyin' all over the place, knockin' holes in the side of that barn where I was hidin'. I couldn't go back to sleep after it was over. I was thinkin' how glad I was to be alive."

Cal was quick to agree, looking at Smoke when he said, "I was feelin' might' near the same way. Not that I ever doubted you'd git us out of that fix, Mr. Jensen, but them slugs sure was comin' close a few times."

Smoke understood both boys' concerns. They were young and inexperienced in the ways of battle. "Leave

Evans and his gunslicks to me. The main thing you're supposed to worry about is those cattle, come tomorrow. Just make sure you keep 'em bunched if there's any trouble. Don't let anybody close to those bulls, no matter what happens."

Now Pearlie was eyeing Smoke. "You expect Evans an' his boys to come after our cattle, don't you?"

"It's a strong possibility. I've never met Jessie Evans, but I know his kind. Some men can't learn a lesson but one way, and that's to teach it permanent."

"You aim to kill him, don't you?" Johnny asked quietly.

"Only if he comes at us again. I won't go lookin' for him, if that's what you mean."

It was Pearlie who said, grinning, "He's done come at us once already, which only proves you've gone an' mellowed some in my opinion. If that'd happened a few years back, you'd have gone lookin' fer Mr. Evans by now."

"We came here to buy Hereford bulls and cattle," Smoke reminded Pearlie.

"So we did," Pearlie agreed, as Maria brought a tray filled with cups of caramel-coated custard into the dining room, which signaled an end to all further conversation as far as Pearlie was concerned.

John Chisum had a small fire going in the fireplace due to a night chill, the house being without most of its windowpanes after the shooting. He had given Smoke a bill of sale for the cows and turned down the lantern while they shared glasses of whiskey while the men went to the bunkhouse.

"I'm also interested in buyin' a good Morgan stud

to cross on my mares," Smoke said, enjoying his drink, and the peace and quiet.

Chisum wagged his head. "This isn't good horse country yet, not by a long shot, however I have a friend in Saint Louis who raises purebred Morgans, and you can trust him. His name is Penn Wheelis. I'll give you his address and you can say I recommended him to you. He'll quote you a fair price, and even arrange for delivery by railroad car as far west as Denver. Wheelis is an honest man, and he'll send you exactly what you're paying for if you do business with him."

"I'd sorta made up my mind to look at one before I paid for it, but if you say this Penn Wheelis is honest, that'll be good enough for me. With those Herefords and cows to tend to this summer, I won't have time to travel to Saint Louis."

Chisum sipped his drink thoughtfully. "A Morgan is a good horse for adding muscle to a common mare. The crosses make good cow horses, I'm told."

"I'll take that address in Saint Louis, I reckon."

Chisum got up and went to a rolltop desk, fumbling through a sheaf of papers until he found what he wanted. He wrote down a name and address and handed it to Smoke. "You won't regret doing business with Wheelis. He'll send you a good horse. You've got my word on that."

"That's good enough for me," Smoke replied, tucking the paper into his waistband.

Chisum took his chair again. . . . There was something else on his mind. "I can send Buck Andrews or Curly Tully along with you for part of the way," he offered. "Both of them have made a name for themselves with a gun."

"No thanks, but I'm obliged for the offer. I handle most of my own problems without any help."

"I can see that," Chisum said. "I'm curious about a couple of things. Where did you learn to fight like that? An ordinary man can't kill almost a dozen men the way you did single-handedly without getting a scratch."

Smoke thought about Preacher a moment. "I had a real good teacher, an old mountain man up in Colorado. If I had to try to explain it, I suppose I'd say he had a born instinct for taking care of himself in any situation. He lived alone in the wildest part of the Rockies. He never depended on anyone else. He survived in a place where all odds said he couldn't, goin' up against Indians like the Crows, Blackfeet, the Utes, and the Shoshoni back when the Indian wars were at their worst. After a spell, most tribes got to where they respected him . . . even made friends with him. Some of the Crow medicine men believed he was a medicine man himself, even though his skin was white and his eyes were the wrong color. He earned their respect as a fighting man, and they left him alone to hunt an' run his traps."

"It sounds to me like you were very close to him, whoever he was."

Smoke felt a slight twinge when the old memories came back. "I reckon we were real close, if that's the right word. He went by Preacher. He told me the last time I saw him his first name was Arthur. I never knew his last name."

"Is he . . . gone now?"

Smoke downed the last of his drink, not wanting to discuss Preacher any longer. "Can't say for sure. He'd be close to ninety by now, if he's still alive. When

I left him, it was at his request. He'd been wounded mighty bad and looked for all the world like he was gonna die. He asked me to dress him in his best buckskins an' a sash, which is the way old-time mountain men want to be buried. Then he ordered me to leave that high country for good, to get clear of the trouble brewin' there. He rode off on his favorite mare. That's the last I ever saw of him, an' I believe it was the way he wanted it, so I wouldn't know if he'd lived or died. Preacher had a hell of a lot of pride, an' I'm sure this was his way of sparing me from seeing him pass on, or as mountain men say, cross over."*

"Haven't you ever wondered what became of him?"

Smoke stood up, stretching his legs. "I owe him too much not to respect his wishes."

Chisum got up, a puzzled expression on his face. "What an unusual story," he said, following Smoke over to the front door to show him out.

"G'night, Mr. Chisum," Smoke said, to end any further talk about Preacher or Smoke's beginnings. "We'll be up before first light to get that herd started."

"My men will help you get them started north," Chisum said as Smoke started for the bunkhouse.

"We'll be grateful," he said without turning around, lost in an unwanted memory, of the day Preacher was dressed in his best beaded buckskins, badly wounded from a scrape with men who had tracked him into the Needle Mountains, putting a rifle ball all the way through his hip, a wound that was badly festered by the time he found Smoke.

The Last Mountain Man

Smoke glanced up at the stars, hoping that somewhere those same stars were shining down on Preacher, perhaps at the high mountain pass Ned Buntline told Cal and Pearlie about. Was the man dressed in an albino buffalo robe truly Preacher?

Smoke knew he would never know, and that was the way Preacher had wanted it.

Twenty-eight

Driving half-wild longhorns away from their home range could be tricky business, Smoke knew from experience, and as they put a few lead heifers in motion northward, some tried to turn back. A cowboy had to ride up at just the right time in order to get the animals moving in the right direction.

The young Herefords were another matter. Gentled by being around men feeding them in corrals, they plodded along at the back of the herd quietly.

Smoke leaned out of the saddle and shook hands with John Chisum. "Pleasure doin' business with you," he said, watching Pearlie and Duke lead the cattle north over the very same hills where he'd killed six of Jessie Evans's men.

"The pleasure has been all mine," Chisum replied. "You be careful, Smoke Jensen. Don't let those owlhoots riding for Dolan jump you."

Smoke grinned. "I'm always careful," he said, urging his horse forward to ride around the herd so he could scout the way for several miles before the cattle came.

Dawn had just come to South Springs, casting golden light over tree-studded hills and shallow valleys. Off to the east, the Pecos River was a thin, distant line of deeper green where cottonwoods and grass were nourished by its waters. It was a peaceful beginning, as the heifers and bulls moved away from the Chisum ranch. Smoke wondered how long it would stay this way.

Keeping the Pecos in sight, he led them over grassy meadows where the cows would have plenty of grazing. Once the herd got settled to the trail, the likelihood of a stampede would be less of a worry.

When he'd scouted ahead for a couple of miles, Smoke turned back to see how the herd was moving, and when he topped a rise he could see them strung out in good trail fashion, traveling along at a slow pace, with the Hereford bulls bringing up the rear, an expected outcome since their legs were far shorter and they would have more trouble staying up with longer-strided longhorn cows.

"So far, so good," he said under his breath. The land they were traveling was empty, no houses or signs of civilization in sight as far as the eye could see.

They were passing through what Chisum called the Haystack Mountain range, little more than foothills to a man who knew the Rockies. Water was plentiful in creeks and arroyos. With so much grass and water, the cattle would have an easy time of it until they reached drier regions to the north.

An hour later, Smoke tensed in the saddle when he saw Duke Smith headed his way at a fast trot. Smoke swung his horse to ride to meet him.

"Nothin's wrong," Duke said quickly, when he saw the look on Smoke's face, "but we did see this horse an' rider way off to the west, an' he didn't stay long afore he plumb disappeared."

It could be someone riding to warn Evans of their

departure from Chisum's ranch, although he didn't want to worry Duke or the others. "Maybe just a range cowboy out lookin' for strays. But keep your eyes peeled anyway."

"Pearlie said to tell you it didn't look right, how this feller rode off that hilltop so quick, like he didn't want nobody to see him."

"Could just be a coincidence. I'll ride over to the west a ways, just to make sure. Keep the cattle moving. Some of those longhorns are a little spooky yet. If one gun goes off, they'll all break into a run."

"I know the ornery critters right well," Duke declared, as he turned his horse around. "Ain't no creature on this earth as likely to run off as a damn longhorn. We'd be tryin' to round 'em up till doomsday if somethin' scares 'em."

Smoke wondered about the rider they had seen as Duke rode off to rejoin the herd at point. Was Jessie Evans keeping an eye on them, planning his next attempt at revenge?

Swinging west, Smoke galloped his horse to the highest hill, where he had a view of what lay beyond. For a time, he sat his horse, motionless, making no effort to hide himself should anyone be watching. A herd the size of theirs couldn't be hidden as it moved northward, no matter how carefully they were kept to low ground, making it pointless to hide his own presence on the hilltop now.

As far as the eye could see, the land was empty. A red hawk soared above distant stands of trees, hunting prey, a sign it sensed no danger from the presence of man in forests below. A hawk's eyesight and hearing were far keener than a man's, and it convinced Smoke they were alone here. For now.

Twenty-nine

Ignacio Valdez came to a decision. Instead of riding back to Bosque Redondo to warn Jessie about the herd moving northward away from Chisum's like Jessie wanted, he would take care of this broad-shouldered stranger called Smoke Jensen himself, and that would please Jessie. The sneaky gringo who'd killed so many of their gang would be dead, and Ignacio would get the credit for it, killing this loco hombre who had done so much damage when he snuck around behind them in the dark, like a coward. Ignacio was sure he could take Jensen down. In Chihuahua and Coahuila he'd been the fastest gun in northern Mexico, killing the likes of Luis Ortega, Manuel Soto, and the worst of them all in a pistol duel, Emiliano Zambrano.

He'd killed Zambrano with his first shot when they drew against each other in Juarez, over a woman. Ignacio remembered how much faster he had been, getting off a shot before the famous Zambrano could level his gun. Stories circulated that Zambrano had killed more than a dozen *pistoleros* in gunfights. He'd had ten notches in the walnut grips of the pistol he carried when Ignacio ended his life with a bullet through the heart.

"I can kill Jensen," he told himself as he spurred

his bay gelding well to the north of the cattle herd. "He is only a man, and I will be quicker, much quicker. I will cut off his head and bring it to Jessie as proof of what I have done. . . ."

He guided his horse down a winding arroyo to a small stream lined with cottonwood trees, lying directly in the path of the herd. Ignacio spent a moment deciding where to hide his horse before he selected a spot to wait for Jensen. Jensen would stop to water his horse, or simply slow down to cross the creek, and this would be when Ignacio would kill him.

Hurrying away from the ravine where he tethered his bay, he trotted down to the stream, where a massive cottonwood trunk would hide his presence. Out of breath, he took off his sombrero and placed it on the ground in the tall grass where Jensen wouldn't see it, before he pulled his Mason Colt .44/.40, checking each load carefully. Ignacio had decided against using a rifle—he wanted Jensen close before he killed him, close enough to see the fear and surprise on his face when he saw the man who would cut off his head for a trophy to give to Jessie Evans.

He peered around the cottonwood, waiting patiently. This would be easy, killing Jensen, almost too easy. It would make up for the lives Jensen had taken in such a cowardly fashion, to creep up behind some of Jessie's men and four of Pedro Lopez's *pistoleros*.

"Adios, Señor Jensen," he whispered, pulling back so that only one eye was visible next to the tree trunk.

Water gurgled softly in the creek, passing over smooth stones on its way to join the Pecos. Ignacio ran the tip of his tongue across his gold tooth, almost grinning with anticipation.

* * *

A horse and rider approached the stream. Ignacio recognized Jensen and drew back out of sight, awaiting the moment when he could be sure of the kill. Resting his right palm on the butt of his Colt, he was eager for things to begin. The sounds made by the horse came closer, very close, and suddenly, they stopped.

Ignacio jacked back the hammer on his pistol, so he only needed to draw and pull the trigger when he killed Jensen. He took a deep breath.

He heard a spur jingle when it touched the ground. *He is down off his horse,* Ignacio thought. *All the better.*

And still he waited for the right moment, when the sounds came nearer, making for surer aim.

Quiet footfalls approached the stream. This was the moment Ignacio had been waiting for. He swung around the cottonwood and spread his feet slightly apart.

"Jensen!" he cried, when he saw a tall cowboy wearing two pistols around his waist.

The man froze in his tracks and Ignacio was sure it was fear that made him so still.

"You called my name?" the cowboy asked, both hands relaxed at his sides.

"*Sí,* and I am calling you a yellow coward. You killed some of *mi amigos.* I have come to make you pay for what you did."

"You'd better be good," the stranger said, his voice relaxed and even.

"But I am, señor. Very good. *Muy bueno con una pistola.* I am faster than you."

"I reckon you're gonna try to prove it now."

"*Verdad.* This is the truth. I will kill you for what you did."

Jensen gave him a one-sided grin, unusual for a man who was about to be gunned down.

"Lots of men have tried it over the years. You can see I'm still here."

"But none were as fast as me, señor." Ignacio raised his hand slightly closer to the butt of his gun. "Of that I am quite sure."

"Only one way to find out," Jensen replied. "Reach for that iron you're carryin' and we'll decide this here and now."

Now Ignacio grinned. "You are a fool, señor. *Un idiota.* You do not know who I am."

"I don't give a damn who you are. Just go for your gun and it won't matter about the name."

Ignacio noticed an odd, icy feeling in the pit of his stomach. "I am Ignacio Valdez," he said, "the man who will put you in your grave."

"I've already invited you to try it," Jensen said. "Any time you're ready."

"You are indeed one loco hombre, Señor Jensen. You are too stupid to be afraid."

"What's there to be afraid of? Some Mexican *pistolero* who calls himself Ignacio Valdez?"

"Are you not afraid of dying, señor?"

"It ain't been proven yet I'm the one who's gonna die when we go for our guns. It could work out another way."

Ignacio stared into the eyes of the stranger to these parts, and he wondered about him. His stare was unwavering, and he was so sure of himself.

Ignacio's hand dipped for his pistol. His fingers closed around his gun grips. As he was pulling the heavy .44/.40 from its holster, he saw a sight that made his blood run cold.

Jensen came up with a gleaming Colt .44 in his right hand so quickly it did not seem possible, and for an instant Ignacio was looking down its barrel, a dark round hole the size of his little finger. No man could be so fast, he thought as his own fist came up filled with iron.

The dark muzzle of Jensen's gun shot forth a beacon of white light that was accompanied by a loud banging noise. Ignacio's finger curled around the gun's trigger, tightening, when it felt like he'd been struck in the ribs by a hammer blow.

The force of the impact drove him backward a half step at the same moment he triggered off a shot into the ground near his boots. He glanced down, seeing tiny tufts of lint arise from a puckering hole in his shirtfront. A trickle of blood came from the hole . . . Ignacio's blood. His ears were ringing from the pair of gunshots.

"Madre!" he cried, trying to keep his feet under him when it seemed the earth was tilting at odd angles.

"You were too slow," a voice said in front of him. "I gave you the first pull."

Ignacio sank to his knees, his mind reeling. He barely noticed when his pistol fell from his hand. How could this have happened, he wondered. How could Jensen be faster than Emiliano Zambrano, the fastest gun in all of northern Mexico?

"Bastardo," Ignacio spat angrily, waves of pain spreading across his chest. He looked up at Jensen, and he found the man smiling again.

"It's all in the wrist," Jensen explained, as if he were talking about the proper way to shoe a horse.

"Your wrist was too stiff. You gotta learn to bend it some, only I don't figure you'll have the time now."

Ignacio saw himself as a small boy playing beside a creek in Torreón, a creek very similar to this one. He had skipped rocks there as a child. He knew his mind was wandering.

"Adios, Valdez," Jensen said. "That slug caught you in a bad place. You're bleedin' like a stuck hog at butcherin' time right now. I don't figure you'll last long."

"Bastardo," he said again, reaching for his wound with both hands to stem the flow of blood.

"I'd take offense to you callin' me a bastard," Jensen said, "if you wasn't already dyin'."

Ignacio's vision blurred. He rocked forward on his knees and fell on his face, wondering if Jessie Evans had any idea how fast this Jensen was with a handgun . . . faster than any gunman Ignacio had ever seen . . . much faster than Emiliano Zambrano.

Thirty

Two cowboys came galloping over the hilltop, their horses at full speed under the punishment of spurs, pistols drawn as they rode for the creek bank where Smoke stood over the body of the Mexican. Pearlie and Duke slowed their mounts when they could see the trouble was over. Both men pulled their horses to a halt a few yards from the stream.

"We heard shootin'!" Pearlie declared, glancing down at the body. "Don't need no crystal ball to know that's one of Jessie Evans's men."

Smoke holstered his gun. "Said his name was Ignacio Valdez, an' that name should mean somethin'."

Pearlie wagged his head and put his pistol away. "Means it's gonna be hard to spell fer some undertaker when he puts it on his tombstone." He gave Smoke a weak grin. "I figure it's gonna be like this plumb to the Colorado border. I knowed we couldn't just drive them cows peaceful all the way to Sugarloaf the way Cletus was hopin' we could. I told Cletus last night to make damn sure his guns was loaded."

Duke was last to rid his hand of a gun. "We heard two shots real close together."

Smoke looked over his shoulder at Valdez. "He damn near shot himself in the foot just a moment ago. Had his pistol in the cocked position when he drew it. I've known a few gents who did without a toe or two the rest of their lives on account of that same bad habit."

Duke chuckled. "I've never claimed to be much of a gunnie, but it don't appear Mr. Valdez was much of one either."

Smoke turned to collect his horse. "He was fast by most men's standards, I suppose. He just wasn't quite fast enough."

Pearlie frowned. "That hired gun of Chisum's, the one they call Buck, said to watch out fer a feller ridin' with Evans by the name of Bill Pickett. An older feller, Buck said. Pickett is rattlesnake mean, accordin' to Buck, an' quicker'n greased lightnin' with a pistol, only Buck claimed Pickett prefers usin' a sawed-off shotgun."

Nothing Pearlie said caused Smoke any worry as he mounted his bay Palouse colt. "A man with a sawed-off shotgun has to be mighty close to a target, Pearlie. Could mean his eyesight is a little on the bad side. If he crosses the road we're takin' to Big Rock, I'll buy him a pair of spectacles so they can bury him with 'em on."

Duke pointed to the body of Ignacio Valdez. "What you want us to do with that corpse, Mr. Jensen?" he asked.

"Not a damn thing. Let the buzzards and coyotes have a meal out of him. Scout around and find his horse. It won't be far, an' I'd hate to leave an animal tied up till it starves to death or breaks its reins. When Valdez don't show up wherever Evans is waitin' for him, he'll come looking for him. And us. We can be sure of more gunplay sooner or later. Evans will likely bring this Pickett and anybody else he can hire. Like it or not, we've gotten ourselves into the middle of the Lincoln County War, just because we bought a herd of cattle from John Chisum."

"I figured all along we'd have to shoot our way out of here," Pearlie said, wheeling his horse away from the stream and the body. He spoke to Duke. "Look fer that horse whilst I git back to the herd. Ain't nobody ridin' point now an' they's sure liable to wander."

Then he noticed Smoke was looking off to the west.

"What's wrong, boss?" Pearlie asked, when he saw a dark look cross Smoke's face.

"I'm thinkin'," Smoke replied.

"Thinkin' 'bout what? If you don't take no offense from me by askin'."

Until right at that moment the attempted ambush by Ignacio Valdez hadn't bothered him. But something changed inside his head in sudden fashion. "Thinkin' about riding back to Lincoln right now to settle this once an' for all, so the rest of you don't have to duck lead all the way out of the territory. I can ask where to find Jimmy Dolan and look him up. I could warn him that if he sends one more gunman after this herd or any of my men, I'll kill him. The more I think about it, the better that notion sounds."

"It could be real dangerous," Pearlie said.

Smoke's mind was made up. A warning was what Jimmy Dolan needed. "You men keep pushing our herd north. Take your time, and don't ride into any tight spots where a bushwhacker could take a shot at you. I'll be back tomorrow. It's time Mr. Dolan found out a thing or two about our intentions."

Pearlie sounded worried. "What'll we do if you don't come back?"

"Keep driving our cows toward Sugarloaf," was all he said as he heeled his horse to a gallop.

The Murphy and Dolan General store sat across from the courthouse in Lincoln. By pushing his horse harder than he wanted to, Smoke arrived in front of the store just before closing time, at five o'clock. When he swung down from the saddle, bone-weary after so many hours of riding, trying to make Lincoln before dark, his legs were stiff.

Smoke entered the store in full stride, walking over to a clerk in a badly stained apron.

"Where's Jimmy Dolan?" he demanded, staring down at the store clerk's face.

"In the back, tallyin' up the day's receipts, only he don't want to be disturbed right now."

Smoke saw a door at the back of the building. "He's gonna make an exception this time," he said, stalking away from the glass-topped counter with his mouth set in a grim line.

He didn't bother to knock, swinging a thin plank door inward as he walked into a small office. A man in shirtsleeves, with a distinctively pallid complexion, glanced up from a ledger book.

"I didn't hear you knock, mister," the man snapped, making no effort to disguise his anger.

"That's because I didn't," Smoke said, stepping over to the desk where Dolan sat before he drew one pistol with his right hand, leveling it only a few inches from Dolan's forehead. "I'm gonna give you some advice, Dolan," he said, glaring down at the store owner. He thumbed back the hammer on his .44. "My name is Jensen, Smoke Jensen. I bought a herd of cows from John Chisum and I'm takin' 'em back to Colorado Territory. Only I'm havin' this problem with a fool named Jessie Evans. He keeps tryin' to kill me and my cowboys. I've been told Evans works for you in this range war you're having in Lincoln County. I don't give a damn about your war, or who you rustle cattle from, or anything else. I want you to send Evans a message tonight."

"You're a brazen man," Dolan said, looking up at the muzzle of Smoke's gun. "I'll have you arrested for threatening me unless you put that gun away and get out of here immediately."

"You don't understand," Smoke snarled. "You weren't listening to me. Call off this Evans and your gunslingers right now, or so help me I'll come back and kill you."

"That's strong talk, Jensen."

Smoke leaned a little closer to Dolan's face. "It ain't just talk, you dumb son of a bitch. I've already killed eleven of your hired guns. I'll kill every last one of 'em, including you, if anybody messes with me or my cowboys or my cattle again. I want you to understand, Dolan. The next son of a bitch who takes a shot at me is gonna start a game between us, a deadly game where you wind up bein' the first to die. I'll blow a goddamn tunnel through your head big enough to toss a tomcat through, and that'll be just the start. I'll hunt down Evans an' every last one of his gunnies, and I'll put 'em all in shallow graves."

Dolan blinked. "One man wouldn't stand a chance of doing what you claim to be able to do."

"Just try me, creep. You can count on one thing bein' for absolute certain. I'm gonna kill you first if a shot gets fired at me or my friends. You won't be around to know if I can make good on the rest of my promise."

"You're crazy," Dolan whispered.

Smoke wagged his head. "I'm just pissed-off. I'm tired of bein' shot at. Tired of having to look over my shoulder to see if any more of your backshooters are behind me. I'm a rancher up in Colorado, but I'm also a real bad enemy to have if you don't pay any attention to what I'm tellin' you."

"I'll go to Sheriff Pat Garrett over in San Miguel County with this," Dolan said.

"I hope you do," Smoke hissed, barely able to control his rage over Dolan's arrogance. "I'll tell him how your boys came gunning for us at Chisum's the other night, and how I killed six of the yellow bastards while they were shootin' at the ranch in the dark. Then I'll tell him how the big-talkin' Mexican by the name of Ignacio Valdez tried to ambush me earlier today, only I killed him too, an' it was easy. Notify this sheriff if you want, Dolan. But remember what I said . . . if just one more bullet comes at us, you'll be as dead as Valdez an' all the rest of your gunslicks."

Dolan swallowed now, and Smoke saw the first hint of fear in his eyes. His message delivered, Smoke wheeled and walked out of the office.

"You may regret this," Dolan warned as Smoke was leaving the store.

Smoke paused in the doorway. "I doubt it. You'll be the one to regret your actions if you ain't been listening to what I said."

"One man can't be all that good, that tough."

Smoke smiled a humorless smile. "One way to find out. Send Evans and some of his men gunning for me."

"I may just do that," Dolan retorted, sounding like some of his nerve had returned.

Smoke kept smiling. "I'll enjoy it, if you do. It's been a long time since I killed more than a handful of men at one time. But I'll enjoy killin' you more than any of 'em, Dolan, because you're a yellow son of a bitch who has to pay to get his dirty work done. Send your boys after me, if you've got the guts for it. But if you do, I'd check on the price of a good casket right after that, and a cemetery plot, 'cause you're gonna need 'em both. And you'll have to hire somebody to dig the hole ahead of time. You won't be alive to attend to your final arrangements."

He slammed the door and mounted his Palouse as the sun was setting on Lincoln. Dolan could have it any way he wanted now, after being warned of the consequences.

Thirty-one

Cal and Pearlie and Johnny were saddling fresh horses at a stream the next afternoon as Smoke returned from Lincoln. Smoke could see the cow herd grazing along peacefully, and that all was well. He waved as he rode up to the creek, just in time to see Cal pull his saddle cinch and step aboard the back of a gray colt they'd brought along to season it to cow work. Smoke's experienced eye saw the hump in the three-year-old colt's back which Cal had apparently overlooked. Before Cal could get his leg over the cantle of his saddle, the gray downed its head and began to buck.

Cal was dislodged from his saddle during the first unexpected jump. . . . He went sailing over the colt's head as if he'd sprouted wings. Arms and legs windmilling, Cal was propelled into the air, suspended above the stream for a moment before he fell headfirst into the water, sending up a shower of spray.

Pearlie was the first to burst out laughing, just as Cal came sputtering to the surface. Smoke chuckled, knowing it was a lesson Cal needed, to watch for a slight rise in a horse's back before he mounted, a warning that the animal intended to buck as soon as it felt a man's weight.

"What happened?" Cal cried, scrambling to his feet in the shallow water without his hat, blinking to clear his vision. His hat floated slowly downstream, unnoticed for now.

"You got your young ass bucked off," Pearlie replied as he held his belly between fits of laughter. "You looked fer all the world like you was tryin' to fly, young 'un, up there with them sparrows an' blue jays. When I seen you way up yonder, I thought I'd just laid eyes on the ugliest buzzard on this earth!" He broke into another series of hee-haws, clutching his ribs.

"It ain't all that funny," Cal mumbled, staggering across slippery stones in the stream bottom to retrieve his Stetson before it floated away. "I just wasn't ready, is all it was. That gray's got a mean streak in him."

Johnny North was grinning. "Wasn't that gray's fault, Cal. You shoulda noticed that hump in his back."

"Wasn't no hump there," Cal insisted, shaking water from his hat, his young cheeks flushed with embarrassment. "It was that damn colt's nasty disposition, is what it was." Cal stumbled out of the creek, his boots full of water, unable to look directly at Smoke or Pearlie for the moment, so deep was his humiliation over being thrown.

"Hell, young 'un, you was needin' a bath anyways," Pearlie said, again breaking into a guffaw or two. "If I'd had a bar of lye soap, I'd have tossed it up in the air whilst you was testin' your wings. That way, you coulda scrubbed clean soon as you landed. You done one of the prettiest dives I ever saw in my life just now. Damn near a perfect landin'."

As Pearlie started laughing again, Smoke swung down from the saddle, exhausted by a long night ride to reach the herd as soon as he could, resting his

Palouse more often on the return trip to spare it any bog spavins or other lameness. "It was a right pretty landing, son," he said to Cal, knowing how the boy must feel with an audience for his mistake.

Pearlie fell quiet all of a sudden. He looked at Smoke for a time. "How did things go in Lincoln?" he asked. "Did you have to shoot Jimmy Dolan? Or was he ready to listen?"

Smoke loosened the cinch on his tired colt. "He didn't pay all that much attention. I warned him what would happen if one more shot got fired at us. He figures I'm bluffing."

"Then he don't know you at all," Pearlie said, serious now. "If he knowed anythin' about Smoke Jensen, he'd know you don't never run no bluff on nobody."

"I'm expectin' more trouble," Smoke told Pearlie. "Dolan is the type who thinks his money will get him everything he's after. He talks big."

"How come you didn't kill him?" Pearlie asked, "Or slap him plumb silly with the barrel of a gun?"

"I'm giving him a chance to think it over. It was probably a waste of time talking to him, telling him what I'd do if Evans and his boys come back. I'm betting they will."

Pearlie shook his head, glancing over to Cal as the boy was pulling off his boots to drain the water out. "Won't be much sleepin' fer this crew from now on," he said. "I can damn near feel it comin' in my bones, like when a blue norther is headed our way."

Smoke cast a lingering look at the herd before he spoke again. "I'm of the opinion your bones are telling you the truth this time, Pearlie," he said, leading his Palouse colt away from the creek to saddle a fresh horse.

Thirty-two

He gave his name in broken English as Little Horse, then he pointed to seven young warriors standing behind him, introducing one as Dreamer, another as Sees Far, then the others, all names Jessie quickly forgot. He didn't care what these Apaches called themselves.

"Can they shoot straight?" Jessie asked Little Horse.

Little Horse nodded once. "Many time kill white-eyes," he said, balancing a badly worn Spencer carbine in one hand. "We kill more if you pay us money." He carried a rusted Colt in a sash around his waist, along with a gleaming Bowie knife. This Indian in particular was always in trouble with the soldiers at Fort Stanton for running off from the reservation to steal horses and cattle, scalping white settlers in the process. Little Horse had just gotten out of jail at the fort, along with the seven men who came with him, when no witnesses could identify them as the killers of six white farmers in the Penasco Valley last year.

"Get the ammunition you need from that store over yonder," he told the Apache. "Then get mounted an' follow us." He gave Jimmy Dolan a sideways look. "That makes eight more. Ten just showed up last night from Mexico, all good *pistoleros,* accordin' to Pedro Lopez. He knows most of 'em."

Dolan frowned. "I hope they're better than Ignacio Valdez," he muttered. "You told me Valdez was really good."

"That Jensen feller probably ambushed him from hidin' some place or another. It sure as hell wasn't no fair fight if he got Ignacio."

"Just make damn sure you get Jensen at all costs," Dolan said quietly, standing in the road where Jessie and more than thirty mounted men waited, all heavily armed. Townspeople were staring at the gang from all over Lincoln's main street.

"You can bank on it," Jessie replied.

Dolan's expression hardened. "Jensen is a cocksure son of a bitch. He acted like he owned Lincoln County. I wasn't carrying a gun, and yet he stuck his pistol right in my face when he came barging in the store. I want him dead. Nobody sticks a gun in my face like that."

"I'll bring you his head in a tow sack," Jessie promised as the Apaches went inside the store to get cartridges. "I'll have forty men with me, includin' those redskins. There ain't but seven or eight with that herd, includin' Jensen. It'll be over before it gets started."

"Kill them all," Dolan whispered, so that citizens of Lincoln standing nearby wouldn't hear. "Don't leave a goddamn one of them alive to tell what happened."

"It's as good as done," Jessie said, resting a palm on the butt of his Colt. He grinned and aimed a thumb at Bill Pickett. "I've done promised Pickett he can make sure every last one of 'em is dead. He gets a kick out of killin' with that shotgun of his. I'm sure as hell glad he's on our payroll."

"Just get the job done this time," Dolan snapped. "I'm paying good money to get results, not a bunch of empty promises like the last time."

"That was on account of Billy Barlow warned 'em. Soon as we get back, I'll find Barlow an' kill him myself."

"Do whatever it takes," Dolan said, walking away with his hands shoved in his pants pockets.

Jessie mounted his horse, waiting between Pickett and Tom Hill for the Apaches to come out of the store.

"Goddamn Injuns can't shoot," Pickett said with heat in his voice. "None of 'em can."

"Maybe they'll get lucky," Jessie replied. "Little Horse, the one who speaks some English, is tough, an' a dead shot when he's up close, accordin' to Colonel Dudley. They've been tryin' to find something to pin on him so they can hang him, only he's smart. He don't get caught very often. They had to let him go this time because nobody would testify it was him murdered them farmers."

"I hate Injuns," Pickett declared. "After we get done with this Jensen feller, I'll do the army a favor by blowin' off that damn Apache's skullbone."

Jessie shrugged. "When we're finished with Jensen, I don't give a damn what you do. You can kill all those Apaches for all I care. That way, Dolan don't have to pay 'em."

"Sounds good to me," Pickett said.

Jessie noticed Tom Hill's color wasn't quite right after he heard what Pickett meant to do to the Indians. Glancing over his shoulder, Jessie took another look at the ten Mexicans who'd ridden in at Bosque Redondo the night before. All were bearded, hard-faced men with crisscrossed cartridge bandoliers over each shoulder. The *pistolero* who led this bunch was named Jose Vasquez, and he had a certain look about him showing confidence. Pedro said Jose was a *bandido,* and a killer who took great pride in his work.

Jessie thought about Smoke Jensen. For a man he'd never met, this Colorado rancher was sure as hell causing a lot of trouble in New Mexico Territory, a condition that was about to end tonight, or whenever they caught up to him and his cow herd. With the odds being over four to one against Jensen, he would be dead by the time the sun went down tomorrow. Jessie was certain of it, as Little Horse and his Apaches came out of the store to climb aboard their scrawny ponies.

"Let's ride," he said to the men around him, wheeling his horse to the east.

"We can't get there soon enough to suit me," Pickett said as they struck a trot out of Lincoln.

Forty-three gunmen followed Jessie into the hills east of Lincoln Township. The rattle of curb chains, spur rowels, and armament accompanied their departure. Dust curled away from their horses' heels.

Jessie noticed Jimmy Dolan standing on the porch of his store watching them ride off. Jessie promised himself Mr. Dolan wouldn't be disappointed this time when he heard what had happened somewhere along the Pecos River.

Thirty-three

Bob and Cletus and Johnny rode slow circles around the herd as the cattle bedded down for the night. The day had passed uneventfully, but when Smoke scouted for a place to hold the herd for the night, he selected it carefully, with defense from an all-out attack in mind, deciding upon the middle of a flat, grassy prairie with no trees or brush nearby where a rifleman would be in range. He knew, once the shooting started, the longhorns would scatter in every direction, making for a difficult time rounding them up, even in daylight. Under the present circumstances, it was the best he could do, to stay out in the open so Evans would have to charge them without benefit of cover. Defenders lying in tall bunch grass would have an advantage over men charging across the flat meadow toward the herd.

Pearlie handed Smoke a tin plate full of beans and fried fatback. He had been watching Smoke use a whetstone across the iron blade of a Ute tomahawk he always carried in his saddlebags. "You figure they're comin' tonight, don't you?" he asked.

Smoke began eating, his face more deeply etched by lines in the light of their campfire. "Hard to say, Pearlie. Best thing to do is be ready for 'em anytime."

"They'll come from the west, from the direction of Lincoln, I reckon."

"Most likely." He chewed thoughtfully a moment. "That's why I'm headed that way, as soon as I've eaten. Those trees way over yonder will give me some cover. I'll go on foot, so I can move around quiet. They may come at us from the south if they've been following our tracks. I want you and the rest to spread out around the herd with rifles and plenty of ammunition. Find a spot in that tall grass where you'll be harder to see when you shoot. They'll have to cross a bunch of open ground to get to us, and that'll cost 'em. Those longhorns are gonna run like mad as soon as the first shot gets fired. I'll try to drop as many of Jessie's boys as I can before they get too close. Main thing is to stay down. I don't want anybody to take chances."

"You'll be the one takin' chances," Pearlie observed.

Smoke continued eating. "I'm accustomed to it, Pearlie. I reckon I've been taking chances all my life, so I've had plenty of practice. The most important thing is that none of you take a bullet, and if you can, protect those Herefords. We can buy more longhorns if we lose a few, but those white-faced bulls can't be replaced very easy. Save as many as you can."

Pearlie glanced across the dark prairie. "Evans would have to be a fool to charge us out in the open like this, even if he done it at night, 'less he's got a helluva lot of men with him."

"I expect him to bring a sizable bunch this time. I'll kill as many as I can before they rush you."

"I noticed you's wearin' your moccasins 'stead of your boots tonight."

"Quieter," Smoke said.

Cal had been listening closely while he ate. "I reckon I'm about to git another chance to kill somebody. It sure does a job on my nerves."

"It ain't affected yer appetite any," Pearlie said.

"I'm eatin' because I'm nervous."

"Hell, you eat all the time anyways. . . ."

Smoke got up as Duke was coming to the fire after tying his horse to the picket rope. He saw the tomahawk in Smoke's hand.

"I sure hope they don't get that close, Mr. Jensen," he said as Smoke tucked the handle under his cartridge belt.

"That's why I'm headed for those trees yonder," Smoke replied, inclining his head to the west, "so I can keep some of 'em from getting close." He looked over his shoulder at Pearlie and Cal. "I'll see you boys at daybreak if nothing happens tonight. Put out that fire soon as everyone's eaten."

Pearlie nodded. "We's all wishin' you good luck, boss."

Smoke picked up his rifle. "You should know by now I never depend on luck, Pearlie." He strode softly into the darkness, his moccasins making no sound.

False dawn came to the eastern sky, making shadows that played tricks on a man's eyes . . . unless he knew a thing or two about shadows in early light. The night had passed without incident, although Smoke continued to circle the herd from a distance, moving from tree to tree, pausing to listen and study the forest before moving on again.

A sound came from an unexpected place, the unmistakable plop of an unshod horse's hoof. He hadn't been expecting Indians, not when Jessie Evans was the enemy. But few white men rode unshod horses in rough country, and the sound of a hoof without an iron shoe was distinctive, easy to recognize.

He hurried toward the sound, dodging from pine trunk to pine trunk, until he crept close to a small clearing, where the outlines of two Apache warriors on wiry ponies moved slowly in the direction of the prairie where the herd was bedded down.

Apache scouts, he thought, by the way they wore their hair under a headband. Smoke continued forward, pulling his tomahawk with his right hand, a pistol with his left.

The element of surprise would be with him if he moved quickly. He crept up behind the pair of Indians, and when the distance was right, he broke into a soundless headlong run.

His first blow with the razor-sharp tomahawk sliced across the back of an Apache's neck, severing muscle and ligaments and tissue all the way down to bone. Jerking his weapon free, he swung at the other Indian just as he was turning to see what had made the wet, chopping noise, then the dull thud of a falling body.

The tomahawk's blade struck the Apache full in the face, entering his cheek and eye socket, splitting bones with a sharp crack. A muffled cry came from the warrior's throat as his pony lunged forward, sending him toppling to the ground with Smoke's Ute tomahawk buried in his brain.

Again jerking the weapon free, Smoke whirled around to dash back into the forest with blood dripping from the ax blade onto his leggings. Where there were two scouts, there could be more. He was certain these were not wandering renegades on the lookout for easy pickings—they worked for Evans, leading his gang to Smoke and his friends. A full-fledged attack was only moments away, coming at dawn, when cowboys who had been vigilant all night would be tired, sleepy, not as watchful.

Smoke knew he had precious little time to reduce the odds against them before Evans led his men charging toward the herd.

The young Apache never heard Smoke's stealthy approach up to his hiding place behind a tree, and when the tomahawk hit the back of his head, splitting it in half like a ripe melon, he did not utter a word or make a sound, crumpling to the forest floor in a growing pool of blood. Smoke knew there were two more Indians watching the herd somewhere . . . he'd found three ponies in a thicket, tied to low tree limbs.

Racing away from his third kill, Smoke saw a shadow move at the base of another oak tree at the edge of the prairie.

"They're makin' it easy for me, spreadin' out like this," he said in a feathery whisper.

Practicing the stalking art he'd learned from Preacher, Smoke came up behind an Apache cradling a Spencer rifle, peering around the oak to see the distant cattle herd. But this Indian somehow sensed something near him as Smoke leaped forward . . . he turned, just in time to see the flash of steel coming at him in a high arc above his head.

The pop of breaking bone ended a total silence in the forest when Smoke's tomahawk cleaved open the Apache's forehead, driving him back against the tree briefly. Then he sank to his knees as Smoke pulled the blade free amid a torrent of blood coming from a wound eight inches deep between the Indian's eyes.

Smoke didn't wait to see the Apache fall. He was running to the south when he heard a muted plop behind him.

He found the last Indian relieving himself behind a bush with his rifle leaning against a piñon pine. There wasn't time to allow the Apache to empty his bladder before he died from a sweeping slash across the side of his throat from a tomahawk severing his head.

Smoke darted behind a tree, listening. Farther to the south he heard the clank of a metal spur rowel.

"Here comes the rest of the army," he told himself. It was unlikely there could be any more killing without gunfire, and the commencement of all-out war.

Smoke trotted back to the fork of a tree where he'd hidden his rifle, passing five lifeless bodies in the soft light of a coming sunrise, the air already thick with the scent of blood.

A lone Mexican squatting behind a thick tangle of thorny brush gave Smoke one more chance to kill soundlessly. A blow to the head by a tomahawk snuffed out the Mexican's life before he realized someone was behind him. He went over on his face in the briars with blood pumping from his skull, oblivious to the scratches on his bearded cheeks and chin where sharp thorns tore into his flesh.

Smoke paused and took a deep breath. His killing instincts had once again overtaken him, pushing everything else from his mind. But just once, before he took off looking for more victims in the forest, he thought about the promise he'd made to Sally to steer clear of a fight, if he could.

"She'd understand," he whispered. He'd done everything he could to warn Jessie Evans and Jimmy Dolan what would happen if they pushed him.

He moved more slowly now, with light beaming over eastern hills that would reveal his presence. Carrying the Winchester in one hand, a pistol in the other, he'd belted the tomahawk, for it had done all the damage it could before sunrise.

Smoke stepped among the trees, halting often to sweep the forest for any sign of the enemy. When it was safe to continue, he moved south, wondering if Evans had split his forces so that some were already surrounding the herd.

Can't be two places at once, he thought, trotting wherever he could, walking where there was less cover.

Then he saw what he'd been expecting all along, a bunch of mounted men waiting in a draw surrounded by slender oaks. He froze behind a tree to count them.

"A baker's dozen," he whispered. Thirteen men would be hard to tackle single-handed. Smoke knew he had no choice.

Thirty-four

A pistol in each hand, his Winchester lying between his feet within easy reach, Smoke straightened up behind a bush at the lip of the ravine—as with the five Apaches, these men would get no warning before they died—this was open war now.

He began firing methodically, one pistol, then the other, sending a stream of lead into the gully while the roar of exploding gunpowder filled his ears. Bullets tore through flesh in a steady stream, snapping bone and gristle, piercing organs and muscle. Frightened horses whickered and reared, plunging to be free of the pull of reins as riders toppled down into a mass of churning hooves.

Cries of pain, screams of agony accompanied the gun blasts and the sounds of terrified horses. Taken completely by surprise, the gunmen merely sought an escape from the deadly hail of hot slugs pouring down on them, but as each one made a dash toward freedom, he was cut down, knocked from his saddle by a bullet. Not a shot was fired back at Smoke until both his pistols were empty, and as he seized his rifle, only two unharmed members of Evans's gang remained aboard their horses. One was able to ride into the trees before Smoke could get off a rifle shot, but the second, a heavy Mexican, met his end as he was spurring his horse behind the first to flee. A rifle slug caught him in the ribs, cracking when it penetrated bone while passing into his chest. He fell sideways, with his right boot caught in a stirrup, so that as his horse galloped out of sight he was dragged along in its wake, leaving a trail of blood through the forest.

Smoke was moving before the echo of his rifle shot faded away, hurrying away from the scene, a ravine filled with writhing bodies and motionless corpses.

He raced back among the trees toward the herd, certain that now Evans would order a full charge toward the cattle. As he was running, he reloaded his Colts, cradling his rifle in the crook of his arm.

And as he expected, he heard the rumble of pounding hooves coming from the south and east. Men came pouring from the pines in every direction, spurring their mounts into a hard gallop, and even a quick count revealed there were far more of them than Smoke had anticipated. It appeared that twenty or more riders were rushing onto the prairie, and now the crackle of guns went back and forth almost in unison.

"The yellow bastard hired every gun in Lincoln County," Smoke growled, running faster, hurrying toward a position where he could help Pearlie and Cal and Johnny and his neighbors by firing from the enemy's flank. Until he was in range, he dared not waste a shot, telling Evans and the others where he was.

Answering fire came from Smoke's friends, only a few shots at a time right then. In his heart, Smoke doubted everyone in his crew could make it through a war like this without a scratch, and the thought saddened him momentarily, until blind rage overtook his sorrow.

"I'm comin', Evans!" he bellowed, knowing no one could hear him in the melee, racing along the edge of the forest with a killing fever burning in his brain.

An unexpected bit of good fortune presented itself just as he was nearing a thick oak trunk. Three riders came charging out of the trees with guns blazing, unaware that Smoke was only a few dozen yards away.

Smoke stumbled to a halt and drew a bead on the first rider with a pistol, firing too quickly, shooting high and wide. He triggered off a second shot as all three men turned toward the sound of his gun.

A man in a dirty brown Stetson flipped off his horse when Smoke's second bullet found its mark. Smoke fired again at another gunman, more careful with his aim now. A Mexican with cartridge belts across his chest went down, his sombrero fluttering away while he fell.

The third rider fired at Smoke, a hurried shot from the back of a moving horse. A molten slug screamed high above Smoke's head. Smoke downed him with a booming pistol, watching another Mexican gunman fly out of his saddle with his face twisted in pain.

Three riderless horses galloped onto the prairie, one with blood dripping from its withers, where its owner had bled before he fell.

The rattle of rifle fire became a din, a constant wall of noise as more than two hundred longhorn heifers scattered with their tails in the air, snorting through their muzzles as the stampede Smoke had been worrying about began. He could see the gentler Herefords milling about, but for the moment they stayed together in a tight bunch.

A rifle popped from a clump of bunch grass near the picketed horses. One of Evans's men floated away from his galloping horse with both hands pressed to his face.

"Nice shot," Smoke muttered, shouldering his rifle to begin dropping as many oncoming raiders as he could.

Leading a moving target with his rifle sights, he fired at a cowboy on a speeding pinto. A miss, and it made him angry as he levered another round into place.

"I've gotta get closer," he said savagely.

Two of Evans's men noticed him for the first time and swung their horses in his direction, bearing down on him as fast as their horses could run.

"Thank you, gentlemen," Smoke whispered, taking very careful aim.

His Winchester slammed into his shoulder, and the report made his ears ring. But mild discomfort did nothing to take away from the satisfaction when a cowboy tumbled into the grass, his horse swerving away from the noise.

Smoke killed the second horseman with a bullet through the crown of his hat, which also sliced through the top of his skull, permanently parting the gunman's hair down the middle before he rolled off the rump of his horse.

"Time to move," Smoke spat, ducking down as he left the tree at a run, heading straight for the middle of the fight.

Thirty-five

Billy Morton spurred his horse relentlessly to catch up to Jessie, and when Jessie saw him angling across the prairie, he wondered where the others were, the dozen men Billy was supposed to lead into the attack from the southwest. Billy was all alone, and he shouldn't have been. Dodging stampeding longhorns, Jessie motioned to Pickett and the men behind him to continue charging Jensen and his cowboys while he reined off to find out what Billy was in such a hurry to tell him.

Billy hauled back on his reins, bringing his lathered sorrel to a sliding stop when he rode up to Jessie. Jessie saw a look on Billy's face that could only be fear.

"He got behind us again!" Billy shouted to be heard above the bang of guns and the bawling of runaway cattle.

"Who?" Jessie demanded.

"That feller Jensen. It's gotta be him. A big son of a bitch with two pistols. I ain't never seen nothin' like it in all my borned days, Jessie. We was ready to charge out here when this big bastard appeared out of nowhere, both pistols blazin'. He killed everybody! 'Cept me. I was lucky to get out with my skin. One man ain't supposed to be able to do what he did. He killed twelve goddamn men, Jessie, in less time than it takes me to tell it."

Despite the battle going on in front of him, Jessie stared at the spot where Billy and a mix of *pistoleros* from Vasquez's bunch and Pedro Lopez's gang were supposed to have entered the fight. He couldn't quite make himself believe what Billy had told him just now. "Had to be some others shootin'," he said, as the crack of a rifle close by made him flinch, a wild shot taken by one of the young Apaches galloping by. Sighting the Apache, Jessie wondered where the other Indians were now. Only two of them were out on the prairie doing any shooting, and their leader, Little Horse, wasn't among them.

"Just him, Jessie. I swear to it," Billy said. "Ain't no man on earth can kill twelve men like he done, only I seen it with my own two eyes while I was gettin' the hell away from there fast as this horse could run."

"How come nobody shot him?" Jessie asked, feeling a touch of worry growing in the pit of his stomach.

"Wasn't time. He stood up behind this bush an' emptied both guns as fast as he could pull them triggers. Men was droppin' like flies." Billy looked over his shoulder quickly as a group of terrified longhorns raced by. "That ain't even the worst of it," Billy continued, his voice with an unusually high pitch. "Just when I was comin' to tell you what happened to us, I saw that half-breed, Raul Jones, come ridin' out of them trees yonder with a couple of Pedro's men. Somebody cut 'em down before you could blink. I figure it had to be Jensen."

It wasn't possible, what Billy was telling him, how

one man could be so lucky. Or was he that good? He couldn't be, not an ordinary cattleman from some place up in Colorado.

Now Jessie looked at the fight going on around Jensen's camp and he saw two more of his men fall from their saddles. Pickett and Tom Hill had already swung their horses around when rifle fire from Jensen's cowboys proved too accurate. Pickett was no coward, but out in the open like he was, he and Tom were sitting ducks.

"Maybe this wasn't such a good idea, Jessie," Billy said, "tangling with Smoke Jensen. He ain't the tinhorn everybody claimed he was. The big son of a bitch can damn sure shoot. I seen it for myself."

"I ain't never met a man I backed down from," Jessie growled, with more resolve than he truly felt at the moment, after finding out how many more lives this Jensen had taken, all in a matter of minutes, before the attack had really gotten started. Now he found himself wondering if Jensen had gotten Little Horse and his four scouts. He could see their assault on the cowboys' camp was doing little beyond running off Jensen's herd. "Maybe it wasn't such a good plan to come at them out in the open like this. We'll pull back an' find another way. Ride a wide circle an' tell the men to head north. It's gonna take Jensen awhile to round up these cattle, an' that'll give us time to come up with a better idea. They're headed north to Colorado with this herd, so we'll look for a place north of here to set up an ambush that can't fail."

Bill Pickett and Tom Hill galloped up as Billy was leaving to give Jessie's order to withdraw. Pickett's face was a mask of hatred.

"Half your damn gunslicks ran off before we rushed

'em," he said. "Look out yonder. There ain't but fifteen or twenty of us, an' we come here with more'n
forty. So few of us can't get close enough to find anything to shoot at. Them cowboys are all layin' down
in the grass where we can't see 'em, an' we're out in
the open."

"Some of 'em didn't run off," Jessie said quietly,
as most of the gunfire stopped when Billy began mo-
tioning men to pull out and follow him northward.
"Billy told me Jensen killed twelve men in that ravine
where they was waitin' for my signal, an' then he got
three more, includin' Raul. He may have killed Little
Horse an' our scouts. Ain't seen 'em since before the
fight started. . . ." As he was speaking to Pickett, he
saw a hatless man carrying a rifle running on foot
toward the cowboy camp. "That must be Jensen right
there. If I had a Sharps buffalo gun . . ."

Pickett saw the running figure too. He squinted to
see him more clearly in the bright morning sunlight.
"He's just one man, Jessie. He may be good, but
there's always somebody who's a little better. If he
done what Billy claimed he did, then he's pretty
damn good. Only, I'm promisin' you I can kill him
if I get to pick the place, an' the time."

"I'm gonna give you that opportunity," Jessie remarked as a final gunshot popped in the distance.
"You can pick the spot. I don't give a damn how you
do it. I just want Jensen dead. We'll skirt their camp
an' head north, the direction they've got to go to get
to Colorado. You can start lookin' for the right place
on the way up."

The man Jessie believed to be Jensen disappeared
into a tall stand of bunch grass near a group of teth-

ered horses still pawing the ground, prancing as a result of loud gunfire coming from all directions.

"I'll kill him for you," Pickett promised again. "You just let me do it my way."

Unconsciously, Jessie shook his head in disbelief when he got a count of the men Billy was leading north, scarcely more than a dozen. Was it possible that Jensen could have killed so many men himself? It went against everything Jessie knew about paid shootists. Even the best of them in tough border towns like Laredo could barely claim a dozen kills over a lifetime. Jensen had killed at least that many in a matter of minutes.

Tom Hill spoke his mind. "Whoever Jensen is, he ain't got any stake in this range war, really. We could let him ride back to Colorado an' git on with rustlin' Chisum out of business, so don't no more of us git killed."

"Are you turnin' yellow on me, Tom?" Jessie asked.

"Nope," Tom replied with conviction. "I've done my share of killin' over the years, but there's always come a few times when I knowed to toss in my cards an' git out of the game. You ain't asked me, but I've got this funny feelin' about tryin' Jensen again. Never was all that superstitious myself, but I've seen with my own two eyes what this feller Jensen can do. Some men are borned with a knack fer killin'. It comes natural to 'em, same as breathin' air."

Pickett's jaw tightened. "He'll bleed same as any man"

"Maybe," Tom said. "First, somebody's got to git close enough to put a bullet in him. Since he come here, that ain't been too awful easy."

Pickett glared at Tom, as though he'd been insulted by the remark. "Ain't nobody with backbone tried yet. These yellow sons of bitches Jessie hired don't know the first thing 'bout killin' a man, seems to me."

Before Jessie lifted his reins to ride off, he caught a glimpse of an Indian riding out of trees to the west. It was Dreamer, if Jessie remembered right. "Yonder's one of them Apaches. If he speaks any English, I'll ask him what come of Little Horse an' all the others."

"My money says they cut an' run," Pickett growled. "I told you a goddamn Injun ain't worth the gunpowder it takes to kill 'em when it comes down to cases."

The Indian came galloping up on a piebald paint pony. He looked at Jessie for a moment as if trying to think of the right words to say.

Jessie grew impatient. "What the hell happened to Little Horse an' the rest?"

"All dead," Dreamer answered, making an odd slashing motion with his hand across the top of his scalp. "Chop head, like this. Come see."

"I don't need to see it," Jessie snapped, when his grim prediction proved to be true.

Tom swallowed. "I didn't know Jensen used a woodcutter's ax in a fight like this. Most Apaches are mighty damn hard to sneak up on, 'specially fer a white man."

"Let's ride," Jessie said, weary of hearing more bad news. "We'll catch up with Billy an' the others an' then we'll decide what to do."

"I've already decided," Pickett said as he turned his horse to follow Jessie. "I'm gonna kill that son of a bitch myself, an' when I blow his goddamn head all to pieces with ol' Betsy here, you'll see Mr. Smoke

Jensen wasn't nothin' but lucky he didn't run into me first."

As they rode around the cowboy camp Jessie wasn't so sure of Pickett's judgment when it came to Jensen. There was a ring of truth to what Tom had said, about some men having a natural gift when it came to killing. He recalled a time down in West Texas a few years ago, when he saw Clay Allison in action. Allison could draw and shoot as quickly as Jessie, and for that reason, Jessie left him completely alone until an offer of a job in New Mexico took him out of Sanderson.

He gave Jensen's camp a last look before he urged his horse into a thin line of trees to the northeast. Jessie couldn't help remembering what Dreamer had just told him, that Little Horse and his Apaches died from split skulls. Tom was right about one thing, that an Apache was hard to slip up on from behind. It was beginning to seem like Jensen was always finding a way to get behind them.

Thirty-six

Smoke crept up to camp and spoke before he showed himself. "It's me. Is everybody okay?"

Pearlie rose up from his grassy hiding place. "Johnny took a bullet in the leg, but it's hardly more'n a scratch. I tied his bandanna 'round it till we could fix a proper bandage. He's lyin' over yonder next to the horses." He pointed north. "All of 'em cleared out, leastways the ones we could see. Wasn't near as many of 'em as I figured there'd be."

Smoke didn't bother to explain how he'd reduced the odds considerably. "Let's get the horses saddled and round up as many of our cows as we can." He examined the bunched Herefords not far away. "One of our young bulls caught a stray bullet in the neck, and we'll probably have to put him down."

"I seen it up close," Bob called from a spot near the bulls, "an' it's in his brisket. Bullet passed clean through. It don't hardly bleed any now, an' I'm bettin' he'll make it."

"That's good news," Smoke replied tiredly, sinking to the ground to put on his riding boots and place the bloody tomahawk in his saddlebags.

One by one, the cowboys stood up, when it was clear Evans and his men were gone. "We damn sure held 'em off," Cletus said, as Johnny limped over to their blackened firepit with pain written across his face. " 'Cept fer Johnny, I'd say we was lucky."

Johnny agreed. "I was also lucky. That slug could have hit me in worse places. I'll mend."

Longhorn heifers were scattered from one end of the plain to the other, while many had run into the trees to escape the loud banging noises.

"We'll be all day gittin' 'em rounded up," Pearlie said, as he carried his saddle to the picket ropes.

Duke was the last to come in from his hiding place in the grass. "I figured they was gonna run over us like a locomotive for a spell. Somethin' must have changed their minds."

Pearlie gave Smoke a knowing look. "I imagine Mr. Jensen can tell us what it was, if'n he's of a mind to talk about it."

"I got a few," Smoke replied, pulling on his boots before he stood up with his saddle and bridle. "Everybody ride careful out there, just in case there's some who ain't dead, or still have some fight left."

Cal's face was ghostly white when he spoke up. "What do we do if we find a wounded man, boss?"

"Leave the son of a bitch right where he is. We haven't got time to be doctorin' men who just tried to kill us. Let 'em rot for all I care."

"I shot one," Cal added quietly, "a big feller in a sombrero with belts on his chest. Makes two so far on this trip. I sure do hope there ain't no more to my credit later on."

"You were doing what you had to do to help protect your friends and the cattle herd, son," Smoke told him. "Don't let it eat on you so hard."

"I'm tryin' not to think about it." Cal lifted his saddle to go to the picket line. "But I seen his face when I shot him. His eyes got big as fried turkey eggs, an' then there was blood all over his face. He dropped the rifle he was carryin' an' put his hands over his eyes just before he fell off his horse. It damn near made me sick all over again."

"I'm bettin' a month's pay you ain't sick enough to keep from cleanin' your plate tonight, young 'un. Don't nothin' make you that belly-sick."

In spite of Johnny's obvious pain, he chuckled. "That's damn sure one thing about Cal, all right. He can eat no matter what."

Cal pretended not to be listening, saddling his horse as quickly as he could.

Smoke was in for a pleasant surprise as the morning wore on, for it seemed the longhorns were willing to gather on the prairie without much urging. Most of them settled quickly and began to graze alongside the Hereford bulls.

As the cow work continued, Smoke thought about the direction the Evans gang had ridden . . . north, making it logical they would try again farther up the trail. He wondered how much convincing Jessie Evans needed.

Pearlie and Duke came trotting over to a grove of oaks where Smoke had just driven out three longhorns, helping him push them toward the main bunch.

"That makes over a hundred an' thirty head so far," Duke said. "This is easier than it looked like it was gonna be when we first got started."

Smoke nodded his agreement as he saw Cletus and Cal bringing five more cows from the east. Two more strays came out of the woods farther north on their own. "Some of 'em are volunteering to come back themselves."

Pearlie shrugged. "Longhorns is the most unpredictable critters on earth. Sometimes they run off fer no reason at all. Other times they won't run if you ask 'em to, an' a few times they stampede an' then come back without bein' asked. The first man who figures out how a longhorn's brain works is gonna make hisself a fortune."

Smoke was keeping an eye on the horizon, and Pearlie was the first to notice.

"You know they'll be back, don't you?" he asked, as the cows took off in a trot to rejoin the others.

"It's likely," was all he said.

"They'll do it different next time," Pearlie assured him a moment later. "They won't come at us straight on."

"Hard to say, Pearlie. About all we can do is stay watchful until it happens."

"It'll happen. You know it as well as me. The way I see it, after they've tried so many damn times, we'll have to kill might' near all of 'em afore it's over an' done with."

Smoke knew there was a great deal of wisdom behind Pearlie's words.

That evening, as Pearlie signaled a pot of beans was ready to eat, only seven heifers remained unaccounted for. Time was more important now than seven cows, Smoke decided, his eyelids heavy from lack of sleep.

He found good news when he climbed down from his saddle at the campfire. The wounded Hereford bull had stopped bleeding entirely, and now it was grazing along with the others, apparently suffering no real discomfort from its injury.

Smoke tied off his horse, carrying his bedroll.

"You gonna sleep or eat?" Pearlie asked good-naturedly.

"A little of both, I hope."

Cletus picked up his rifle. "I already ate all I could stand of Pearlie's beans, so I'll take the first watch along with Cal. Cal's young enough not to need as much sleep as the rest of us."

Smoke tossed his bedroll over a stretch of soft grass before he came for a plate of beans. "Suits me, Cletus. I'll relieve you before midnight. Ride as close to the herd as you can without spookin' 'em. They're still a little jittery after all that happened today."

"So am I," Cal said softly, leaving his beans mostly untouched to saddle the gray colt.

Pearlie straightened up from spooning more beans onto his plate. "Well I'll be damned an' hog-tied. We just witnessed a miracle, boys. That young 'un hardly touched his food tonight, an' that's like seein' a man walk on water without gittin' his feet wet."

Thirty-seven

North of the Haystack Mountain range, Jessie led his men to a fork in the Pecos River coming from the west, a shallow body of sluggish water only belly-deep on their horses. Pickett seemed to be interested in a spot north of the crossing, where big rocks and tall cottonwoods lined the river.

"This is it," Pickett told Jessie, while Jose Vasquez and four of his remaining *pistoleros* made it across, followed by Billy Morton, Tom Hill, Pedro Lopez, and the two members of his gang left alive after the fight with Jensen. The last rider to cross was the Indian called Dreamer, who kept glancing backward as if he expected them to be followed.

"This is what?" Jessie asked, still brooding over their resounding defeat yesterday morning at the hands of Jensen.

"The perfect place," Pickett replied, his voice turned to ice. "I'll kill the son of a bitch while his horse is crossin' this river. I can hide in them rocks yonder, an' I'll be close enough to use my scattergun. Betsy'll cut him to pieces at this range. Probably kill his horse too."

Jessie looked things over. "He may get suspicious when he comes to a spot like this where he can't see if anybody's hid on the other side. Might not work like you planned."

"He has to cross here to make sure there ain't no bogs or quicksand that'll trap his cattle. He's a rancher, an' he'll know the risks if he don't test this crossing."

"We can have the rest of the men spread out up and down this riverbank to cover you."

Pickett wheeled on Jessie with fire in his eyes. "That's what was wrong every goddamn time, Jessie. These idiots you hired don't know the first thing 'bout killin' a man out in the open. What you've got is a buncha saloon-raised gunmen who've got no experience bushwhackin' a man who knows wild country. He'll come real cautious down to this river, bein' as careful as he knows how. That's why I'm gonna do this my way, so none of the rest of these fools tip my hand on what I aim to do."

"Suit yourself, Bill," Jessie said. "The only thing I care about is findin' Smoke Jensen dead."

Pickett jutted his jaw. "You won't find nothin' but pieces of him. I give you my word on it. He'll be twenty yards away when he's in the middle of this river, an' that's close enough to shred every piece of meat on his body with a sawed-off shotgun like mine. You leave Jensen to me. The sumbitch is as good as dead right now if he crosses this river."

Jessie wondered. However, Pickett's reputation for killing his victims any way he could made him the perfect choice for this job. Jessie could never have admitted it to anyone, but after yesterday's defeat and the incredible number of men Jensen had killed single-handed, he'd begun to experience twinges of doubt that he could do the job himself. Jensen apparently had some uncanny ability to move around without detection. How else could he have slipped up behind Little Horse and four more experienced Apache warriors, chopping their heads open with some kind of ax, not the sort of weapon the average man used in a war being fought with guns.

"I don't give a damn how you do it, just make sure it don't backfire," Jessie said, as his grim-faced gunmen sat their horses around him, listening to his exchange with Pickett. Jessie knew the others feared Pickett, and rightfully so. Pickett was a madman, more than slightly out of kilter when it came to killing other men, even as they lay dying from other bullet wounds. Roy Cooper had been much the same in that regard. Only somehow, Jensen had been able to kill him along with all the others that night, and it still worried Jessie some.

Pickett turned back to Jessie. "Tell that Injun to ride back and see how far they are behind us. An' tell the dumb son of a bitch not to let 'em see him. All Injuns are good at bein' sneaky, so tell him to be careful."

Dreamer apparently understood every word. At first he gave Pickett a chilly stare, then he swung his pony around and went back across the river, resting a very old Henry repeating rifle across his pony's withers.

"Dreamer's liable to double-cross us now, after what you just said about him," Jessie remarked, watching the Apache ride out of sight around a bend in the trail.

Pickett made a face. "He won't do it, because he's after a payday. The rotten bastards will do damn near anything to get their hands on enough money to buy whiskey. Never saw an Injun who wasn't drunk, or plannin' to get drunk. That's why you can't trust 'em."

Jessie looked north, where the trail climbed to the top of a ridge between two low mountains. "We'll ride on over that rise yonder an' make camp wherever there's water. Find a spring or somethin', a feeder creek. We'll be listenin' real close for gunshots."

"Won't be but one," Pickett said, "when little Miss Betsy gives Jensen her ten-gauge loads." He drew his double-barrel Greener from a boot tied to the pommel of his saddle, and for a moment it seemed he almost caressed its dark walnut stock while his face visibly changed. He glanced over at Jessie and now a glint flickered in his pale eyes. "This here gun has ended a hell of a lot of men's lives. Only this one's gonna be special, because Jensen thinks he's so god-damn tough an' clever."

"He is clever," Jessie said. "But like you say, he'll die the same as any other man if a load of double-size buckshot hits him in the right places."

"He can't be all that clever," Pickett assured him. "A man makes mistakes now an' then. The biggest mistake Jensen made was comin' to Lincoln County at the wrong time. Now he's gonna pay for it with his life."

Jessie reined his horse for the top of the ridge. There was no point in discussing it with Pickett any further. If Pickett was as good as his reputation, and what Jessie had seen of him in action during several attacks on Chisum's cow camps, all their troubles with Mr. Smoke Jensen would soon be over.

Tom rode up beside Jessie as they were trotting up the ridge to look for water and a campsite.

"This is liable to be one helluva mistake," Tom said under his breath. "I've got a real bad feelin' about it."

"You worry too much, Tom," Jessie said, although he shared some of the same nagging doubts about Pickett's planned ambush.

Tom looked up at a clear spring sky. "I worry when a man's already proved he's hard to kill, an' I'm sidin' the bunch who aims to kill him. Pickett ain't never seen Jensen close before. When he gits a good look, he may change his mind."

"That's damn sure a fact," Billy Morton said, riding along Jessie's left side. "If I live to be a hundred years old, I won't forgit what it was like when Jensen jumped up from behind that bush with both pistols spittin' fire. It was the same as facin' the devil himself."

"Bill Pickett's a proven killer," Jessie argued.

It was Tom who said, "So's this feller Smoke Jensen. I've never heard of him before he came here, but I'll tell you one thing fer sure . . . he's about as mean as they come, and this job ridin' for Jimmy Dolan don't pay enough to be worth gettin' killed. If Pickett don't kill him when he crosses that river, I'm quittin' this outfit fer good. There's gotta be easier ways to make money, an' live long enough to spend it."

Billy didn't say anything, but Jessie was sure he was of the same mind. "Give Pickett a chance to prove himself before you start quittin' a good-payin' job with Dolan," said Jessie. "There ain't all that much work to be had for a shootist in this part of the West, an' I'm sure as hell not askin' to be taken off the payroll till I know there ain't no other choice."

Thirty-eight

Cattle were strung out for half a mile when Smoke turned to look back at the herd. As they had from the beginning, the short Herefords brought up the rear. Cal and Cletus were riding drag at the back of the bunch. Bob and Johnny held the flank positions, keeping wandering strays driven back, while Pearlie and Duke rode point on either side, aiming lead cows in the right direction. A peaceful day had passed, with no sign of the Evans gang. Smoke had been reading their tracks every now and then, counting horses when the prints crossed barren ground. Between fifteen and twenty men were a day's ride ahead of the herd, judging by the freshness of the tracks, the edges of the clear prints that were still sharp before wind and time had made the dirt crumble.

According to a crudely drawn map he carried in his saddlebags, they were a couple of days' drive from old Fort Sumner, an abandoned army post turned into a small community where sheep men and Mexican goatherds lived in empty army barracks. The herd was managing fifteen or twenty miles a day, slower because of the short-legged bulls.

Smoke swung his horse away from the trees, where he'd been keeping an eye on the herd's progress. He was staying closer to the cows than before, in part because the tracks left by Evans and his men continued due north, with no sign any of them had turned off to launch another attack or take up snipers' positions when they came to high ground.

Still, Smoke was nagged by the dull certainty that Evans would try again. Arrogant men with high opinions of themselves rarely ever gave up completely, not until someone convinced them they had no other choice.

It appeared to be a small fork leading to the main body of the Pecos River a few miles to the east. Lined with cottonwoods and jumbles of limestone boulders swept aside by previous floods, it looked to be shallow, easy to cross. Smoke sat his Palouse on a high bluff above the river, watching things carefully from a considerable distance before he rode down to test the river bottom for treacherous sand pits and bogs.

Examining the branches of each tree, he was troubled when he found no birds perched on any of the leafy limbs near the crossing. As with most of his experience, reading this sort of sign had been taught to him by Preacher. Most all types of wildlife exhibited behavior that was as good as a signpost, if a man knew how to read it. The sudden flight of birds from a particular spot was a warning to knowledgeable men. The direction a deer ran when it was frightened, sensing danger, was as meaningful as the angry charge of a grizzly protecting her newborn cubs. Even a lowly cricket gave off excellent warnings in the dark, simply by suddenly growing silent when it felt another presence close to its hiding place. The absence of sparrows or blue jays in trees beside the river alerted Smoke to the possibility of danger.

He reined his Palouse around and tied it off in a thicket where it could graze, pulling his rifle, taking a single thin blanket from his bedroll, and wrapping it around his forearm. The sun was almost directly overhead. A soft breeze came from the west, thus he began his approach to the crossing from the east, up-wind, in the fashion of all seasoned mountain men stalking prey. He had a possible use for the blanket, a trick, just in case someone was down there gunning for him.

Pickett had grown bored with all the waiting. Last night, as he rested on thin blankets with a pint of tequila for company, his impatience had lessened somewhat. But today his nerves were on edge more than usual. . . . It was this damn waiting, even though he fully understood the necessity of it. If Smoke Jensen was the trained killer everyone else believed he was, he'd be smart and cautious.

He checked the loads in his pistol, a Colt Peacemaker, for what seemed the hundredth time, then he holstered it and after he took off his flat-brim Stetson, he peered above the rocks, where shadows from nearby cottonwoods covered his hiding place. Again there was no sign of a horseman approaching the river. He then clamped his jaw in frustration and ducked back down.

"I'll bet the gutless son of a bitch headed another direction," he said softly, angrily. "He's liable to ride plumb to Nebraska to get back home." Pickett took another swallow of tequila, listening closely for the sound of a horse in the distance.

He'd gone over what he meant to do a thousand times, not raising his head at all when the rider got close, waiting until he heard a horse in the river. Jensen would be looking for any kind of movement, and there would be none until he was in the water. Then he might catch a split-second glimpse of two shotgun barrels flashing in the sunlight just before they exploded, too late for any man to draw and shoot.

"C'mon, you yellow bastard," Pickett whispered, resting his head against a rock, his shotgun held loosely in his left fist with both hammers cocked . . . he didn't want the click of metal to alert Jensen just before he killed him.

He wondered what was keeping Jensen. According to what the Apache told Jessie, they should be nearing the river by now. He took a bite of jerky and washed it down with tequila. "Hard on a man's nerves, all this waitin'."

He let his gaze wander upriver, then downstream, examining every rock and tree, when suddenly he saw a shadow dart among the cottonwood trunks.

"It's him," Pickett hissed, whirling around to hide himself behind the boulder. Jensen wasn't as clever as Jessie thought. Pickett was sure what he had seen was the outline of a man coming upstream, already on the north side of the river.

He left his horse somewhere, Pickett thought, so he'd make less noise. Peering cautiously around the rock, he aimed his ten-gauge and drew his Peacemaker, ready for anything, every muscle in his body tensed.

He saw the movement again and almost fired at it, until he caught himself. "Not till you're closer, you bastard," he whispered as his grip relaxed on his pistol. Pickett wanted to shred the Colorado cowboy with his scattergun if he could.

Now nothing moved, and only the quiet gurgle of the river passing over stones reached his ears. The second time he saw Jensen he'd been closer, yet not quite close enough for Betsy to do her best work.

"C'mon, turkey," Pickett mouthed silently, as beads of sweat formed on his forehead. He could almost taste the moment when he would kill Jensen, a thickening of his tongue with a slightly sweet taste on the tip. He found himself longing for the sight of a bullet-torn body oozing blood from hundreds of pellet wounds, and he imagined the coppery smell of Jensen's blood. He hoped the first twin charges didn't kill Jensen instantly. . . . It would be far better to stand over him, to see the fear and pain in his eyes just before another shotgun blast tore his head to pieces.

More waiting made him more impatient, until a heavier gust of wind blew down the river, rippling its waters, and at the same time Jensen moved again, darting around the base of a cottonwood, rushing toward him.

Pickett straightened up quickly and fired both barrels of the Greener, jolted by twin explosions that deafened him briefly. He saw the shadow swirl, twisting when a wall of lead struck.

"Gotcha, you son of a bitch!" Pickett cried as he took a step away from the rock, holstering his pistol to reload the ten-gauge for a sure kill when he reached Jensen.

"Not quite," an even voice said behind him.

Pickett froze, twisting his head to look over his shoulder. He saw a man standing beside a rock pile less than twenty yards away. Pickett's mouth fell open.

"You shot a blanket draped over a limb," the man added, an evil grin widening his lips. "But the blanket does belong to me. I'm Smoke Jensen. I reckon you've been waitin' here a long time to ambush me."

Pickett only had one shell in the Greener, and its breech was open. His Peacemaker was holstered. "How'd you get behind me?" Pickett asked, buying time until he could think of a way to get at his pistol without being shot. Both of Jensen's pistols were holstered. . . . He carried a Winchester, muzzle aimed down at the ground.

"To tell the truth, it was mighty easy. I suppose you're the feller named Bill Pickett, on account of that short shotgun. We were told you fancied yourself a man-killer. So far, the only thing you've shot holes in was a blanket."

"You're gonna shoot me in the back, ain't you?" Pickett asked.

"My conscience might bother me, so I'm gonna let you turn around and reach for that Colt. I'll give you plenty of time."

"You're lyin'," Pickett replied. "You'll kill me soon as I move"

Jensen nodded. "I'm gonna kill you either way, but if you want a chance to see how good you are with that six-gun, make a move for it. But do it quick, or I'll just kill you now an' be on my way. That shotgun blast is liable to bring Evans and his men any minute."

Pickett felt he had no selection. He dropped Betsy to the ground and made a slow, deliberate turn, expecting Jensen to draw a pistol before he could square himself. To his surprise, Jensen remained motionless until Pickett had his feet spread slightly apart and his right hand hovering above his Peacemaker.

"Reach for it," Jensen said, as calm as could be.

Pickett didn't wait for a second invitation. His hand went clawing for his gun.

There was a flash of gun metal in sunlight, then a booming noise.

Thirty-nine

Jessie and Billy Morton were the first to scramble aboard their horses when they heard gunshots, with the others mounting right behind them.

"That was Pickett's shotgun!" Jessie cried, spurring his horse to cover the half mile down to the river crossing as rapidly as he could. "Pickett got the son of a bitch!"

Billy galloped up beside him. "I ain't gonna believe it till I see it!" he shouted back over the clatter of iron horseshoes on rock.

Jessie drew his pistol, just in case, and as if it were a signal, every member of his gang was fisting guns. Riding as hard as they could, they covered the distance in only a few minutes, until Jessie reined to a halt on a knob above the river.

"Yonder he is," Jessie said, as soon as the others came to a stop alongside him. "Pickett wrapped his body in a blanket so's we can bury him."

Billy kept looking up and down the river. "Where the hell is Pickett? I don't see him nowhere."

Jose Vasquez pointed to a distant horseman on a ridge on the far side of the crossing. The figure appeared to be watching them.

"*Quien es?* Who is that?" Vasquez asked.

"Probably just one of Jensen's boys," Jessie answered. "I'm ridin' down to have a look. You can see Jensen's dead from here, 'cause he ain't moving, all wrapped up in that blanket like he is."

Tom said, "I ain't all that convinced it's Jensen."

Jessie ignored the remark and rode his horse off the knob to reach the river. But as he got closer, he felt something was wrong. He heard the others following him, but at a slower gait.

He rode up to the blanket-clad body and jumped down, in a hurry to set eyes on Jensen's corpse. He knelt and pulled back the dark blue blanket, riddled with pellet holes, and what he saw made him draw in a quick breath.

"It's Pickett," Billy Morton observed without leaving the back of his horse.

Jessie's hand, the one holding the blanket, began to shake. He dropped the woolen cloth quickly and stood up, gazing at the mounted figure far across the river. "That is Jensen," he said with a dry mouth.

"He's prob'ly laughin' at us," Tom said. "One thing's for damn sure—he's gotta be the toughest hombre I ever ran across, an' if Bill Pickett was still alive, he'd be sayin' the same damn thing. You can count me out of this, Jessie. I'm pulling stakes while I still can."

"That goes fer me too," Billy said, looking up at the man watching them from the ridge. "I knowed when he killed twelve of us back in that draw there was somethin' about him that damn near wasn't human. If you're smart, Jessie, you'll let that feller go wherever the hell he aims to go with his cows."

Jessie whirled to Jose Vasquez. "How 'bout you, Jose?"

"I see enough," Vasquez replied. "This man be *muy malo,* one bad hombre. Maybeso he is no man, *un espíritu.* He kill three of my cousins, also many of *mi compadres.* I don't want no more to have fight with him. We going back to Mexico."

When Jessie looked at Pedro, Pedro shrugged.

"Is no good, Señor Jessie. We no can kill him. He kill Ignacio and Roy and now he kill Señor Pickett. He make killing look easy. He kill us also if we don't leave him alone."

Jessie turned back to Jensen, scowling. "Mr. Dolan ain't gonna like it when I tell him."

Tom spoke. "Tell Dolan to try an' kill him hisself. He'll find out damn quick it ain't easy done."

Jessie's jaw clamped angrily. "I wonder who he really is. I can guarantee you he ain't just some cattle rancher from up north."

"No lo hasé," Vasquez said. "It make no difference to me. I only know one thing about him—he don't get no more chances to kill me or *mi compadres.* We go home now."

Billy rested his elbow on his saddle horn. "That don't leave nobody but you, Jessie. We've knowed each other a long time, an' I'm givin' you good advice. Leave that Jensen feller plumb alone or you'll wind up like Pickett an' Cooper an' all the rest."

"He's just sittin' there watchin' us," Jessie said, with his gaze still fixed on the ridge.

"He's waitin' to see what we'll do, I reckon," Tom said. "If we act like we're comin' after him, he won't be sittin' there in plain sight very long."

Jessie's hands unconsciously balled into fists, then they relaxed.

"C'mon, Jessie," Billy said quietly. "Let's git the hell outa here afore Jensen changes his mind."

"It ain't my nature to run," Jessie replied, still frozen to the same spot above Pickett's corpse.

"It's any man's nature to wanna stay alive," Tom suggested. "We got no quarrel with Jensen."

Jose Vasquez was done talking. He gave a silent signal to his men and reined away from the river, riding off in a cloud of dust swirling in the breeze. Pedro and his two remaining men were not long in following Vasquez, swinging their mounts around after the other *pistoleros*.

Jessie's shoulders sagged. He finally took his eyes off Jensen to look at Billy and Tom. "We can't tell Dolan what really happened, boys. It'll make us look like fools."

Billy wagged his head. "The only way we'd look like bigger fools is to stay an' tangle with Jensen again. We can tell Dolan a bunch of Chisum's riders showed up, leavin' us outnumbered. If you agree to leave this Jensen alone, I'll stay on with Dolan's outfit. Otherwise, I'm cuttin' a trail for parts unknown."

"Same goes fer me," Tom said, as Jessie finally mounted his horse.

Jessie gave Smoke Jensen a final stare, then without a word he wheeled his horse around to head back to Lincoln. It damn sure wasn't going to be easy giving Dolan the bad news, and it could cost him a good-paying job as Dolan's ramrod.

Forty

Approaching the lush green mountains and meadows south of Sugarloaf range brightened everyone's mood. The cattle were fat and had proven to be trailworthy, even the short-strided Hereford bulls. It had been two weeks since the last confrontation with Jessie Evans and his paid guns, a peaceful two weeks of guiding cows across good grazing and plenty of water.

Smoke had all but forgotten about the battles with Dolan's gunslingers, until they neared Sugarloaf. He'd have to come clean with Sally about what he'd done, the men he killed, and he feared making the admission more than he'd ever feared the risks when bullets were flying.

"She'll throw a fit," he said one clear, crisp spring morning less than a dozen miles below Sugarloaf.

"You're talkin' about Miz Jensen, ain't you?" Pearlie asked with a grin. "I understand. I'd rather face the Shoshoni tribe on the warpath than Miz Jensen when she's got her feathers ruffled."

"I'll make her understand," Smoke said without conviction, "even though she'll keep reminding me of my promise to stay wide of difficulties."

"We tried to avoid 'em," Pearlie remembered.

"They was just too damn hardheaded, an' wouldn't leave us alone."

Cal came riding up as the herd wound its way through a valley leading to Bob Williams's ranch. "We're home," Cal said with unconcealed excitement. "Means we'll be havin' some of Miz Sally's good cookin' afore too long."

Pearlie made a face. "I see your appetite has done returned to its usual."

"I'm sick of beans an' fatback. A big bearclaw drippin' with melted brown sugar sure would be nice. Maybe two or three of 'em."

Smoke was hoping all had remained quiet at the ranch while they were away. "Before she cooks up a bunch of bearclaws, I'm afraid she's gonna fix me a dish of my own words, when I tell about all the troubles we had."

"You hadn't oughta promised her nothin'," Pearlie said. "I reckon she knows you well enough to know such a thing just wasn't possible."

"She'll have her say-so about it," Smoke said, with all the assurance of experience.

"It'll soften her some when she sees them good bulls," Cal remarked. "That little one with the hole in his chest is doin' just fine. He don't hardly notice it now."

Pearlie spoke again. "Me, I'm lookin' forward to sleepin' in my own bed, 'stead of this hard ground. It's damn sure gonna be good to be back home fer a change."

Smoke looked back at the herd. Some of the Hereford bulls had already mounted heifers coming in season during rest stops. "Next spring we'll have pastures full of white-faced crossbred calves. And I'm gonna wire that feller Chisum told me about down in Saint Louis, and have him ship me a good Morgan stud by rail this summer."

"Sounds like you've got things all planned out," Pearlie said. "Maybe things will settle down now. We've burned a hell of a lot of gunpowder lately."

"For a fact," Cal added quietly. "I still dream about them two fellers I killed, the Indian an' that *pistolero.*"

"It'll pass, young 'un," Pearlie assured him. "Besides that, if you didn't spend so damn much time sleepin', you wouldn't have time to do all that dreamin'."

Bob Williams and Duke Smith rode up when they came to a fork in the valley leading to Smoke's ranch. "If it's all the same to you, Mr. Jensen, me an' Duke will take a couple of those bulls, an' head for home. I'll bring the purchase money over in a few days, if that's okay."

"You're a neighbor and a friend, Bob. Pay for 'em whenever you get ready."

Bob extended a handshake offering. "Thanks again for takin' us along."

Smoke nodded. "As it turned out, we might not have made it if it hadn't been for the two of you helpin' out with your guns once in a while."

Bob grinned. "Always glad to help a neighbor," he said as he swung off to pick out two bulls.

As soon as Bob was out of earshot, Pearlie said, "Hell-fire, I never saw Bob or Duke hit nothin' whilst we was shootin'. Bob couldn't hardly hit the side of a barn with a rifle."

"They did the best they could," Smoke replied,

not really caring either way. Marksmanship was a low priority when it came to picking good neighbors.

He saw Sally waiting on the front porch as they drove the herd up to the corrals. She smiled a beautiful smile and waved to him.

"Best you put yer lyin' britches on afore you tell her about this trip," Pearlie said, stifling a chuckle.

"I won't lie to her," Smoke replied. "She'd know right off I wasn't telling the truth anyway."

"You can tell her part of the truth. Say we ran into a bit of trouble but it didn't amount to nothin'."

"She'd know," Smoke told him.

Now Pearlie laughed out loud. "Miz Jensen is the only two-legged thing on earth Mr. Smoke Jensen is afraid of."

"That's about the size of it, Pearlie. I wouldn't do anything that might cause me to lose her."

He kicked the Palouse colt toward the house while the others pushed the cattle toward the corrals. When he got to the front porch, he swung down and took her in his arms.

"I've missed you," he said, kissing her lips. "Have things gone smoothly here?"

"No problems," she told him, smiling. Then her face changed to a serious look. "But I can tell you had a few problems. I can see it in your eyes, and the fact that Johnny's wearing that bandage around his leg."

"There was some shooting," he told her. "I had to discourage some hard cases who didn't want us to get these cows to Sugarloaf."

"You can tell me about it later," she said. "Right now I want to see those Herefords up close."

"I'd rather see you up close for a while," he replied.

She gave him a taunting turn of her head. "That will come later, Smoke, if you behave yourself until the sun goes down."

"I may not be able to wait that long."

"Then find yourself another woman. I'm not that easy, to just take my clothes off when a man comes riding up to ask."

"Even if he's your husband?"

"I'd forgotten I had a husband, you've been away so long."

"I got back as quick as I could."

He held her in a powerful embrace, something he'd been thinking about for several long days on the trail. "You always win arguments, don't you?" he asked.

"We are not arguing. I won't let you take me to bed until I see those Herefords. End of discussion."

"I suppose I should have looked for another woman on the trail."

"Suit yourself, Mr. Jensen. But you won't find another woman who loves you the way I do, and you'll never find a woman who's any better in bed."

He looked down at her in mock surprise. "You've got a very high opinion of yourself, young lady."

"I've earned it, for putting up with you. Now, show me the new bulls or you may wind up sleeping in the barn tonight."

He let go of her and took her by the arm. "They're just what you said they were. Beefy, and I've seen Chisum's crosses on longhorns. They'll be perfect for the markets."

She squeezed his hand as they walked side by side down to the corrals, where Pearlie and Johnny and Cal were driving the Herefords into a separate pen.

She looked at the bulls a moment before she said anything.

"Those bulls are the future of this ranch," she said. "I've never seen so much meat on one animal before."

"Some of them have already bred some of the heifers on the drive up here."

She looked up at him with a twinkle in her eyes. "I'm sure there's much more to tell me about the drive," she said.

"A few minor details," he admitted.

"Like the gun battles you got into, and how many men you had to kill to get them here?" she asked.

"I did have to shoot a couple, maybe more than one or two, but I didn't have a choice."

She stood on her tiptoes to kiss him. "It seems you never have a choice when there's a fight," she told him. "I do wish you'd learn to turn your back on them."

"Somebody might have shot me in the back if I'd done that," he argued feebly, knowing he would have to tell her everything. It was because he loved her so deeply that he couldn't hide the truth from her.

"You can tell me all about it after supper, Smoke. I'll do my best to understand. There's something inside you that won't let you avoid taking a side in things, and I suppose that's also one of the reasons why I love you. Some men would ride right past a one-sided fight. I've come to know you well enough to know you never would." She examined the young bulls again, then she said, "Just remember, one fight you'll never win is a fight with me."

William W. Johnstone
The *Mountain Man* Series

Complete Your Collection
William W. Johnstone
The *Mountain Man* Series